A BRIDE WITHOUT
A WEDDING NIGHT

Lady Eleanor rejoices at being free of the ruthless warrior she'd married by proxy but never met, yet when she arrives to claim his castle as her new home, she finds it abandoned and in ruins. And as she explores the dim tower, a tall figure demands she leave—immediately! Who is this compelling man with the burning gaze? And why does he make her heart pound so strangely?

Nicholas Bayard is stunned to discover he has a bride who is very much alive. But painful experience has convinced him there is no room in his heart for a wife, so he disguises his identity. Yet nothing can disguise the passion he finds in Eleanor's arms. With her joy in life and belief in miracles, she is a temptation he cannot resist. But what will happen to their fragile love when his innocent wife discovers the truth?

If You've Enjoyed This Book,
Be Sure to Read These Other
AVON ROMANTIC TREASURES

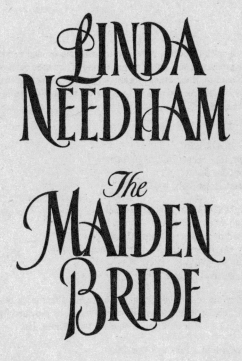

LINDA NEEDHAM

The MAIDEN BRIDE

An Avon Romantic Treasure

AVON BOOKS ◆ NEW YORK

This is a work of fiction. Names, characters, places, and incidents either are the product of the author's imagination or are used fictitiously. Any resemblance to actual events, locales, organizations, or persons, living or dead, is entirely coincidental and beyond the intent of either the author or the publisher.

AVON BOOKS, INC.
An Imprint of HarperCollins*Publishers*
10 East 53rd Street
New York, New York 10022-5299

Copyright © 2000 by Linda Needham
Inside cover author photo by Expressly Portraits
Published by arrangement with the author
Library of Congress Catalog Card Number: 99-96443
ISBN: 0-380-79636-8
www.harpercollins.com

First Avon Books Printing: April 2000

AVON TRADEMARK REG. U.S. PAT. OFF. AND IN OTHER COUNTRIES, MARCA REGISTRADA, HECHO EN U.S.A.

Printed in the U.S.A.

WCD 10 9 8 7 6 5 4 3 2 1

Chapter 1

*The Northwest Coast of England
May 1351*

"Pardon my sayin' so, Lady Eleanor, but this late husband of yours left you the sorriest damned castle I've ever set eyes upon."

"Aye, Dickon, Faulkhurst is a mite frayed about the ramparts—but it's our home now." Eleanor Bayard muzzled the curses she wanted to rain down upon William Bayard's blighted, unlamented soul.

At last, home. And hope, and three of the dearest companions in the world to care for. This was not the time for letting regrets and recriminations gain a foothold—not when she'd come so far.

"I like it, Nellamore."

Eleanor laughed and lifted little Pippa into

her arms, bird bones and feathers, a breeze captured inside an eider pillow. "I do too, Pippa. Very much."

"It needs buckets of paint, my lady." Lisabet battled the sea wind for balance atop the stubby wall of the overgrown kitchen garden.

"Needs a hell of a lot more'n paint, 'Bet." Dickon snorted and cast his young sister a skeptical frown. "A mason, for a start."

Aye, and a carpenter and a smith and so many other things that Eleanor didn't have and didn't know where she would find anytime soon.

May your eternity be blazing hot and sticky with gnats, William Bayard.

No, she would not allow her very wicked, very dead husband to ruin this fine moment.

"Above all else, my loves, Faulkhurst needs the four of us. Desperately." *And we need Faulkhurst.*

"An' the ghost, Nellamore, don't forget." Pippa's gamin little face needed scrubbing, despite last eve's streamside wash-up and another that afternoon.

"Faulkhurst needs a ghost?" Eleanor nosed a kiss against the gilded curls at Pippa's temple.

"It has one already. A huge grey one." Pippa's dark eyes grew round and earnest. "I

2

saw him myself. Over there, walking on the sky."

She pointed toward the roiling storm clouds and the grey tower that rose a full four stories out of the seaward wall. It was the highest point in all of Faulkhurst, overwhelming the stocky keep and the tiny, deserted, tumbled-down village and the seaswept cliffs beyond.

A tower wheeling with gulls. "Sweet love, did your ghost by any chance have wings?"

Pippa shook her head gravely, casting Eleanor a glance that belied her six years. "It's not a bird, Nellamore. A spirit. Like my papa's and my mama's, too."

God rest them both, whoever they might have been.

"If it is a ghost, Pippa, we'll put him to work fixing the roof of the bakehouse first thing in the morning."

"He'll like that, he will."

"As for now, 'tis high time we made ourselves at home."

Dickon let free a battle cry and then took off toward the keep with Lisabet fast on his heels.

But for all their eagerness, Eleanor found them waiting for her and Pippa just inside the dim portico, staring into the bleak vastness of the great hall.

"Do you smell it, Lady Eleanor?" Lisabet

captured Eleanor's hand and held it tightly, trembling. "A hospital."

Unmistakably. That cold, lonely smell of suffering and sorrow: the aromatic pinch of charred juniper and thyme—futile remedies against the pestilence. Too familiar and terrifying.

"Aye, it must have been, Lisabet. Once."

Where were you then, husband, when your people were perishing in their agonies? Hiding in your fortress across the sea?

But William Bayard kept silent, as always: her blackhearted, proxy-wed, sight-unseen husband, who'd at least had the good timing to die of his sins—or of the plague itself—before she'd had to meet him face-to-face.

Before their marriage could begin in truth.

"I'm hungry." Dickon's stomach howled, and Pippa giggled.

"So's the squirrel in your tummy, Dickon."

"I hope it likes dandelion pottage," Eleanor said, sweeping them all into the hall. "Lisabet, Dickon, we need firewood. A bonfire's worth, to light the night and tell all the ghosts that we are here."

A full pantry in the kitchen, or even a small chest of grain, proved too much to ask from the departed Lord of Faulkhurst. Their wilted

4

carrots and dried peas would have to do once again.

But at least they'd be cooked in her very own home tonight—not by the side of the road, or under a bridge.

She and Pippa sang their favorite melodies to keep away the shadows while they assembled the kitchen trestle in front of the hearth in the great hall. They added benches, and then a roaring fire as Lisabet and Dickon rushed in and out with armloads of firewood, and tales of rusted locks.

"Massive ones, my lady, on every door!"

And deserted sheds. "As if the smithy was hammerin' away on a horseshoe one moment and a blink later he was gone."

And sometime during the noisy chaos of settling into their new home, Pippa disappeared.

"She's vanished, my lady!" Lisabet's eyes spilled over with tears.

"Just like the blacksmith an' the wainwright." Dickon's face was pale.

"She can't have gone far." *Please, God.* Eleanor's heart failed every other beat and thudded loudly against her ears. "She was here talking about that grey ghost of hers. I only turned my back, and—"

The ghost.

They'd been nearly a year together, the four of them, abiding Pippa's fearless adventuring.

"The tower," Eleanor said in relief as she grabbed her cloak and bolted toward the door. "You two stay here in case she comes back."

Trying not to panic, she dashed up the shadowy incline of the inner ward toward the tower, then through the labyrinth of deserted buildings.

Around every corner was another disturbing vignette, as though ordinary castle life had been tragically interrupted in the midst of a workday. Carts littered the bailey, burdened with kindling and wool sacks left to stand out in the fierce weather. The farrier's apron danced at the end of its ties in the ceaseless wind, and a picket of lances waited for war, their blades rusted beyond use. A cookpot, yearning to be warmed over a bed of glowing hot embers; a saw craving the sweet taste of pine—all of the parts and pieces waiting for life to come again.

Perhaps Pippa was right: there were ghosts at Faulkhurst, her husband's among them. Though he had died on one of his estates in far-off Calais, he seemed close by, as though he watched and waited, too. But then, some spirits had more reason to be restless than others.

And needed evicting if they didn't behave.

Eleanor ran up the tower steps. The fist-thick, ironbound door was open just wide enough for a determined little girl to slip through.

"Pippa?" She shouldered the door a half foot wider and entered an octagonal room, utterly dark but for the pale light slicing through the arrow slits.

The perfect place for Pippa to go looking for her ghost.

"Pippa?" she called again, but only the wind replied, sighing far up inside the tower, beyond the spiral-stacked shadows of the wooden staircase that drilled its way through the center to another floor two stories above.

She hurried up past the first landing and then the next toward the open doorway above, a pale rectangle of grey.

And Pippa standing just inside, bathed in sunset-tinted amber, staring up in open-mouthed, wide-eyed wonder at something across the room that Eleanor couldn't yet see.

All this intrigue for a roosting gull.

"I found him, Nellamore." A ragged whisper, gentled by awe. "I found our grey ghost."

"Oh, Pippa—" Breathless with relief, Eleanor climbed the rest of the stairs to the landing and entered the room.

7

But as the shadows shifted, an enormous shape moved against the high, half-shuttered windows—a looming barrier of darkness that dwarfed Pippa and the arching hearth and everything else in the cold room.

Her heart stopped and went icy with dread and the rawboned scent of bleakness.

Ghost or ghoul or nightmare, the monster was peering down at Pippa, poised to strike, held at bay by the child's simple curiosity, which had obviously disturbed its sorcery.

Terrified that she'd come a moment too late, that Pippa would be gone in the next breath, Eleanor whispered, "Pippa, come here!"

The dark eyes that found Eleanor were terrible, forbidding. Her heart started with a cold thump, then drummed madly as he stared down at her from the advantage of his great height.

"Do you see him, Nellamore?"

"Oh, yes, Pippa. I see him." *I feel him.* In her bones and in her breast, in the dizzying lightness that whirled and eddied in her stomach. A rogue breeze lifted her hair, sending a chill from her nape to her toes.

He was death poised on the edge of midnight, arrested on the wing. The beast turned toward her fully, his shoulders as broad as the rafters, his great wings furled but ready to envelop them both if she didn't shake free of the spell he'd cast.

"Come here, sweet." Keeping her eyes trained on the beast, prepared to throw herself in his path if he took a single step toward Pippa, Eleanor reached out her hand and inched toward the child.

But Pippa was utterly transfixed, studying the beast as though he were a fox cub she'd come across in the forest.

"He came out of the wall, Nellamore. I saw him."

Those fathomless, unreadable eyes shifted their darkness to Pippa's eagerness and then sharply back again to Eleanor, as though he didn't trust her.

Dear God, he was huge and feral, and there was so dreadfully little room to maneuver Pippa to the stairway behind her.

"Reach for me, sweet. Take my hand."

"My papa is a ghost too, isn't he, Nellamore?"

"Please, Pippa! My hand." Her fingers trembled uncontrollably.

But Pippa took another inquisitive step toward the silent, seething intruder, and said, "Are *you* my papa's ghost?"

"Leave here." It was a voice grown dark and deep with disuse, an untamed resonance that paralyzed Eleanor's breathing and made her want to weep. The boards moaned beneath her feet, a mournful sound that made the room seem to tilt. The meager light from the tall windows went away completely as he straightened to strike.

"Come away, Pippa! Please!"

A thunderous bellow roared out of him, rattling the shutters, scattering her strategies into motes. "What are you doing in my castle?"

"*Your* castle?" Oh, wonderful day! A madman holed up in her turret. She had an insane, terrifying thought: that the castle was deserted because he'd *eaten* everyone, chewed them up with those gleaming white teeth.

"Be gone from here, woman. *Now!*"

Knowing better than to stand in a tiny room and debate the ownership of Faulkhurst with a lunatic three times her size, especially one who was bearing down on her, Eleanor grabbed up Pippa and raced down the spiraling steps.

"Hold tightly to me, Pippa!"

But the girl was straining back over Eleanor's shoulder, waving and squirming, throwing her off-balance. "Good-bye, grey ghost. Come see us tomorrow!"

"Pippa, please!" Eleanor heard a swooping sound—which might have been her cowardly stomach—felt her hair swirling upward in a sulfurous breeze, the stairs lurching behind her.

They would never make it to the room below, let alone to the bailey. Sweet Pippa would be ripped from her, and both of them would be broken to bits, their brittle bones cast into the sea. And then brave Dickon's and dear Lisabet's, leaving the beast to lie in wait for his next unwitting victims.

And William Bayard would have won at last.

Not while I have a breath or a bone left in my body! With no other course but to sacrifice herself to the monster's mad chase, she stopped short and sent Pippa scampering down the turn of the stairs.

"Run Pippa! To Dickon." *I love you dearly!*

"I'll bring Lisabet, too!"

"Noooo! Don't—"

But Pippa was safely out the door, and the monster was on Eleanor in the next breath, clamping his ironbound arm around her waist, lifting her backward against his massive chest as though she were a rag poppet, squishing the air from her lungs and the mettle right out of her heart.

His threat seared itself against her nape. "I

11

give you one fair and final warning to leave here as you came, madam."

Steamy heat poured off him, melting swiftly through her cloak and her woollen kirtle, surrounding her like a chastening flush; he smelled of a sea-misted sunset and the powdery grit of stone.

Though her teeth chattered and her breath came in ragged gasps, she was suddenly, blazingly furious at the man: for threatening Pippa, for his savagery, for thinking himself master over her castle and all her hard-fought dreams.

"I don't need your warning, fair or otherwise. I am—Sir!"

She was suddenly in the air, and then she was standing on the floor below, free of his manhandling. He leveled that demon-dark stare down on her again in his doomed campaign to terrorize her into leaving.

"Do you know, madam, what I do to thieves and intruders who disturb me?"

Her wanton, runaway imagination ambushed her with thoughts of his curling smoke and his battle-bronzed hands, of his insolent heat and artful terrors that had her grasping for her wits.

"For the last time, sir, I am not a—"

"Thief, madam?" He made a satisfied rumble in his throat, pleased with his own judgment. "Ah, but you are."

"I'm not—"

His laughter stopped her denial, as cold as the stone that braced against her back. His eyes never left hers for a moment of peace, hungry for something she couldn't give him, growing darker still until she saw hot fires flickering there. "In truth, madam, I roast thieves, and then . . . I eat them."

"Do you?" An absurd question, but her knees had turned to custard, her lips to sun-warmed honey, because he was carefully charting them with his eyes.

"Aye, madam thief, then I toss their scrawny bones over the seawall for the crabs to scavenge. Now, leave here."

As though she could, even if she wanted to; he was as close as he could possibly be. The nostrils of his long nose flared, no doubt sniffing out his supper. Next he'd be weighing her for roasting time.

"I'm not a thief, sir. I am—"

"Trespassing." He rolled the word around in his throat, letting it hiss against her ear, a sound that tumbled along every nerve and lighted startling little fires and improbable expectations.

"No." He was too close. "I'm not!" Too

astounding. " 'Tis *you* who are trespassing."

He lifted the corner of his darkly mous-tached upper lip in a mockery of a smile, and seemed to grow larger.

"In case you misunderstood me, madam—" his breath was soft against her cheek, laced with a deceiving sort of spice; bayberry or ju-niper, as though he'd been prowling an exotic forest, sampling sunlight by the handfuls "—you have as long as it takes you and your child to walk across the bailey and through the gate to be gone from my sight."

He waved a dismissive hand toward the door, turned his broad back and started up the stairs with his weighty tread, having exiled her, having gotten the very wrong idea that she would give up her home—the only place she had in the world—without a fight to the death.

"I will not be gone today, sir, or any other day. I have legal claim to this castle by right of marriage. I am Eleanor Bayard, wife and widow of the late Lord of Faulkhurst. And make no mistake, sir, from this moment on, *you* are here at *my* leave!"

It was as though all the world stopped as he did—the clouds and the gulls and her heart as well, the sun and the moon, all of them spellbound as the man turned slowly and stared down at her darkly.

"What did you say?" She had expected another resonant roar, would have preferred that to the piercing sharpness of his whisper that stole the lightness out of the air.

"I said, sir, that you ... That I am Lady—" She swallowed, her throat as dry as a handful of autumn leaves. She hardly looked the part of a lady at the moment, and hadn't for the better part of the past two years. Her kirtle was homespun russet and hanging loose, her cloak only a woollen blanket fastened by a bit of stick through a convenient hole; her feet clad in boots that Dickon had found on a cobbler's table in an abandoned village.

But blast it all, he had no choice but to believe her, *and* to obey her orders. She squared up her pride, shoved her fears behind her courage and leveled her best glare at those censuring eyes.

"I am the widow of William Bayard, the Lord of Faulkhurst." Feeling bolder because he still hadn't moved—though one should never fully trust a mountainside of solid rock—she took three unsteady steps up the staircase toward him, clutching the railing.

"This is *my* castle to command. Not yours. It never has been, even if you found it abandoned, or if you stayed behind when everyone else left. I intend to rebuild Faulkhurst, to make it a far better place than it ever was under my husband's indifferent care. That being the case, sir, you will do as *I* bid from now on—should I decide to allow *you* to stay."

There.

And yet he remained still—a stone gargoyle, perched precariously in that edgeless space between the air and the solid earth, between heaven and hell. They were mythical, menacing creatures, transfixed in their motion, kinetic carvings of sinew and claw imprisoned for eternity in limestone.

She'd studied many from the ground, her neck craned and aching as it was now, imagining that one of the creatures might spring down upon her if she stared too long, if she caught its unseeing gaze. But this one had eyes of living embers; had thick, seething muscles that were even now shifting dangerously beneath his woollen cloak.

He was on her in the next breath, pinning her arms behind her with his great, hot hands wrapped round the railing, bending her backward so that her entire world became nothing but him and the raging flight of her heart against her chest, close enough for her to see the tiny flecks of grey in his eyes.

"Again," he said, surrounding her with his heated scent of fresh-hewn oak and seafoam.

"Again, *what*?"

Don't come now, Pippa. Stay away.

He snapped off a growl, then bellowed, "Your *name*, madam."

It took her two tries to find enough air, and then only enough to whisper. "Eleanor."

"Eleanor—" he said instantly, taking in her name with a gasp, tasting the sound of it on his tongue. Then he said again, slower this time, "Eleanor," with such care, such profound desolation, that it made her ache inside, made her stomach flip and her heart fall wide open when she ought to be wary of him.

"Aye, sir. Eleanor." She would have reached up and brushed that wind-whipped, darkly falling hair off his brow if he hadn't still had her hands pinned safely behind her, where they couldn't betray her. "I am the late lord's—"

"Christ—" He made a horrible snarling noise, full of anguish, then lifted her, grabbing up her kirtle and cloak, and flew with her up two flights of stairs, out the door to the wall-walk, and into the piercing gold of a sun that had won a last squint between the lowering clouds and the sea.

"I am your lady, sir! Put me down!" She felt

17

like an ungainly bird who'd forgotten how to fly. Her skirts tangled in his cloak as he wedged her against the breast wall overhanging the seacliffs, where the waves looked small and far, far away, the rocks huge and sharp and clamoring for her bones.

"Proof, madam," he said, roughly grazing her hair off her face with both hands, then tilting her chin to him with his thumbs, as though he would lean down and kiss her with that very hard-sculpted mouth.

"Proof of what?" Her heart battered her rib cage, out of control with fear and some unnameable fluttering low in her belly. She could see him better now, the raven black of his hair striped copper by the sun, cut roughly to his shoulders and slashed by the wind; a weeks-old beard, black as the night and shimmering. Eyes of deepest indigo now focused, in all their madness, on *her*.

"Proof that you are Bayard's wife."

A long shudder rolled down her spine, a deep and dark knowing that lodged in the pit of her stomach. Something of the raw earth connected her to this man, something anchored them both to the bedrock, to each other, forever more.

"I'm Bayard's *widow*: he's long ago dead of the plague. Though I don't have to prove anything at all to you." She struggled to free herself, but he held her fast with his grip around her upper arms. His hips pressed her thighs against the stone, a molten and unyielding trap that made her look up into his harshly angular face, into all that intensity.

"Married where?"

Dammit all, she didn't want to recall that ignominious event. Her father, Bayard's lecherous ambassador, and a leering, tippling priest—what a mockery of wedded bliss that had been. "You will let me go. I am the lady here and you are—"

"Where?" His breath mixed with hers and the mist from the storm-driven waves, and made her struggle harder to be away from him.

"I was married at my father's manor, damn you. At Glenstow." As though her answer could mean anything to the brute whose eyes reflected the devilish orange of the sunset. "In Cornwall. How many more details do you need? The rain was falling in cold sheets. I wore a green worsted kirtle and a hempen snood."

His voice tumbled low right through her, a leveled threat. "When?"

"Two and a half years ago. On the eve of St. Cecilia." A wicked night, much like this had become. "I was married by proxy, sir. To a scroll of unyielding vellum and a pot of indigo ink."

The man's eyes darkened to raven and the wind whipped harder at his hair, at his shoulders. He bent to her as though he would share a secret just between the two of them, out here at the tattered edges of the world.

Nay, madam. Not to vellum and ink.

You were married . . . to me.

Chapter 2

William Nicholas Bayard stuffed his dark confession back inside his chest like the malediction it would become if he let it loose between them.

Wife? Impossible. She could *not* be alive. Eleanor Bayard was safely dead of the plague, along with the rest of her bloody family. They'd told him so. Someone had—a hundred years back, when the world had been growing dark and indistinct. When things mattered.

Yet here she was with her proof: this ghostly wife who smelled of bread and nutmeg and bedstraw, of sultry kitchens and the murmur of the living, the exquisiteness of her scent caught up inside the folds of his cloak, in his hair, and on the riffling wind.

"Have I convinced you, sir?"

That I have gone utterly mad? Oh, yes, madam, you have.

Though he had expected the madness of hellhounds and slathering demons to beset him in these last days of freedom in the carnal world, a plague of doubts and a parade of soul-tempting delights.

How the hell was he to know that those temptations would come for him all at once in the guise of a wife, one so very breathtaking in her rumpled rags and her outrage?

She was looking up at him without a hint of her earlier fear, waiting for him to answer; her new-fawn eyes softly unflinching, her wildly red hair whipping at the edges of her hairline and streaming out in the sea wind to snag the fading light of the day.

She was magnificent.

And mine.

Buttermilk skin and keen-edged tenacity. The very sort of perfection gleaned from his dreams, by an omniscient and highly skilled God who faithfully practiced his art of conspicuous damnation.

The God who knew the best way to break him, one blow, one unbearable loss at a time.

Why not this one, too?

A blackened soul, a shattered estate, a dead son. And now a dazzlingly, home-scented wife returned from the grave.

"Christ, woman, why did you come?"

Yet he already knew the answer: *to bedevil you, husband; to call up your shame and revel in it—to make you pay for your blasphemies in the only coin you understand.*

"I came, sir, because Faulkhurst is my home now—my widow's dower, granted to me by King Edward only last month. So, you will unhand me."

Or bed you, wife, as is my right.

And his desire, to bend and taste the pale damson of her ripe mouth.

Aye, to take her here at long last, on the crumbling ramparts of his castle, where the wind tugged as madly at her skirts as he would do in his revel between her pale, precious thighs. As he might have done in those long, dissolute ages past, the vile creature he used to be—would always be, in the depths of his heart.

In the eyes of God.

Aye, she was that kind of a temptation. The sort he ought to let go before he lost control completely. She was eddies of warmth curling round him, tempting him to call her wife, when he could not.

For he had other, weightier debts to pay.

"I don't know or care who you are, sir. Faulkhurst may look abandoned and available to the first vagabond who ventures past and takes a fancy to it, but it's not. It's mine. I mean to sow the fields and graze sheep on the hills. And dig the village out of the ashes."

Do you, wife? That single word—*wife*—taunted him to speak it rashly and close by her soft ear. If he did, he would be husband and lord then, alive once more.

William Nicholas Bayard risen from the dead. No. That was no longer possible. He was beyond that now, beyond caring, already condemned and buried deeply in his self-imposed penance, sworn everlastingly to a solitary life with no provisions for wives or titles or estates.

Less than a month from now, he would enter the cloisters of St. Jerome, and be quietly done with the world.

Certainly done with this wife.

"Be gone, madam." Still, it hurt to whisper the words; it left him more hollow than he'd ever known. He shifted his shoulder aside and she swiftly shoved away from him in her escape, running along the curtain wall, her ragged skirts flying out behind her, leaving all that heady fragrance to tug at him.

From the tower passage she spared him a glowering glance, with a relentless finger leveled at him. "Mind your ways and your temper in my home and among my household, sir, else you'll find your*self* outside the gate come morning."

Then she disappeared into the darkness, as though she had never been.

Her *home?* She still misunderstood him completely, this wayward wife of his. He could not possibly let her stay here, no matter how loudly she made her claim, or however royally it had been decreed.

Faulkhurst would beat her down, would smother her in its corruption, if it didn't crush her first beneath its precarious arches. He hadn't room for the weight of her life on his soul if she died here of his negligence—not with all the other lives settled there like lead. He would be rid of her tonight, if she weren't already running toward the gate with the child, and the others she mentioned. He'd fill her fool head with fiery visions of hell and send her on her way before she could settle in.

And should she refuse to leave, he would tell her . . . what? That *he* was William Nicholas Bayard, and very much alive?

Christ in heaven—there was his towering dilemma, the teetering balance between this life and the next. He couldn't banish her with the power of the truth. Not without ungodly consequences to her, and to his monkish vows. His soul was already pledged.

To exert his lordship over Faulkhurst, over this untimely wife of his, would mean a stark confession of everything, would mean that she would learn of the sins and the heathen soul of Nicholas Bayard. His past, his present, and the unalterable fact that he had no future at all.

And what then? She had that innocently meddling look about her; a conquering angel who would steadfastly stay if she knew the truth of him. Who would demand a merciful household, chests of sun-washed linen, spice merchants, holy days, and children.

Sons.

If she knew.

He drew a careful breath, guarding against the grip of his heart around his throat, against the sting of the salt-thick wind behind his eyes.

And the memories. He wanted nothing to do with them.

He went to the curtain wall and watched her cross the shadowy inner ward, darting inexorably between the taunting ghosts and rotting carts. Though he willed her and her defiance toward the gates that would speed her away from this place of desolation, she went deeper and deeper into the castle until she was only another insolent phantom, dashing up the

26

steps of the keep and disappearing into the great hall.

My *great hall*, *wife*. Where the windows glowed with a pale tinge of orange, where a thin spiral of smoke slipped from the chimney into the unwary stillness before the storm blew in off the sea.

He had been well warned of her coming to the cliff tower; had tasted her delicate fragrance as it climbed the stairs ahead of her, slipping unseen past the little pale-haired ghost to wreathe the rafters and cloud his senses. He should have lashed out immediately and sent them both scurrying away in terror.

But he'd lived so long without feeling the tread of another across the floor, so long without the melody of another voice in the room with him, that a drunkenness had settled into his marrow, had warmed and slowed him, had stopped him entirely.

And made him listen for too long to the heady whisperings.

Reach for me. Take my hand.

He'd thought she'd been talking to him.

Nellamore. Such a little voice. His hand ached to be filled again, for that gentle tugging.

Jackstraws, Papa? Oh, please!

A raging sorrow wrung his gut raw. The ache, the monumental loss was still larger than his chest; it pressed at his ribs, sizzled against his eyes, and thawed out in that single moment of confusion, in the blinding glare of the woman's impossible announcement.

I am Eleanor Bayard.

Wife.

And in that clever guise, she was an ordeal designed for him alone. An immutable lesson to those who ignored a vengeful Heaven, to those whose sins were legion, the stuff of living legends. Whose redemption had come too late.

Much too late to appease an exacting God.

And in the end, far too late to save his own son.

I love you, Papa.

Nicholos swallowed back the harrowing sob and sought the soothing coldness again, conjuring it out of discipline, stuffing brittle fistfuls of it back into his chest, where its comfortable chill settled again into his bones, back where it belonged.

She had been wholly right on one count: William Nicholas Bayard was dead, had been for a very long time. A surprise to the deceased, but not wholly unexpected and hardly mourned—by anyone, it seemed. The king

28

had decreed it, had declared his wife to be legally widowed, his estate forfeit to her, to her grandiose plans to graze sheep and restore a tiny village that God's anger had shaken to its foundation.

The rotting fields, the village and the ashes, the false promises, fallen skies, deserted streets, the pounding seas, the tyrannical shadows.

The graves and the staggering sorrow.

Well then, Madam, take Faulkhurst exactly as you found it.

All of it gladly hers, for he would be gone from here someday soon. He remained only to finish the chapel roof.

And the boy's grave marker.

Then he would keep the last of his pledge: to take his vows of penance and poverty, and be done with the world.

Though he shouldn't care what became of the woman, he made his way along the cold passages of the undercrofts, past doors that he'd locked for good, past barricades of tumbled archways, and up a set of hidden stairs into the murky shadows of the gallery in the great hall.

Allying his own darkness with that of the moonless night, he became a part of the stonework colonnade that overhung the darkly vaulted hall. A single torch flame wobbled against the blackened stone wall opposite, battered by the age-old breeze that seemed to come from inside the earth itself.

He hadn't been inside the great hall for a year, since he'd scrubbed it clean of the pestilence and closed it up. He'd thought he had evicted all the ghosts that day. But they had returned, alive in the clatter of pots and spoons and the dancing disorder of footfalls.

"But, my lady, please—"

"I do understand that you are worried, Dickon. But you needn't be." It was his wife's voice, a silken sensibility that took hold of his chest and tugged at him.

"If he touched you or Pippa, I'll—"

"He didn't."

He'd done far more than touch her yet she was defending him?

"And I've taken care of the problem," Eleanor finished.

"You killed him?" The young man's voice cracked with newness and his callow admiration.

"Not even close, Dickon." She laughed, a smoky, sinuous sound that inched him closer to the railing, toward her gentle reassurance. Just enough to see her this one last time—so that he could remember. "Murder was my late

30

husband's way, not mine. I merely put him in his place."

Ah, she would have been the tussling sort of wife, opinionated and unflinching in every part of her life.

"Bravo, my lady!" A fist thumped down on a table—the boy's, no doubt, as his voice slid back to its rocky depths and stayed. "But still, he threatened you, this ghost. I'll run him through the next time I see him."

"You won't, Dickon. And I tell you again that he isn't a ghost, any more than I am." She laughed again. "More like a gargoyle—"

Gargoyle, indeed!

"Truly, my lady? Like that huge, snarling gargoyle we saw hanging over the lady chapel at St. Oswald out Ramsay way? Remember that, Lisabet? Hideous, he was."

Hideous?

"Oooo! I do remember, Dickon," the young girl said with a trill of laughter. "I'll bet this one bays at the moon."

Bloody hell. He'd never bayed at anything in his life.

He could see them fully now, hovering with their opinions at his wife's elbow while she chopped a pile of greens: the girl-child, the older girl, shaking out a blanket with her whole reed-thin body, and a young man, bear-like and tall in his unchained prowling.

Surely there were others, if she meant to mount a full-scale invasion against him: hired thuglings who were even now skulking round his castle, rattling his bolts and bars, finding the doors locked tightly against their larceny.

Not that it mattered what the devil they found or stole. Let her have the place and all its peril. She would soon enough find the land barren and impossible, and then she would leave on her own, to apportion her fancies elsewhere.

"Enough speculation, Dickon, and you, too, Lisabet. He's neither ghost nor gargoyle; just a man. He was, in fact, plainly...." The woman paused and tilted her head, tapped the arching heart of her lips with a finger that must have smelled of the fresh dandelion she'd just dropped into the kettle, deciding upon just the proper word for their inauspicious first meeting—wife to gargoyle, husband to comely thief.

He waited, unbreathing, to hear the candid truth of himself as seen through the discerning eyes of his wife.

"Plainly...."

Forbidding, she would say of him. And barbaric.

"—lost."

Lost? *Lost!* Bloody hell, *she* was the one who'd stumbled into his castle, assuming him dead, who'd nested herself in the middle of his great hall, commandeering *his* kettles, *his* well water, burning kindling from his stores as though he were running a wayfarer's inn.

Damnation!

"His name is Graystone, Nellamore."

Graystone?

The woman seemed as surprised as he. She turned from hooking the kettle handle on the hob and knelt in front of the little ghost child, who sat cross-legged on the tabletop, walking a straw poppet around a landscape of chunked onions and assorted greenery.

"What did you call him, Pippa?"

"Graystone."

"Is that his name, sweet?" His wife shared a bemused smile with the others, tucked some of that curling gold behind the child's ear. "Did he tell you his name before I found you in the tower?"

He hadn't said a bloody word to the child.

"No, Nellamore." The little girl captured his wife's chin between her small hands. "But he needs a name, don't you think?"

His wife pressed a smiling kiss on the girl's nose. "I do, Pippa. Graystone's a fine name.

We'll call him that until we know the truth of him."

That can never be, madam.

Even as he loosed the thought, she stood and raised her eyes to the gallery. Cinnamon and red clover. The clear force of it hit him straight on, splintered through his chest like rays of summer sunlight.

He stood in the utter darkness, unmoving, inhaling her scent even from there, feeling her hair as it swept across his face in the wind and through his fingers, her heat still caught up in the wool of his chanson, in his chest and at his groin, where her lithe hips had so softly opposed his as he held her trapped on the battlements. He'd only vaguely noticed the fine shape of her at the time, the sleekness of her thighs against his, her belly, the smoothness of her cheek, the stubborn line of her jaw in the bowl of his hands.

So abundantly alive, and so late in coming.

He stilled his ragged breathing, ignored the delinquent racing of his pulse at the memory of her searing softness, denied the head-spinning scent of her, and that utterly unanswerable quickening in his groin for this bountifully beautiful wife—whom he could never touch or taste or embrace because of the promises he'd made in his son's name. He dropped more deeply into shadows.

But she knew, this prying wife of his. Or thought she knew. Suspicion and that deft self-possession raised her chin higher and brightened the flush across her brow, her mouth contracting impatiently into a glistening, unfurled, untasted rose.

Then she looked away from him, and the gallery grew chilled, emptied of the light.

"We've plenty of work to keep us busy toward the harvest, Dickon. We'll take stock of the castle stores in the morning, room by room, from undercroft to attic. Then we'll go to work on the keep to make it livable enough, and then the bailey, and the village."

An endless inventory of pointless labors: scrubbing, sweeping, laying cobbles, thatching roofs, restoring stone walls. The woman must have brought along an army of skilled craftsmen: masons, carpenters, a cadre of blacksmiths. Though the devil only knew where she'd encamped them.

They weren't anywhere in the castle. He'd have sensed the altered sounds: a change in the icy whispering of the wind in the corridors as it mourned through the towers: an echo of the living who still haunted him.

Not that it mattered anymore. There was righteousness in that, and relief.

The young girl coughed and then sneezed as she shook out another well-used blanket. "But we're only four of us, my lady. We'll be stretched as thin as a spittle of milk, don't you think?"

A cold, sharp stone dropped into his chest. What madness was this? Just a child, a young girl, a beardless boy, and a lunatic woman with a taste for the impossible?

Hell and damnation.

"We may be only four right now, Lisabet." His guileless wife stuck one of his spoons into one of his kettles and stirred blithely. "But we've got room enough for a whole castleful if they come."

Only four.

Christ—there it was, blinding in its brilliance: his final obligation. A test of his endurance, of his resolve.

There would be no leaving his wife here to find her way alone—to starve, to freeze in the winter in his ruin of a castle. She and her misfit band would perish within the week, and he'd have four more demon souls to battle him on his way into hell.

Damnation. Why did you come, madam? Why now? Another month and he would have been safely gone from here, would never have

36

known that she still lived, or that he was so damnably obligated to her.

But she was as alive as the sun, breathing fire and fury. And that changed everything.

As surely as it changed nothing at all.

Nicholas slipped away from the dancing lights into the familiar closeness of the undercrofts, grateful for the secret dark passages that led from under the castle, up his private staircase, and into the hush of the scaffolded chapel perched on the edge of the sea.

The moon had dodged the storm and shone through the open rafters to shadow the stone floor of the sanctuary with sharp-edged chevrons of pale blue and midnight. Why he'd come here, where the ghosts were so plentiful and his damnation so vivid, he couldn't fathom. Habit, perhaps.

He'd started to rebuild the long-neglected chapel when he'd first returned from the endless bloodletting on endless battlefields. He'd been damned arrogant to have believed he could so easily make amends for the hundreds of churches he'd sacked, for the lives he'd claimed with his insatiable blade.

For that beggarly boy he'd nearly run his sword through in the nave of St. Justin's, when the full meaning of his life had come crashing down on him.

And in the end, for the most selfish motives of all: to finally claim his bastard son and shore up his darkened soul with good works.

But God had devised a more pointed penance for his lifetime of brutal sinning, a retribution that had laid waste to all who'd had the misfortune to come near him, innocents and devils alike. Though he'd tried to protect them with his life, they'd all been struck down—by plague and famine and a sunless winter—until he was left finally, utterly alone.

Until now. Until Eleanor—wild-haired and unbending in her impossible dreams. And he feared her most of all.

Separation was the only way.

And so you are annulled, wife. Dismissed by me, here and now, witnessed by the sea and the hissing rocks. If not in the eyes of the law, then surely in the stark impossibility of a marriage between them. He would see the matter closed in secret: one last indulgence purchased with his plunder. After all, a marriage never begun was no marriage at all. It was—

Impossible.

The sterile coolness of distance had always served him well in the past, had muted the metallic stench of blood on his sword and armor, had deafened him to the shriek of steel through living bone, had allowed him to see past the carnage to the numbness.

Yet that distance had failed him completely when he needed it most of all.

I'm so cold, Papa. Hold me.

He would keep his distance from the lady of the castle. It was for the best. He would set immovable boundaries around their dealings and look upon her merely as another charge against him, a penance to be quickly done with forever.

The Lord of Faulkhurst was no more.

Chapter 3

After dinner, Dickon had stationed himself in the portico with all the pomp and pride of the king's own bodyguard. "Not beast, nor thief, nor anyone else shall pass me and live, my lady."

But he was fortunately fast asleep in his threadbare blanket now, which was far safer than having the quick-tempered lad meet up with the prowling night shadow named Graystone.

Possessive beast! This is my great hall, not yours.

Eleanor had sensed him in the gallery earlier, had felt an unsettling sense of being studied from afar, of her eyelashes ruffled, her nape sniffed and blown hot.

Graystone. Her gargoyle.

Or her husband's wicked, restive ghost.

Trouble in either case—and unfinished business, for no amount of bellowing or chest beating was going to evict her.

Or keep her from her bath.

Though the kitchen was dusty and dark and nearly empty of pots and utensils, it contained one true blessing: a hot spring that bubbled and steamed unchecked through a pipe that jutted out of the wall near the outside door. The water swirled merrily around inside a long limestone trough and then drained out through another pipe into the kitchen garden.

She'd thought of little else through supper: a steaming, skin-pinkening soak and blissfully scented solitude.

When all was finally quiet, with Pippa and Lisabet snoozing on pallets in front of the hearth, Eleanor filled the half barrel in the pantry with water from the spring, barred the door from the inside, then stole a quietly magnificent half hour to wash her hair and soak herself to wrinkles, steaming away the memory of too many baths taken in near-freezing streams, wondering all the while how a gargoyle-infested, tumble-down old castle way out here on a forgotten spit of land had so quickly become a part of her breathing.

"Because it's mine."

There. She'd said it. Felt it all the way through to the marrow, as thickly hot as the

41

lavender-scented steam rising off the water.

"My home. My castle." Where she needn't ask permission of anyone to plant what she pleased in her fields, or to endow a village school for girls and boys, or to one day marry a man she actually liked—

Or loved. Because marriage was a good and holy undertaking, if entered into with an honorable intent—with an honorable man.

Aye, marriage had to be a partnership, a fact she'd never fully realized until a few hours ago on the ramparts, while her gargoyle was testing her, making her defend her marriage to Bayard.

Her marriage, indeed. She hadn't been his partner, by any measure. Neither in sickness, nor in health, nor anytime at all—because he'd never given her the chance. He'd never even come to claim her as any husband would. Hadn't sent for her, or bothered to dispatch a message or an edict, or even a simple query as to her welfare, let alone her dearest wishes. He'd used her—as her father had always done—for his inscrutable purposes, and then he'd set her aside, forgotten her entirely while all hell was breaking loose upon his lands.

While she was turned out of her home and away from the people who needed her most, by her own uncle.

And by a king who made bargains with devils like William Bayard.

Mother Mary, what sort of union it would have been? A wife ought at least to respect her husband, the father of her children. It was difficult to find anything to respect about a man who lived only to loot and plunder and kill.

The misbegotten blackguard.

But here was her chance. She'd show him exactly what sort of life he'd missed out on: a wife with brains enough to resurrect his castle and his village with her bare hands, to plant his fields and cart his goods to market. To swell his stores and defend his house.

And God knows she'd have been an excellent lover to the man, given the chance. A willing one, because she had a wickedly passionate imagination, which had been working just fine in the close presence of her gargoyle—working overtime, in fact. She could smell him still, the heat of him, that electrifying connection.

God only knew what sort of wantonness she'd have heaped upon a husband that she loved.

The poor man.

The ruthless bastard.

She might have lounged in the steaming water until morning, if she didn't have hours of work yet to do. A map to make of the fields, strategies to devise against those who would try to steal Faulkhurst from her because they might think her lacking.

She dried and dressed in her only clean night shift, and stepped from the pantry with her cresset lamp into the pooling dimness of the deserted kitchen.

She was just setting the lamp on the table when a shiver crept across her shoulders and prickled down her chest like fingers. Knowing exactly what—nay, who—she'd find there, she blinked at the shadows directly across the table, though she couldn't quite see him.

Her gargoyle. The shifting, smoke-scented image of him coalesced into dark robes and brooding shoulders. And as he stepped closer, a face that would remain in her dreams forever. His cheeks were cleanly shaved to his moustache and the edge of his jaw, his hair blown wildly and long, making him look larger and more wrathful than ever.

And completely untamable.

"Were you born in shadows, sir, or do you just find them pleasant company?"

The man had a devilish way with his silence, letting it spool out until she thought he hadn't heard, his gaze wavering from hers only to track the length of her gown to her knees, then to linger indulgently at her breasts, at their very tips, until he raised his eyes to her mouth and made her knees weak.

"My name is Nicholas Langridge, madam. Not Graystone." He leaned forward into the lamplight and said, without the slightest hint of deference, "And as of this moment, I am your *steward*."

Chapter 4

The woman laughed merrily. Fearlessly, in fact, leaning against the pantry door, crossing her arms perilously beneath her breasts, uplifting them to him, like a gift of sweetly warm, just-risen bread.

"After all you said to me, Master Nicholas? I'd sooner trust a starving wolf at a lambing than trust you as my steward."

Trust? Bloody hell, he'd just granted her full reign over his entire estate, from cellar to roof. She could hardly ask for more than that.

Yet here she was in her insolence, standing unabashedly barefooted, with her coppery hair still damply curling from the bath she'd just taken in *his* pantry.

The soft flame of her cresset lamp lit that lovely face and the sultry length of her, sporting all kinds of curves and shadings that he could see through her night shift—a thready

linen thing that was too big for her and had
seen too many bouts with the laundress.

And *she* couldn't trust *him*?

A woman of great wisdom, for this was
monumental restraint on his part. 'Twould be
the simplest thing he'd ever done to banish his
good intentions and let his hands wander
where they might, to let his mouth take hers
and find her hidden softness.

And why not? He was already damned to
the hellfires of eternity; he might as well just
confess all and let their doomed marriage begin here.

For he wanted her deeply, wanted to claim
her fully, selfishly, and damn the consequences. He'd thought of little else since she'd
come.

*You are my wife. Whether you like it or not,
madam.*

His chest ached like fire from not breathing;
his too-long-celibate tarse throbbed as it hadn't
in years, standing in full and rigid agreement
that his wife was the most magnificently pro-
vocative woman that God had ever created.

She would be the rarest of heavens to hold,
to kiss, to lose himself inside.

But at this moment she was glaring daggers
at him in this cramped, lavender-scented
kitchen, bristling with her innocent pride, her

pointedly accurate opinions of him.

It was on his tongue to tell her everything, to take back what was and had always been his. But she was purity of the flesh—his eternal torment. He would only sully her if he dared touch her. He couldn't. Not ever. He could only hope to save her—from herself and from him.

She needed a steward, a keeper—not a husband. At least not this one.

So he damped his anger and his untoward lust for his wife's soft and sultry places and said, *damned* pleasantly, "Whether you trust me or not, madam, you'll have me as your steward."

"Why?"

"Why?" He'd spat the word, and realized his error when she set her chin firmly and narrowed her eyes at him. He'd never had the patience for negotiation, hated sitting out a siege on his backside while stubborn, otherwise prudent citizens patiently starved to death. But he said evenly, "It should be clear to you, Lady Eleanor, that you need a steward to save you from your own follies."

"My follies?" She snorted through a sumptuously smug grin and went to a plate chest near the pantry door, then lifted the slope-lidded box sitting on top. "And you believe that *your* particular stewardship is just what I need."

His jaw ached from holding in the bellow that thundered around inside his chest. "I am your only chance in the world if you mean to survive the week, let alone prosper here."

She studied him with a good deal of heat. "Not a half dozen hours ago you were threatening to roast and eat me if I didn't leave. Now you're offering your assistance? Hardly the sort of behavior I should trust in a steward. The moment I step out of the castle, you'll shut the gate on me."

He couldn't now if he tried. Though he could lean down a few inches and taste her mouth. "Madam, I didn't realize who you were at the time."

That made her laugh, bringing a pair of dimples to her cheeks. "Well, Master Nicholas, that soothes me tremendously. Because when you finally *did* realize that I was Lady Eleanor, you dangled me over a cliff and threatened to feed my bones to the crabs. How am I to reconcile your helpful intentions with your deeds?"

"You were nowhere near the cliffs, madam. And never at risk from me. Nor will you ever be." He'd never in his life harmed a woman. Condemn him for greed and vengeance and blasphemy, but never for that sin. "Instead of

49

doubting my intentions, you'd best heed my warnings."

"And cede my castle to you?"

"I don't want your castle."

"But you want to be my steward?"

"Yes." He was failing miserably here—because she made no bloody sense. It wasn't like talking to a man in the same position. He'd have simply run the bastard through with his sword and sent his head back to his family in a wooden coffer. Faulkhurst was *his*, by God. As it would remain, until he left it legally behind. But he could hardly wrestle her to the ground to gain his title. He yanked the bench out from beneath the trestle table and stomped his booted foot down on the seat.

Yes. Casual. Pleasant.

"What did this cataclysm of a castle cost you?" He'd been sharper than he'd meant to be, caused her to narrow those light brown eyes and sniff at him.

"Only my pride and my dignity. Beyond that, Faulkhurst cost me nothing at all. It had belonged to my husband before he died."

Her pride? This suddenly stank of Edward Plantagenet.

"Your husband must have had other estates than this—ones in far better shape than Faulkhurst." The woman was indisputably discriminating, not in the least stupid or acquiescent, and he had plenty of more profitable manors, other castles, that she could have chosen instead of this one. He'd purposely neglected his estate in the last year, not caring what Edward did with it—not until now.

"Faulkhurst suited me perfectly." She unlatched the lid of the small box. Writing works, all tumbled together from her travels. "King Edward granted it to me quite happily."

"I'll wager he did. It cost him little enough: a broken fortress, an uninhabitable village, the fields grown wild. You haven't even a chicken to lay you an egg, or a cow to milk. Did this generous-hearted king grant you a household staff that hasn't arrived yet?"

She ignored him, though her brow flushed as she dug around in the box.

Nicholas rounded the corner of the table. "You have no livestock, no game. Have you masons to rebuild the bakehouse?" A step closer gained him a distracting view of the lamplight threading its fire through the silky strands of her hair, and the altogether disastrous need to bring an overflowing handful of it to his nose and sniff there while she still rummaged. "Carpenters? A brewer?"

"You know that I haven't. Nor have I a blacksmith, or plow horse, or baker. But I do pray for them, regularly." She stopped and clapped her hands together firmly, then squeezed her eyes shut. "Please God, send me a baker—and if you don't mind, I'd prefer that he be riding a horse for plowing."

Her eyes were bright when they found his again, her cheeks tinted rose. "As simple as that, sir—they will find us. It takes a bit of faith. I'm sorry if you can't see it."

But he could, and felt quite suddenly and fiercely embraced in her imaginings, against his better judgment and all possible logic. He couldn't let that happen, any more than he could allow himself to revel in the scent of her, in the pounding of his heart. She needed to see the danger in her situation, and he needed to practice his distance.

"So, madam, in lieu of a skilled household and suitable allotment of chattels, the king granted you vast sums of money to aid in the rebuilding."

Her jaw tightened before she turned sharply from him, sat down on the bench, and went to work trimming a quill nib.

"King Edward did apologize to me—repeatedly, almost charmingly in fact—but he had nothing to give of his treasury. And my husband's was empty by the time it came to me."

"It bloody well was—" *not*, he'd nearly said. The Bayard holdings included three enviable titles, four rich, black-bottomed estates in Brittany and two others in England, which by rights ought to have been completely uncontested in his premature death. They should have gone directly to his widow. But Edward and his thieving barons had passed off this wreck of a castle to his wife without a sou, and expected her to survive the winter.

Blackguards. Aye, here was his penance: to instruct and protect her, no matter the cost to his own causes or his pride.

"It bloody well was what, sir?" She was blinking at him, waiting for him to finish his outburst.

"You were cozened, madam." He straddled the bench, rocking it as he sat down beside her, leaned over her shoulder, and came up sharply against her deeply pouting frown, those engulfing eyes, the delicious scent of her recent bath. Lavender, liltingly sweet.

That quickly, he was fully roused again, his pulse thrumming hard enough to be heard by her.

"Cozened of what?"

His mouth went dry, his brain dull-edged. He'd made a grand mistake, sitting so close to her in the way of his old, libertine habits: one

thigh aligned against hers, the other across her
backside, there to keep her in place. But she
wasn't a tavern wench or a coy-eyed milk-
maid—and he was a monk-to-be.

And just now he was noticing spriggy curls
at her temple, her honey-golden skin, and a
light spray of freckles that wandered off between her breasts to some exotically scented
land. Of sandalwood and ginger.

He came off the bench like the seat was afire
and strode toward the garden door, hoping
she couldn't identify a man in rut, for he was
fully charged.

And she bloody well shouldn't know of
such things—she was a virgin.

His virgin at the moment. No other man's.

"You were cozened of a fortune, madam,"
he bellowed, unreasoningly jealous of some
future husband who would know her secret
places, her sated sighs, as he never would.
"Cheated of a decent home, at the least. William Bayard was a wealthy man."

"How do you know this?" She turned fully
on the bench to scan the length of him, suddenly very interested, it seemed. Then she
cocked her head. "Did you know him? My
husband?" The quiet, painfully naked question made her sound suddenly vulnerable.

Christ, what to do now? This was an opportunity for the truth to trip him up. A test.

"I knew him somewhat." Faithless warrior, then a joyously reformed heretic. A father too late. An unredeemable sinner. And now an unsuitable husband.

Husband, still.

"How did you know him? Are you a soldier?" He could see the bedeviling questions in her eyes, and the caution that he'd put there long before he'd met her. "Were you one of his household knights?"

He rolled bitterness around inside his cheek. "No. I was with your husband at Crécy."

"I see." She hesitated, as unsure of herself as he'd ever seen her. "Did you ever hear him speak of—"

Me, she'd been about to say. He could see it in those doe-soft eyes as they blazed briefly, hot curiosity dissolving into cold contempt. He felt looked through, to the image of the man he had once been, distorted in age-rippled glass and her questing imagination.

Then she shook her head. At herself, it seemed, and the absurdity of their marriage and all that had brought her here to him. His widow. His wife.

She gathered her dignity once more, and her determination. "Then, Master Nicholas, if you knew my husband somewhat, you knew him far better than I ever did. I never met him."

Distance, Nicholas, or you'll compound your many wrongs against her.

"Then William Bayard must have been the grandest fool of all."

Surprise lit her eyes, and the corners of her mouth turned up slightly. "I believe that with all my heart, Nicholas. That he missed out on many things."

Her candor would surely kill him, if his guilt and shame didn't first, or his craving for her.

"But to answer your question, sir: I knew nothing about my husband's estates when the marriage began." She turned away to unstop a horn of powdered ink. "I didn't care, because my opinion didn't matter. The venture had been made between my father and my husband. I assumed that I would learn of Bayard's holdings after he sent for me to join him in Normandy or wherever he might be warring." Though she was intent upon tapping a small measure of the black powder into a bowl, her mouth was set firmly against the memory of him. "But that never happened."

How could he let her know that his callousness had been for the best in the long run? She'd have found only heartbreak in his house, would have been caught in the same retribution as all the others.

"I knew enough of your husband's reputation, my lady, and of the laws of inheritance to know that you were entitled to much more than this pile of rubble in your widow's grant."

"I don't want anything more from my husband. I'm delighted with Faulkhurst as it is, with all of its flaws. And with no help from Edward's royal treasury. I knew very well that Faulkhurst was abandoned and in terrible shape, so I let Edward and his council think me a simpleton—for the less I involve the king, the more easily I can evade his influence."

He suddenly felt vastly proud that she was so wise for a woman with so little experience in the world. He sat on the edge of the table, enchanted all over again. "Where did you learn your politics, madam?"

She smiled up at him. "At the hands of my late father and the king and my unlamented husband."

The little jabs hurt most of all. They would keep him in his place, and aching. "Ah, yes."

"My life has been ill served by the politicking of men, but only because I was innocent of its power and its vanity. I am wiser now, and use my guile to my own advantage." She drew her fingers along the rib of the quill. "As you say, why would the king be interested in a tattered old castle on the verge of tumbling into the sea?"

"But guile alone can't guard you against your enemies. How will you defend yourself? With sticks and flaming arrows?"

She laughed with a brightness that caught him round the heart. "Look around you, Master Nicholas. There's nothing to defend at the moment."

Preposterous! "There is *yourself*, madam." She cast him another wry and worldly glance, as though she knew great secrets and kept them proudly. "You and your little brood are as lambs staked out for a pack of hungry wolves."

"Believe me, sir, we are far more secure here than we've been for many months." She wielded a small pestle against the crumbled ink, pressing it into a finer powder.

"Safer here? What do you mean?"

"We're quite used to bedding down in the open, under a tree, a bridge, or in a cave—whenever we were lucky enough to find one."

Hell and damn, he'd left her to wander the countryside like a vagrant. Well, no longer, by

God. He would give her this damned castle, even if it killed him.

"Faulkhurst isn't a cave; it's a fortress that needs defending, constantly."

She raised a brow at him and pursed her lips. "Of course it does."

"That's another reason you need me as your steward, madam: to see that the postern door in the main gate isn't left propped open by some fool as an invitation to every thief for miles around."

She stopped grinding and met his gaze directly. "*I* am that fool. I left it open purposely."

"The postern door?"

"Aye, sir. For anyone to come through at anytime, God willing. How else can they get inside with no one to open the gate when they knock?"

He hoped to hell she was jesting. "Thieves don't bother to knock, neither do raiding Marcher lords."

She stood, looking fierce with her fists planted against her hips. "Please tell me that you left the door standing wide."

"Are you mad? Of course I didn't." He shook his head, disbelieving the course of this entire conversation. "I closed and barred it."

"Blast it all," she huffed as she left the table, frowning at him as though he had just unloaded the full weight of the world onto her shoulders. "Master Nicholas, you're *not* recommending yourself very well to the position of steward." She lifted her cloak from the back of a chair and stepped into her boots at the same time.

"Where are you going?"

She picked up the cresset lamp. "To prop open the gate, just as I left it."

"Absolutely not! You're not doing anything of the kind." But he'd bellowed his command to the hem of her shabby cloak as it swung round the corner of the kitchen doorway and out into the great hall.

Utterly, wholly mad. "Madam!"

The woman frowned a quieting finger at him as she made a detour to the guttering hearth and the two girls sleeping there, tucking a threadbare blanket around a stray foot and landing a fond kiss on a chin before she was off again, stepping around the angular boy sprawled and snoring across the entrance to the portico.

Nicholas followed her, chewing on his silence until they reached the wide stairs in the dark bailey, unable to think of a single thing to say or do—beyond tackling her—that would stop her bullheaded progress.

"I'll only close and bar it again, madam."

But she tromped on, her lamp a bobbling outrider to her bracing strides, which seemed overlong for a woman whose head barely reached his shoulder. That bespoke long legs— fine, curving legs, if this chastening God had construed his dreams correctly.

And never to be seen by you, Brother Nicholas. He would spend his eternity in hell, burning with desire for her.

"You will *not* prop the gate open, madam." He easily met her stride, increased it by the length of a step, and took the lamp from her so that he could stare down at her. "Are you listening to me?"

"Convince me that I should do that, sir, that I should trust you as my steward—the man who will be charged with my daily accounts, with the running of my castle and fields. The one who will do my bidding without question. Why should I choose you?"

"Because, madam," he said between his teeth, "I am your only bloody choice."

Chapter 5

Eleanor wanted to cry, to stomp her foot—
though she had to keep a level head and
a steady heart. The man was right, of course.
He might be quick-tempered and opinionated
and highly possessive of her castle, but that's
exactly the kind of man she needed in a steward.

But how the devil was she going to contain
his fierceness within the smallness of the title?
He seemed so much more than that, larger
than life. Larger than her will—which terrified
her.

He needed gentling, needed to know that
she was the master here, not him. Despite his
prior claim, despite the fact that he knew William Bayard, however marginally, despite the
very puzzling matter of his being here at all.

"How long have you been living at Faulkhurst?"

THE MAIDEN BRIDE

He caught her elbow and turned her as they reached the low wall of the kitchen garden, and peered down at her with a midnight scowl. "Long enough to know the castle better than any man living."

"How long?"

"I don't know." He circled his hand in the air as though to pluck an answer from the darkness. "Months, I suppose. Which makes me the logical choice for steward."

Good God, he was handsome; impossible to look at without her mind wandering into places it had never wandered before. That was surely a strike against him, this ability to muddle her thoughts.

"Why do you want to stay here, Nicholas? You despise Faulkhurst to its foundations."

"I—" he seemed to gather his temper before he continued "—don't despise it."

Liar. "Perhaps not, but you do believe me a silly fool—"

"Hardly that—"

"You just said as much."

"When did I, madam?" He seemed truly indignant, initially matching her pace when she started across the bailey, then increasing it until she was nearly running to keep up with him. She finally slowed to her own stride.

"Do you truly believe, Master Nicholas, that

63

I ought to welcome you as my steward when I know right well that you would subvert my plans? You are trying to at this very moment."

"Not if your plans are sound."

Aye, he would think that way in his vast male arrogance. She stopped by an empty wagon and swung her lamp toward him to better see how he played the truth.

"How do you plan to measure that soundness, sir? By whose standard? A tyrannical, condescending soldier's ... or *mine*?"

His eyes became shards of indigo, hot in the lamp's flame as he mulled her question carefully. His mouth was so perfectly crafted— even in his thwarted scowl—that she wanted to follow the curving lines of it and its dampness with her finger. He smelled cleanly of leather and smoky thyme in the cocoon of the night.

"Try me—" he leaned down and whispered, so warmly, so near to her brow that he ruffled her lashes and the hair at her temple, and made her tilt her mouth up to catch the rest of his intoxicating words, "—my lady Eleanor."

Try him. His mouth on hers. Oh, yes; she'd like to. But oh, my, he was large. And wholly distracting. Her heart pounded so loudly she couldn't hear herself think, let alone recall the subject, though she knew it was of grave importance to her future.

"Try you, sir?"

"Aye, madam." He caught her chin with his thumb, then brushed her lips with it, watching them as though gauging her answer. "Tell me your reasons for keeping the damned gate open."

Oh, yes, that. She stepped safely away from the man, to a place where she could regain her thoughts. Because no matter how she explained them, her reasons wouldn't satisfy him; they only made sense to her because she had risked everything already and had little left to lose.

Except hope, and she refused to allow him to steal that from her, nor to shake it in any way. No man would ever do that to her again.

"Whatever your low opinion of me, sir, I am not an unsuspecting innocent—"

"My opinion of you isn't low in the least." He took hold of her sleeve, wrapped his fingers in the loose linen, and tugged her into his delicious heat.

"I am deeply, *dreadfully* familiar with what it takes to manage a castle, in good times and in times of unthinkable evil. Like the years just past." The horrors nudged at her as they did

65

so often, wanting airing, but she shook her head and they vanished.

"Then you know that you'll need three hundred people at the very least." He was nodding impatiently, that black mane of hair emphasizing just how tall he was and how well he favored his own opinions over hers.

"I need people of every sort if I'm to vanquish my husband's memory and redress his uncaring policies. Tenants and crafters and villeins. That's the very reason I can't afford to let a single person pass us by because they think Faulkhurst unoccupied and unwelcoming."

He snorted and sat back on the open wagon-gate, his arms crossed defiantly over his broad chest, those tremendously long, knee-booted legs spread out on either side of hers. "My dear lady, only thieves and highwaymen travel about in the dead of night. And they look only to take advantage—"

"Which makes them an enterprising group of people, don't you think?" Of course he wouldn't. Couldn't possibly.

He went still. "*Enterprising?* Is that what you just said?"

"Aye, enterprising. Terrifically skilled at making a profitable something out of absolutely nothing. Have you ever watched a mountebank at work at a faire?"

"Hell and damnation, I believe I am watching one right *now*. Are you mad, woman?" He was up again, pacing away from her into the blurring shadows and back again into their shallow pool of light, making her hope suddenly that he wouldn't give up on her, because that would feel too much like defeat.

"I'm not mad, sir. I've only done in my life what needed to be done. And on that course I've become acquainted with dozens of outlaws in these past few years—"

"*You* have? With outlaws? How?" He took hold of her forearm and turned her, fully horrified by her confession, as though her welfare in the past meant something personal to him, a private outrage. "What the bloody hell have you been doing since your husband died? Making covenants with brigands?"

"And kings, sir. And priests, and merchants. Whoever would listen to me, whoever would talk freely. And I learned that every man and woman who managed to live through the horrors of the last few years wishes a better life for himself—and a far better one for his children."

Nicholas tried to unscramble the woman's logic, but it was impossible. No matter how many ways he twisted it, not if he tried for the next hundred years—and he hadn't nearly that much time, else he might well enjoy the task. He sat down again on the back of the cart, its creak a bitter echo of the way his bones felt just now—aged and hollow.

And utterly confused. "What the devil are you talking about?"

"Opportunity, Master Nicholas." She gave a sharp, satisfied nod and threw out her hands, as though that clarified everything for him.

"What?" He wondered if he'd suddenly gone stone deaf and stupid.

"I will leave the castle doors open as an opportunity for the enterprising." She took an impatient breath when he couldn't make himself respond with the bellow of outrage that seemed crammed inside his chest. "Very well, sir. I offer you Dickon and his sister as an example."

Clarity at last, God help him. "Do you mean to tell me that the lad snoring his head off in the great hall is an outlaw?"

She stepped between his knees, a stunning temptation as she bent closer to him, as though she were keeping a great secret, or protecting the boy's feelings. "Dickon was a highwayman. He's been entirely reformed for a whole year. Nearly monkish."

68

Nicholas knew that state intimately, was suffering that very moment from its exacting dictates, aroused again. His wife's hair tangled itself up in his fingers and her mouth glistened too near his own as she whispered on about reforming thieves and vagabonds.

"You're a gullible innocent if you believe that the boy has changed one whit in his heart, madam." He couldn't breathe with his pulse slamming around inside his chest.

"I believe in Dickon, sir, to the end of time. I have to. His sister, Lisabet—the young woman you saw from the gallery while you were eavesdropping on us—had been a pick-pocket. A very good one. Now she reads and is learning to write."

"What are you saying exactly?" He closed his hand over hers, suffered the heady shock of it as he brought the lamp closer to her face, looking for the hazy madness in her eyes. But he found only the stalwart, clear divinity of hope. The sort that would land her in Edward's dungeons if he wasn't careful with her life, or in a shallow, unmarked grave in a ditch. "Do you truly think you're going to populate Faulkhurst with outlaws?"

"Outlaws? Good heavens, no." Her eyes glistened with the misguided compassion that caused her to place her hand on his shoulder, to draw him closer. "With people like you and me, Nicholas—who yearn to be better for their tragedies, who have grown wiser in their sorrows, who are grateful for this day and for the next."

She was holding his hand tightly, this resurrected wife of his, searching the depths of his eyes for a sign of the hope she'd never find.

"Ah, Nicholas, we can't give up. Not even God can save the fool who stands willfully in the path of a team of runaway horses, unless that fool uses his brain and leaps out of the way in time."

Unless he has no choice in the matter of where he stands. "You may believe that, madam—"

"I do. I'm not going to just sit here whimpering in my barren castle and pray for a baker to come trotting up to the gate on a plow horse."

The image was so absurd that it forced a smile out of him, filled the hot hollowness in his chest. She, of course, took the smile for his assent. "Good, then." She tugged him to his feet, then let go of his hand, stealing away her warmth, and continued across the bailey, trailing her scented dreams behind her. "I have a strategy."

Good Christ, woman. He followed, already

planning his own strategy against her outlaws. "Tell me," he said evenly.

"We will rebuild the village and plant all the fields this spring for a grand harvest come Michaelmas."

"This spring? It can't be done." An annoying spot between his eyes had begun to ache.

"It can, with enough labor." She strode through the barbican, past dark arrow loops on either side of the narrow passage, and beneath the perilous portcullis that he'd foolishly neglected to lower just before she and her brood had arrived.

God, had that only been this afternoon?

"How the devil are you going to attract enough labor way out here, on the last gasp of the earth?"

"They'll come, as I said."

"Do you mean to collect them one by one as they pass by on the low road, thirty miles from here? You'll be years finding yourself a village full of tenants. Every able-bodied man and woman in the kingdom fled the countryside to the nearest town or city long ago, the moment their lord's back was turned."

"Aye, just as they probably did from Faulkhurst the first chance they got. Though I can hardly blame them for fleeing from my husband and his wickedness in great, rolling multitudes." She frowned when she came abreast of the postern door. "But, thankfully, William Bayard is no longer lord here."

He is, my lady. Or would be until he could straighten out the mess he'd left to her.

"Labor can't be bought anywhere, madam, for any amount of gold. Even if it were legal to treaty with another lord's servant."

"I'm not offering gold—I don't have any." She slid the upper bar to the side, and then the middle one. Nicholas stood there, illuminating her foolishness with the lamp, resolved to sleep here in the gatehouse tonight—at least until he knew that she was safely asleep, and he could lock the damnable door.

"What are you offering then in the way of your 'opportunity'? Schooling? Great piles of broken lumber, handfuls of crumbled daub? You have that aplenty."

"A cottage in the village."

He snorted. "In *that* village?" He pointed beyond the gates.

"Scoff if you wish, Master Nicholas. But each man who comes to live and work here will have a cottage for himself and his family."

"And this is what will bring your outlaw baker galloping through the gates of Faulkhurst."

"It will, sir. But only if the gate is left *open.*"

She shot the last bar and yanked the door wide.

And there, just beyond the portal, in the pale yellow spill of light from Nicholas's lamp was the long, thin muzzle of a droopy-eyed horse, and beside it, the weary face of a withered, white-bearded old man, whose bony fist was raised to knock.

"Your pardon, milord, for disturbing your fine evening. But we saw the light in your tower."

Nicholas met his wife's glance, a dazzling pageantry of angelic innocence and devilish cunning that made her eyes sparkle and upturned the corners of her mouth.

He warily turned to the old man, all too aware of the sort of God he was dealing with.

"Are you a baker, sir?"

"Ah, no, no, no. 'Fraid not, milord." The man's leathery frown drew up into a smile somewhere inside the fall of his scrappy moustache.

Nicholas turned to offer his opinion of wild-ass miracles to his wife when the old voice rattled on, "But m' wife here was the best baker in all the Marches. Weren't you, Hannah, dear?"

Nicholas followed the old man's adoring gaze inexorably upward to the ghostly face that appeared out of the darkness as the horse stepped forward.

A baker. On a bloody horse.

"Bloody hell."

He steeled himself for his wife's chortling "I told you so," but she was deep into her beaming welcome, gathering up the horse's reins and the old man's hand and coaxing them both over the threshold of her castle and into the midst of her wayward dreams.

Worst of all, he wanted to laugh. For the first time in long years, a great, rolling belly laugh slammed around inside his chest, wanting out, wanting freedom. But that would be a mad sound, indeed.

Absurd woman.

Wild-hearted vixen.

Wife.

"You must be hungry after your journey, and cold to the bone. Here, Mistress Hannah, please wear my cloak."

On she went in her lavish welcome as he helped the spry woman off the mare. "I'm Lady Eleanor Bayard, and this is Master Nicholas." She flashed Nicholas a smile that any man would die and die again for. "My steward."

His heart thumped, proud, pleased, famished for her, for her touch.

"Is he, then, my lady?" Hannah turned back toward Nicholas, her wrinkled brow creased, a deep chuckle in her throat. "Imagine me, my dear—thinking the handsome lad was your husband."

Bloody, bleeding hell.

Chapter 6

"**A**n honest error, Hannah." By the look of appalled horror on Nicholas's face, though, the old woman might have been suggesting that he be drawn and quartered. Surely he could imagine a more miserable fate than being mistaken for her husband.

She'd never been a ballad-inspiring beauty, but she'd never lacked for a partner at May dances, and had fended off more than her share of eager embraces.

She'd even been soundly kissed a few times, and had liked it quite well.

And *he*, Master Snort and Growl, was hardly a prince himself—not in the husbandly sense. Not the sort to snuggle close to on a wintry night. Though he certainly radiated enough heat to warm a chamber.

Perhaps that wasn't quite so unthinkable—snuggling against him. Beneath a counterpane, on a feather bed, mounded with lavender-scented pillows. She'd probably kiss him.

Oh, hell. Hannah's impression had been a simple misunderstanding; there was no reason for him to grimace and start unlashing the panniers from the horse with such determination. He was taller and broader-shouldered than anyone she'd ever known, fashioned of timber and stone, and could bellow as though he had commanded his share of battlefields. Easily mistaken for the lord of the castle.

Too easily.

He was a powerful, compelling presence she'd have to guard against, if she were to contain the man's judgments.

"Go, madam. Take your new *tenants* to the keep, if you wish. Out of the cold." He dropped the pannier into a small wheelbarrow, his suspicions of her as plain as his lordly overreaching. "I'll see to the mare."

"And you'll mind the gate as I asked you, steward."

He studied her overlong, with that raking gaze that shoved her off-balance and stole her breath. "Milady."

He said the last with a nearly imperceptible bow, then disappeared into the darkness beyond the barbican. The old mare followed him like a stray pup, nudging her nose into Nicholas's hand, finding an idle caress there.

A friend.

Insufferable man. Well, stubborn at least. Yet she shouldn't be complaining at all. She needed a steward, and he was perfect in many ways.

All in all, a remarkably well-spent day, considering how it had begun. Whatever Nicholas's opinion of her plans and the role he would be forced to play in them, he could hardly doubt that Fergus and Hannah and their agreeable bay were anything but one huge miracle.

"Did you come a long way, Master Fergus?" Eleanor gave him the lamp, then lifted the barrow handles and started toward the keep.

"From up Berwick way. But I'll push that, my lady." Fergus took hold of her elbow with his trembling, bony hand and stopped her. "We already owe you so much."

"You don't, Fergus."

"But we do," Hannah said, alongside her husband. "Tell the lady, Fergus." The lamplight caught Hannah's weary smile, and her cross-hatching of wrinkles. "She needs to know why we come here. Honestly."

"It wasn't the light in the tower?"

They both looked shamefaced. "Nay, your light only gave us hope that the rumors were true, my lady. Them being unbelievable tales."

Rumors and tales of Faulkhurst? Already! Eleanor wanted to shout with delight, wanted to find her steward and share the news with him. Aye, and to gloat just a bit.

"What sort of rumors?"

"Hardly creditable, my lady." Hannah drew the cloak around her and huddled up against Fergus's insubstantial chest, an enviable place of love and comfort she must have known for decades. Her partner. "But the tattle was that the lady of Faulkhurst was giving away a cottage to every man."

Eleanor tried not to laugh out loud. "Well, it isn't tattle, Hannah. It's true."

They both gasped. "A cottage for us, Fergus!" The pair shared a married glance, took hands as Fergus continued, more agitated now.

"There were also wild rumors of shops and the rights to a guild craft."

Eleanor's heart was racing madly. That too! They'd heard about Faulkhurst all the way up in Berwick. "Aye, Fergus. A craft and a virgate of tillable land."

"Oh, Hannah!" Fergus sat down hard on the wheel of the barrow. "Could you ever have imagined it?"

"Never at all, my love." Hannah took

Eleanor's hand in hers. "Oh, my lady, the towns are filled with outlaws in the guise of lawful burghers. Terrible prices for goods. And the barons do prosecute those unwilling to work for them."

"Prosecute?" She'd never heard of such a thing, not in town, where freemen lived. "And they get away with it?"

"They need every hand at the plow and forge, yet they take greater advantage than before the pestilence."

Here was her skeptical steward's answer as to why she would have no trouble attracting tenants. But there was one enticement that even she was apprehensive about, one that he would surely balk at when he learned of it.

"There was something else, Lady Eleanor," Hannah said. "A false rumor, to be sure, impossible to credit. You may even laugh, for you know how swiftly gossip travels and grows till it swamps all truth."

"What gossip is this, Hannah?"

"Well—that come next year's harvest, the Lady of Faulkhurst—you, my lady—would be tithing to her tenants." Fergus and Hannah both laughed uneasily, as though they had pushed the limits of her hospitality and feared she would send them packing.

But it only made her grin. "That is true as

well, Hannah. I will be tithing to my tenants—but only for the next five years, and only if they work hard."

"Oh, my. We shall." Hannah clutched her laced up hands to her bosom. "We're home, Fergus. God bless and keep you forever safe, Lady Eleanor."

Eleanor grinned all the way through the dark bailey, her fears banished for a time.

As they entered the portico, poor Dickon woke into a scrambling start.

"Ho, there, scoundrels!" he shouted. "Stop where you are!" He clapped at his chest and then at his belt as he searched in vain for his long-bladed dagger, his highwayman's reflexes gone thankfully dull in this new life of his.

"It's all right, Dickon."

"Ah, my lady! 'Tis you. And—" Dickon blinked at the newcomers with sleep-bleary eyes.

"Hannah and Fergus. They brought a horse with them, Dickon."

Dickon snapped his mouth shut in the middle of a yawn. "A *live* one?"

Fergus laughed. "Her name is Figgey."

"You found a grandmere, Nellamore!" Pippa came racing out of nowhere to grab

81

Eleanor's hand, but hung back shyly among her skirts. "Hello."

"Pippa, this is Mistress Hannah." Eleanor knelt beside the girl and took her sleepy warmth into her arms. "And her husband, Master Fergus."

"Do they stay with us, Nellamore? Please, can they?" she asked in a noisy Pippa-whisper.

"I hope they will stay forever."

"Me, too!" Her delight uncontainable once again, Pippa slipped her hand into Hannah's and tugged the startled woman toward the hearth. "Lisabet, come look what Nellamore brought for us!"

The great hall clamored with noise for the next hour, and only settled down after the fire was once again banked and Eleanor had seen the newcomers tucked in among everyone else in front of the hearth.

Everyone but Nicholas—though he certainly didn't need tucking in. He was probably prowling the ramparts with his sword drawn, watching for dangerous outlaws like Fergus and Hannah to come swarming through the gates and over the walls, now that he was steward.

She had sprung the news on him rather abruptly, and without thinking the matter through completely. She ought to find him and make his appointment to the post official. She owed him that much, for his mostly civilized patience while she tried to make him understand that most people only needed the chance to start over.

She also needed to set down a few rules.

It hadn't been anything he'd said, exactly, that made her decide to take him on as steward; the man was as opinionated as a mule with a toothache, and would fight her at every turn.

Nay, it had been the smile that he'd tried so vainly to hide when he saw Hannah sitting on old Figgey. That and his gentleness as he lifted the old woman down from the saddle.

A man who was that frightened of his joy needed all the clemency she could bring him. Whether he wanted it from her or not.

Where and how have you been living all these months, steward? And why did you stay? He was part of the castle itself, as craggy and windblown.

And so terribly lonely.

Eleanor took up the lamp again, and a small sack of sugared plums that she'd been holding for a special occasion—never ever expecting that she'd use them to tame a gargoyle—and made her way to the stables.

Figgey had been carefully unsaddled, curried and blanketed, and now stood dozing amongst tall weeds and newly sprung grass in the middle of the neglected enclosure.

Her steward had paid the mare every courtesy, down to a freshly filled water trough. But—damn his eyes—the main gate was closed and barred.

"You'll learn that I mean to win this round, Master Nicholas. And every other one that rears up between us through the years." Even if she had to lock him in the cellar and sleep against the gate door all night long.

But when she reached to unseat the upper bar, she noticed that a thick rope had been threaded through the grated spy hole high in the door, outside the gate. It draped heavily across the center of the barbican, then looped upward into the dimness of the ceiling and disappeared.

Whatever kind of device it was, it hadn't been there an hour earlier.

Leaving the mysterious rope hanging there, she climbed the circling stone gatehouse stairs until she was standing in a round room, amid the jumbled workings of the chains and pulleys that had once operated the portcullis. They were badly fouled now and in need of repair.

The rope from below passed in front of the raised portcullis like the thick strand of a giant spider's web, draped over a rafter, then vanished into a place above that her lamplight wouldn't enter.

And beneath all this tangled mystery lounged her steward, fast asleep in a tipped-back, leather-slung chair that seemed far too small for him. The heels of his tall boots were propped on a rust-frozen gear, and his broad chest rose and fell in a steady rhythm.

Hannah had called him handsome. He was that, indeed. Extraordinarily so, though not in the perfection of his features, for they were rough-hewn and angular. It was the overwhelming sense of him that drew her, that made her think astonishingly of the children she would never have with her husband.

It made her think of just ... leaning down and kissing him. This cold-cast man whose hands were broad and strong and enchantingly warm—and which spoke so powerfully of possession and tightly stoppered passion. The memory of them wrapped roughly, eloquently around her waist, of his fingers raking through her hair, made her face flame to the tips of her ears, made her heart zip along, dancing like a honeybee beneath her breasts.

Jesu! Where the devil were these thoughts

coming from? These utterly capricious fantasies about a man whom she'd just met, who had the power to level her world in one stroke if she didn't monitor his every move. She'd never had so much trouble with her wicked imagination as she was having today, when she ought to be planning her strategies, setting unerasable boundaries between them. She took a deep breath, leaned over, and tapped him on the knee.

"Nicholas?" She got her hand trapped tightly for her boldness. He opened one eye slightly, a sliver of dangerous moonlight breasting a hill.

"What, madam?"

Such a low and craggy voice, tucked here among the rafters. The roughness of it hummed and shimmered along her forearm and lodged low in her belly.

"What?" he said again, because she was staring and her face must be red as new clover.

"I—" His hand was larger than her memory of it and startlingly heated, holding hers fast against his knee. "What are you doing here, sir?"

"I was sleeping." He released her hand abruptly, and she pulled away, her fingers blithely tingling, wanting more, telling other limbs and locations about his wonderful

86

touch. "At least, attempting to. What do you want?"

Seeing the glint of lamplight on his moist mouth, she nearly forgot why she'd come: to tame the man.

Their rules of engagement.

"First of all, sir, I want to know what the devil this apparatus is." Her resolve renewed, she tugged lightly on the rope and set a cascade of bells ringing above their heads. "Bells?"

"A caparison bridle." He lowered the chair sharply, brushed bits of wood from his hauberk, then stood up in reluctant courtesy, as though every muscle in his body were already cramped from sleeping folded into the chair.

"A caparison bridle, tied to the end of a rope? Whatever for?" He seemed even taller, standing among the hatchwork of the thick wooden rafters that supported the portcullis and the roof—overpowering, with the restrained gentleness of an appeased bear.

"That I might know when someone is at your gate, my lady." He bowed slightly and her heart took a long, skimming leap toward the remarkable man.

"You did this for me? Fashioned a welcoming bell?"

One of his brows arched wryly, along with

the corner of his smile. "An alarm, madam."

Ha! A compromise, my dear steward. But she wouldn't say that aloud. Let him think that he'd bested her in his quiet sedition. The gate would be opened to anyone who wanted to enter the castle, one way or the other.

"Whatever your reasons, sir, it was clever and obliging, and I thank you for it." There—a compliment where it was due.

He shrugged off her gratitude, and her wariness of his motives rose precipitously. "Nothing more than my dutiful effort to guard and increase your property, madam. To defend your rights and franchises. To be prudent, faithful, and profitable."

"I am much obliged to you, sir." And hugely suspicious, that he'd so thoroughly conceived his steward's creed in such a short time.

The blackguard. Trying to carol dance around her, while he kept his own ways.

"I am, after all, your steward, my lady."

"Aye, sir, and *not* my husband—"

He went utterly still, and her innocent bit of humor thudded to the floor between them like a block of limestone pushed from the cliff tower.

"No, madam, I'm *not*." The flat echo of silence followed, like a door slammed on an argument.

So—her steward was entirely humorless on the subject of marriage, and not exactly given to flattery, blast the man.

"I didn't mean to offend, Nicholas." She smiled, meaning none of it if he was going to be *that* stoneheaded. "I merely wanted you to know how grateful I am that you're my steward."

"Are you?"

"Yes—" *dammit*, she wanted to add. "I'm glad that you persisted when I put you off so squarely. I didn't want to turn you out of my home, though we did step off on the wrong foot."

He leaned toward her. "Much more than a foot, my lady."

"Indeed." There went her thoughts again, completely distracted by his gaze. "You were my best and only choice all along—short of giving up altogether, which I will never do."

"You've made that patently clear." Pronounced like another judgment on her sanity and a sacrifice to his patience.

"Let me make this just as clear: though I'll consider your warnings and your advice and your guidance with great care before I make any decision, you must understand that my word will reign here in all matters. And you must abide by it."

"Fine." Too quickly said.

"So you agree to this very basic rule?"

"Yes." That was said a breath too late for her to believe him completely.

He looked suddenly weary and irritable, as though he had a long, regretful journey ahead of him, and Eleanor felt oddly responsible for disturbing his lonely peace. After all, Faulkhurst had been the man's home for some time. His solitary refuge from his own secret tragedies, it seemed.

"Where do you sleep, sir?"

He took a long measure of her and then tapped the back of the chair. "Here."

"You can't sleep in a tiny chair. I'll send Dickon with a pallet."

"No. Send me nothing."

"But you'll be aching by—"

"The chair will do." She couldn't possibly have softened his abruptness with any amount of argument or eider ticking. He seemed bent on his discomfort—a mendicant monk in the guise of a soldier.

Who are you, Nicholas Langridge? But it was far too late in the evening for that kind of question; tomorrow would be soon enough.

"Where have you been sleeping these

months since you arrived here? Surely in the keep somewhere. If you have a chamber there I can bring—"

"It doesn't matter, madam. I am fine here."

Fine? Sleeping among the chains and gears? An ordinary man would have quartered himself in royal splendor, given an entire castle full of appointments, would have gathered together the riches of the late lord's bounty and reveled in them. Or packed the lot off to the nearest town and sold it all. But her steward seemed as spare in his living as he was grand in his honor—a far better man than the one she had been so briefly wed to.

He'd been protective when he could have pillaged at will. A steward in fact, if not by title.

Oh, my—she'd been a complete dunderhead not to have realized from the start what he'd been doing here all alone at Faulkhurst. "You've been steward for months, haven't you, Nicholas?"

"What do you mean?" The question was asked quickly, ripe with suspicion of her motives.

"First in my husband's absence, and then in my own." No wonder he'd taken possession with such vengeance.

Nicholas's heart was thudding again against

his chest, his pulse again under siege from her innocent arrows that forever hit him dead on target and pierced deeply.

"I lodged here only, madam. For a few months, because it has been convenient for me. Make nothing more of it than that."

She settled closer to him, a hand on her hip, puzzling over him, over some bit of unlikely logic. "Whether you meant it so or not, your skulking has kept Faulkhurst from being picked clean."

Ah. "By your enterprising outlaws?"

She laughed generously, as though he'd caught her in a misstep, and touched the hollow of her throat, exposed in that sloping, alabaster breach above her night shift. "Aye, sir. You saved me from those very outlaws, locked everyone out until I could come. Why?"

Blasted woman. He would never be ready for any of her stunning questions. He hadn't thought ahead that far into his story—the whys of his being here, of his staying. And he sure as hell couldn't judge—at the mercy of her gaze, of her fingers smoothing the edge of his cuff—what this falsehood or that would mean in the coming months. Would a simple detail eventually trip him up when he least expected it?

"Why? Nothing I had planned," was all he

could manage. For that smallness of spirit he got another of her enigmatic smiles. And his privacy, his distance.

"Well, sir. How can I ever thank you for all you've done for me thus far?"

She put out her hand for him to shake, which scared him brainless—because he couldn't stop himself from taking it, any more than he could stop himself from raising its slim paleness to his mouth and pressing a kiss to the back of her fingers and between.

Yes, fresh dandelions and lavender and soap. A new fire in his cold hearth.

"Oh, my." She watched his dangerous, forbidden courtship with open fascination, with eyes that sparkled with curiosity and invited much more exploring than he dared imagine.

"Well. Thank you, Master Nicholas," she said, with a magnificently erotic hitch of her breath that flushed her cheeks and her throat, and made his skin ache, his chest burn.

He let go of her hand, regretting few things more in his life. "You will thank me most effectively, my lady, by keeping yourself safe at all times."

"From . . . ?" Her mouth glistened, pouting as though he'd just kissed her and she was asking for more.

From me—from your husband's outrageous lust for you, for it is hot and close by.

He sighed. "Your bloody outlaws, my lady."

"And the bloody king."

Oh, she was very good, this wife of his. Forbearance became her, and generosity of heart. So very tolerant of an interloper's arrogance, as masterful in her mercies as she was in her unwitting malice.

"My husband may have been a neglectful monster, but we'll make amends for his wickedness, you and I. We'll finally put Faulkhurst aright."

"Fine. Good." Damned little else he could say, outside of "So glad the bastard's dead."

"We'll meet in the great hall in the early morning, if you will, sir. The seven of us. Do sleep well."

God help him, he craved the choking sting of the battlefield as he never had in all of his life—it was far safer there than here beside his wife. He'd been arrow-shot and sliced through to the bone a dozen times; he'd suffered broken limbs and festered wounds, had been stitched up with catgut and rusted needles in the thick of a brawling fray.

But he'd never felt so mortally wounded, so dazed and confused as he did now at the end of this interminable day.

"Good night to you, madam."

"And to you, Nicholas." Her voice was pillowy and warm, and he feared she would cup his jaw with her hand and leave a kiss on his cheek. She was that kind of woman, and he was just the kind of sinner to let her.

But he could never stop there—not at a kiss. He'd gather her into his embrace, and meet the dawn all tangled up in her skirts and in the lushness of her arms.

He stood unmoving as she turned away, feeling coarse-muscled and slow. Then she stopped, studied the floor beside his chair for a moment with that keenly tender brow of hers, then stooped and picked up a partially carved block of pine—the upper half of the standing bear he'd been working at with his knife.

"Is this your carving, Nicholas?" She turned it in the lamplight, raptly studying the details, unaware that his heart had stopped for more reasons than he cared to admit: fear and flattery and the desolate yearning for a better man's life.

"It is mine." He could hardly deny it. There were bits of shavings on the floor, and, he suddenly noticed, on the sleeve of his tunic. He brushed at them, stark evidence of his melancholy distraction. That tenuous connection with his son.

"Why, it's—" she laughed in pure delight, lighting the room with the lilt of it "—oh, Nicholas, it's absolutely wonderful." She sent a quick, assuring glance to him with those clear, painfully lovely eyes, then she went back to studying the bear from all its angles, caressing the small nose and the back of its head and neck as though it pleased her as nothing ever had.

"Whoever is it for?"

My son, Liam. Your son, wife, if I'd been a better man, a better father.

His mouth went as dry as the wood shavings, leaving him feeling exposed, lacking an explanation for the very simplest, the truest, the purest, part of his life. Though he burned to confess it, he could never tell her this particular truth either—because she might understand, might absolve him, and ask more of him than he could give her.

He'd crammed eight years of fatherhood into a single, astonishing summer of joy, when all around him had been collapsing. He'd found the boy abandoned to poverty and neglect and had courted his trust, carving dozens of animals for his son, his heart filling up, spilling over with every chip he'd cut away.

A clumsy, aching attempt at making amends. Toys and trifles to catch his son's fancy and rest his fears—not much to recommend him after years of absence and deliberate denial of the boy. But Liam had fallen for the carvings.

For the badgers and the bears and the kennel full of hunting hounds.

I like the pony best of all, Papa.

Nicholas could hardly breathe for the memory of all the grinning, the skipping and hooting that the boy had done so often in the simplicity of his joy. And now his wife seemed just as taken with the unfinished bear, beaming with admiration that he didn't deserve.

"The toy is for no one in particular, madam," he finally managed, though she must have heard the rasping of his voice. "A passing of time, is all."

Her eyes sparkled with a starry dampness. "I never would have guessed at your secret, Nicholas. Never in my life." Her smile for him was tender and compelling, the affection in her voice, devastating. "And that would have been a sorrowful loss indeed."

She nestled the bear into his hand, lifted high onto her toes, and pressed a warm, lingering kiss against his bristley cheek. With a small, startled sound, she lowered her lashes and whispered hoarsely, "Good night, steward."

Then she was gone down the stairs with her lamplight—leaving his heart thumping with equal parts of longing and terror and rampaging lust.

Christ, she'd kissed him. Just like that. Felled his resolve with the single pressing of her lips against his heated skin.

That close to his mouth—a slight turn of his head and he would have been lost for days in the scent of her, lost for eternity in the fires that would come later.

Bloody hell. That's just what he needed, a wife who touched and embraced at every turn.

Thank you, Nicholas. Good night, Nicholas. He scrubbed at the brand she'd left, but that only warmed his hand, spreading heat down his arm into his chest to scatter through his loins like torch fire, making him long for her in the fragrance she'd left in the cool air.

He prowled the gatehouse for a time, wanting to follow her, wanting to run for his life. He would stay on his guard at all times. Not only against her outlaws and her lunacy, but against her random embraces.

Belling the damned gatehouse had served him nicely; he would override all her decisions with stealth.

He had no sooner folded himself into the torturous chair again when the bells in the rafters began to ring: a cloud of annoying jingles that sent him caroming down the gatehouse stairs to the gate, where the taut rope continued the clamoring.

"Wait just a bloody moment!" Damned impatient outlaws. He had a mind to toss them out on their backsides.

Enterprising, Nicholas.

Aye, madam, but you'll never know about the derelict ones that I got to first.

It wasn't until he was throwing open the postern door that he realized it wasn't barred or latched, though he'd left it that way not an hour past.

Damnation, that could only mean this was—

Eleanor. "My God, woman. Are you mad?"

"Your welcome bells work perfectly, Master Nicholas. I could hear them from here."

She was grinning at him from the other side of the doorway, clearly proud of something. Of him or herself or the bright moon that shone down across her shoulders and the broken-down village beyond, God only knew.

"Very clever indeed."

"You doubted me?" He leaned hard on the open hinge, blocking her way, thinking how

99

easy it would be to close the door against her.
To start the day again.

"Only to see it for myself, sir." She touched
the middle of his chest and stepped through
the opening. The hem of her night shift
snagged on the tall sill, pulling her off-balance
enough to make her grab hold of his belt and
then his arm.

"Have a care, madam." He caught her waist,
then stooped and tugged her gown free, only
to catch the scent of her bath again and the
shape of her hip as he stood up slowly, resisting the urge to lift the linen hem and run his
hand, his mouth, along her bewitching calves,
the backs of her knees, her thighs, and over
her softly rounded bottom.

*She's your wife after all, Bayard. Who would
stop you? Or blame you for it?* The devil's voice,
or God's—a luscious temptation, nonetheless
enticing for its source.

He wanted another kiss from her as he held
her—wanted far more than that, more than his
fingers threading through her hair as they
were doing now, or her cheek fitting so perfectly, so persuasively into the curve of his
hand.

"Do you like sugared plums, Nicholas?" She
let go of his arm and pulled a small bag from

her sleeve, capturing his wrist as she put the bag into his palm.

Sugared plums—his weakness. Deeply red, overripe, and darkly sweet. How could she possibly have known? A wife's instinct to satisfy her husband, to tempt him to sample her as well? "I do, madam. Thank you."

"My pleasure. And good night again, sir. I shall pray tonight for a carpenter, and a mason, too. I hope that you do as well."

As it always was, his prayer would be for peace and salvation—both of which seemed more impossible than ever as he watched her leave the barbican with her bobbing lamp. Aye, and her lushly bobbing breasts.

He followed her, well out of her hearing, just to be sure she made it all the way to the keep, his heart rambling the passages ahead of her, wondering where she would sleep, wishing it could be in his arms.

Bloody hell. Barely half an evening with the woman and he was already making love to her fingers, making marvels of her casual kiss.

And imagining so much more.

Chapter 7

E leanor had dreamed through the night of
a prowling, red-eyed gargoyle and awak-
ened before dawn, thoroughly rested and eager to organize the day well ahead of her
steward's prejudgments.

That would remain her creed in her dealings
with him: to take firm control of the reins and
never—

Dear God, I kissed him! Out of habit, because
she kissed all sorts of people, regularly. Pippa
and Lisabet and Dickon, the abbess, Father
Clyde and . . . well, *everyone* whom she cared
for, respected.

Nicholas's carving had charmed her completely. *He* had charmed her. She'd meant only
a simple kiss of appreciation, but she'd ignited
flames and yearnings instead. She'd lingered
like a thief, tasted the surprising black softness

of his beard. His scent of bay and woodsmoke swept round her still.

But these were hardly the kind of thoughts she needed with a castle waiting to be rebuilt.

She shook Dickon awake at the portico door. Rubbing his eyes and yawning, he got to his feet.

"Dickon, what do you know of horses?"

"I've stolen more'n my share." She loved the bumptious slant of his grin, mostly because he wore it too rarely. And too quickly his face flamed beneath all those freckles, and wariness filled his eyes. "But I've given up stealing, ya know."

"I would never ever ask you to go raiding for me. But since we now have a horse, would you know one end of it well enough from the other to feed and saddle and shoe Figgey?"

That smile came again and stayed. "My lady, I know horses well enough to do all you ask, on a moonless night, at a dead gallop, with a legion of Edward's English bowmen on my arse. Why do you ask?"

She couldn't help her own smile. "I'd rather the king's men never again have reason to follow you so closely, Dickon. And I doubt Figgey could raise a trot, let alone a gallop. I'm asking because I want you to be the constable of Faulkhurst."

"Me, my lady?" His face grew unaccountably surly. "Why the bloody hell would you do a thing like that to me?"

"A thing like what?"

"To tempt me to sinning." He crossed his arms and ankles and leaned stubbornly against the arch jamb. "I *am* a highwayman, ya know."

"*Were* a highwayman."

"Aye. *Were* one—but sometimes I still get the itch to—" He shoved his fingers into his belt as though to trap them away from temptation.

"To jump out of the hedge and rob a passing merchant of everything, right down to his garters?"

Dickon's mouth hung open for a long moment, and then he nodded fiercely. "Exactly right, milady."

"And does this itch pass you by an instant later?"

"God be praised, it does."

"Then, love, it's only the prickly remains of a bad habit. The feeling will fade completely one day—like mine has for sugared ginger." A tiny falsehood, but only to gain the point that he had will enough to decide rightly and to get on with his future. "You will be the very best constable."

He still looked stunned and afraid and unreasonably angry, with his sturdy arms fused to his chest. "What would a constable have to be doing?"

And there it was: opportunity. In its most divine splendor, offered to those who needed only to reach out and take it.

Just as she had offered throughout the towns and villages on her way to Faulkhurst. A rumor of opportunity whispered into a hungry ear. To an apprentice cobbler, a beleaguered smith, or a reformed highwayman.

Or a stubborn steward too, with a little coaxing.

"You'll mind the gatehouse and the stables, take inventory of the armory, round up the carts and wagons that are scattered all over the bailey, make ready for—"

He snorted. "For your garrison of ghosts and gargoyles."

"Aye, Dickon!" Eleanor rounded roughly on the boy, her patience scattered, that ever-present fear whispering harshly of her folly, her conceit. "We'll make ready for whoever will fight on our side. For anyone with hope enough to start again. You'll stand with me, won't you, Dickon? I need you."

His clear eyes reddened and watered, but he steadied his chin. "You know that I will follow you into hell, my lady."

That made her smile and warmed her bones, made her take his hand, and say quietly, "We've already been there, Dickon, and stayed far too long. Now I'm ready for an ordinary view of earth. What about you?"

He made a broad swipe across his eyes with his ragged sleeve and snuffled back a sob. "Ah, yes, my lady."

Tears filled Eleanor's eyes as her freckled champion went down on one knee in front of her.

"Your staff of office, Master Dickon." An old ladle was the only thing near enough at hand for an instant naming. "And my abiding love."

Blushing far up into his hairline, as he always did at the slightest kindness, Dickon took the honor and the ladle with a gigantic smile and an all-the-way-to-the-ground bow.

"Did you just dub Dickon a knight, my lady?" Lisabet and Pippa had been watching in rapt silence from their pallets in front of the hearth, and now surrounded their new constable, Pippa holding fast to his neck, Lisabet absently twirling a hank of his hair.

"If I were queen, Lisabet, I'd grant Dickon a dozen knighthoods for his bravery. For now he'll have to settle for constable here at Faulk-hurst."

"It'll do, my lady." Dickon stood amongst his fondly clinging admirers, squared his shoulders, and offered one of his engaging grins. "For now."

She found Hannah in the kitchen, powdered to the elbows in flour and bread dough and looking happily frazzled, her grey hair caught up in a cap that was missing a tie on the right side.

"I've only enough for three more loaves after these two, my lady. After that—"

"You'll be baking in the kitchen with Faulk-hurst grain tonight, Hannah. And tomorrow, in the bakehouse. I will find my husband's larder, store of grains, and winter fruit supply if I have to break down every door in the castle with my bare hands."

Meanwhile, Nicholas would start on the bakehouse.

She spent the next hour before breakfast forcing William's stubborn locks: picking some cleanly, whacking others when they wouldn't budge.

"Fie and damn you, Bayard, to a hell filled with insatiable lice and poxy harlots."

She cursed her way down the passages and

up the tower steps, adding to the growing map in her head of a castle rich with possibilities and risk, retreating only when a corridor was blocked by a dangerous stone fall.

Her husband's obstacles stood guard over all manner of rooms, from vaulted chambers to dank undercrofts to small metal coffers. But each finally gave up its secret cache to her, opening to a startling discovery of one kind or another, from echoingly empty to absolutely captivating.

"How do you fare down here, my lady?" Hannah found her just as she broke into a well-stocked spinning room.

"It's like finding treasure, isn't it, Hannah?"

"Oh, yes, my lady."

They ogled and speculated as though they had been let loose at a mile-long market faire, with a bottomless purse and all the time in the world. Restraint was difficult, but Eleanor's plan was to open every door and save the exploration and cataloging for later in the week.

Food stores were the most critical, and she offered a grateful prayer when she finally found the larder: long and low, cluttered to its square, squat vaultings with a mottled mix of furniture and chests, barrels and casks, and odd things hanging from the ceiling.

"Dried peas, my lady," Hannah called.

"And persimmons, Hannah! And walnuts, combs of honey, chests of barley and wheat-berries." And crossbeams hung thickly with smoked fish and beef, and shelves of green-rimed cheeses. "And a spice chest for you, Hannah." A flurry of exotic scents wreathed the tall cabinet, even before Eleanor had its door unlocked and one of its small drawers pulled out to show the woman.

"I've never seen such a thing." Hannah stuck her nose into the drawer and sniffed so hard she came up sneezing fiercely, nearly dislodging the new bright green-linen cap Eleanor had found for her in a small wardrobe. "What is . . . is . . . it?" Another, bigger sneeze made Eleanor laugh.

She sniffed the airy yellow powder lightly and sighed in pure pleasure, then recited from memory, "Roasted capon stuffed with bread crumbs and ground almonds and currants and spiced with saffron."

"This is saffron, is it? Oh, my aching bunions." The woman looked horrified and clutched the drawer to her thin bosom. "God's dusted gold, and I just sneezed a handful of it all over my apron."

"It's all right, Hannah."

"Saffron's so dear that I never smelled it before, or tasted it." She replaced the drawer with a trembling hand and pulled out another, sniffed at it, and shook her head. "And this, my lady? It's got the sharp pinch of ginger to it."

"Zedoary. I know the scents and tastes well, Hannah, but I haven't the least idea what to do with them in the kitchen."

"Though I'm a baker by trade, my lady, I'd like to offer my hand at the kettle, too." Hannah smiled hesitantly.

"Then a cook you will be."

They stacked three boxes of kitchen things and carried them up the stairs and into the pantry. "If you don't mind me asking, my lady, what happened to your husband? Was he taken in the pestilence?"

Aye, taken straight to hell by the devil himself. Or so she had imagined the scene—with a great deal of cursing and cowering and gnashing of teeth. "Aye, he was, Hannah."

Hannah clicked her tongue in unwarranted sympathy. *Don't waste your prayers on him, Hannah. Please.*

"I am sorry for your loss, my dear." Hannah rubbed Eleanor's back in just the right place to make her sigh and detest her husband that much more. "Such a ferociously wicked time, it was."

"Aye." William Bayard hadn't been the cause, but he'd surely been a symptom, his phantom shape always at the head of her nightmares—the fifth Horseman, a demon of his own making, always chasing her.

"My Fergus and I . . . we lost every one of our children, milady. The grandchildren, too."

Eleanor's heart collapsed. Tears crowded her throat, brimmed her eyes, and fell swiftly. "Oh, Hannah, no. How awful."

"A dozen they had been, my babies. All grown-up and healthy to a fault, every one of them. Then all of them lost in the course of ten days. Such horrible anguish they suffered, one after the other. And me not being able to do a blessed thing to help, don't you know?"

"I do know, Hannah." *So well, so deeply, that I'm too much a coward to let myself remember too thoroughly.*

So she dodged the horrifying memories again—of a malady so accursed and anguishing it had sent good fathers and mothers running from their dying children, priests from their flocks, the starving into the homes of the dead with the dogs.

Sent her into the places of the dying, where she did her best to give comfort and peace, yet failed so often.

Save me, my lady. But of course, she couldn't. No one could.

And so she shoved aside these horrifying,

111

paralyzing memories and all the others that pursued her when she wasn't planning or writing or humming—exchanged them for better, safer ones. She slipped into Hannah's sagging arms and held tightly to her as they clung and rocked each other in the kitchen pantry.

"As unrighteous as it seems, my lady, I prayed that God would take them quick."

"As I did, too." Hundreds of times. "There's no divine penance to be found in that kind of torment." There couldn't be.

"They're all with God now, don't you think? Together and feasting on candied ginger, like they never had in this world." Hannah laughed sharply and fanned at her reddened eyes. "And me, my lady, as old and useless as I am, was left behind instead of my little Timothy. For what reason, I don't suppose I'll ever know."

Eleanor could hardly see the woman through her streaming tears as she held her away. "I know the reason, Hannah."

"Do you?"

"Aye. You stayed behind to rescue *me*."

Hannah chuckled and waved away the notion. "Oh, ho. Me, my lady? Rescue you, after all you've done for us? Nonsense."

"I need you sorely, Hannah. And Pippa

does, too. And Dickon and Lisabet." And a particularly prickly steward. "Your children were well loved, and like it or not, you have a new brood to care for, and we do love you already."

"And I love you, dear girl. Right from the start." Hannah's smile was watery as she opened a drawer of peppercorns and sighed with joy. "You must miss him greatly, mi-lady."

A question from nowhere at all. "Who is that?" Eleanor snuffled back her tears and dropped to her knees in front of another trunk, fishing around with her iron pick inside the interior of the flat-faced lock, feeling for the catch that would spring the hasp on the sugar safe.

"Your husband, my lady. Do you miss him?"

"Do I—" She stopped, only because she might have laughed heartily, and that would have sounded bitter and selfish.

"I've known you only these few hours, but you seem the kind of woman who loves fiercely and forever."

She missed William Bayard like she would miss a boil on her backside. But Hannah had suffered unfathomable loss, dear family that she must ache for with every breath. She deserved a softer truth. "To be honest, Hannah, by an odd twist of fate, I never actually met my husband."

"What? How does that happen?" The woman sat down on a cask, brushed her palms together, and sniffed at them. "Was he an old man and didn't quite make it up the church steps to take you?"

"No. He was thirty and a bit, or so I was told. And able enough to climb any church steps he came across in his pillaging—to sack the sanctuary and the altar beyond. I doubt the man ever heard a full mass in his life, marriage or otherwise."

"Dearie me. A scoundrel?" Hannah looked too stunned for Eleanor to go into the gruesome details of her husband's blighted career as Edward's Holy Terror.

"A soldier. William Bayard and I were married by a proxy arranged by my father. After which the pestilence came, and then the next thing I heard about my husband was that he had died. In Calais, I believe."

"You don't know for sure."

"I know of a certainty that he's dead. But I can't really say that I miss him when I never set eyes on the man, or communicated with him in any way." A fact that rankled more with every cloud of dust she stirred.

Hannah was as persistent as she was insightful. "So you and your husband never shared a marriage bed?"

"No, we didn't." All the heavens be praised. Then a jangling unease rolled across her shoulders, and became a nagging fear that settled like a snake in her stomach.

A marriage unconsummated wasn't quite complete in the eyes of the church or in the common laws of the country. So if she'd never been completely married to Bayard, how the devil could she still be his widow?

And if she wasn't his legal widow, then her claim to Faulkhurst was—

Invalid? No. It couldn't be.

Oh, bloody, bleeding hell, to quote her steward.

Chapter 8

E very muscle in Nicholas's body ached as he crossed the sun-drenched bailey toward the keep. He was too old to be sleeping in chairs—though he welcomed the chance to practice. A monk's cell couldn't be any less sterile or uncomfortable. Not that a pallet on the gatehouse floor or even a plush feather bed and all the silken trimmings would have left him any better off, or in a less abused mood.

Against all of his convictions, and twenty years of expertly overrunning ill-fortified castles, he had dutifully opened the bloody gate wide, had checked on Figgey—his wife's new plowing marvel—and had steeled himself to face her willful crusade with one of his own.

One whose sole intent was to repair her castle, *his* castle, and then be gone to the monastery and to solitude—as swiftly and as distantly as possible.

Distant seemed more possible in the broad light of day. She'd hardly left him alone all night, had ambushed him round every corner of his dreaming, feeding him ripe plums and warm-skinned peaches, beckoning him, kissing him again and fully, breaking his will a hundred times. A stunning temptation that had roused him near dawn to a brisk walk on the ramparts.

Aye, today would begin their separation, and his solitary walk toward his monastic calling.

He was already practicing chastity with a vengeance. He was serving the less fortunate well enough with her wayfarers, and as for poverty, he hadn't a coin to his name.

Not so impossible, after all.

He climbed the portico steps and entered the great hall, expecting to find it chaotic, stuffed with the child's rambunctious squealing and the lad's blustering. But the hall was empty of people, and as still as a crypt. A strong, familiar silence slipped lead through his veins and slowed his breathing, thickening the cool air with weighty memories.

Of clouds of thyme and juniper collecting in the timbered ceiling, of pungent, medicinal smoke billowing from dozens of braziers round the clock, stationed like hellish sentries between the cots and the pallets, between the dying and the newly fallen.

He'd called on every resource that he could buy or beg or build, anything that would ward off the terror that seemed to slip over the ramparts on the wind: first, vinegar and rose water to wash the floors and the walls. Then, unshuttered windows to let in the unaffected air. Then sealed windows to forestall the invading miasma. He'd prayed on his bare knees, he'd sopped brows, dug and filled grave after grave, had blackened the daylight with burning linens from the pallets of the dead.

He had offered up every prevention prescribed by the priests and the scholars and the doctors—everything but flight from the carnage or seclusion. This battle had to be played out in the open and to the death—between himself and his God.

He'd had little time to learn their names, had come too late to know their dreams, and they had all been too close to death to understand his gratitude for tending his crops and filling his coffers through the years, while he'd been out cutting his way through other villages, sieging and sacking other castles, spending other lives.

And just when he had begun to believe that he'd served his penance, when he'd had nothing left but the son that he'd come to love so late, he discovered the true price of sin.

The boy had lasted a night, and went so quietly that Nicholas hadn't known he was gone until those small, precious fingers had slackened around his own. The loss still ached like fire in that burnt-out part of him.

Faulkhurst had been totally deserted by then, by God and by any goodness that had ever dwelled there. The village was a shambles, its commerce as bankrupt as his soul.

He'd locked the gates, and every storeroom, every door. Then he'd tossed the ring of keys into the sea.

He'd spent a year of private atonement here on the edge of the world, finishing the chapel in his son's name, preparing himself for a life of penance in the brittle solitude of a monastery.

And then she had come flouncing through his castle gates, bringing her hopes and heresies and her irresistible anarchy.

It was the lack of that now, the silence, that disturbed him even more than the echoes ever had.

It ached of loss and nothingness.

Yet there was a sweet scent curling about him, slipping from the kitchen hall to scrub away the remembered reek of the hospital, a scent as foreign and familiar as moondust.

He was drawn down the passage toward the kitchen by the fragrance of newly baked bread, and the muffle of soft laughter.

He saw his wife first, standing at the end of the cook's table, dawn-fresh in her determined joy as she cut a thick slice of bread and placed it in Pippa's upturned palms.

"For Fergus, sweet."

"Here's for you, Ferguuuus!" The girl ran with her offering to the end of the table and plopped the bread in front of the old man, who smiled with his grandfatherly eyes.

"Thank ya, child."

"And for Dickon, Pippa." His wife had animated his kitchen with the sounds that he was certain he'd never hear again. And it frightened him to death.

As he stood in the doorway he wondered if he were invisible to them, if yesterday's haunting had been only a figment of his imagining, the lonely dreams of a madman.

If none of this was quite real. Not even the kiss that still scorched his cheek.

But that unthinkable possibility came apart in the next breath by his wife's uplifted gaze as it found him, by the startling tenderness that he saw there, and the surety that her prayers were being answered as quickly as she could pray them. That he was one of those she had waited for.

"Good morning, steward."

His heart leaped and the words 'good morning, wife' hung in his chest.

Dickon stood abruptly, scraping the bench against the stone floor, and took up sentry duty beside Eleanor, his hand on the hilt of a fine-bladed dagger—stolen no doubt off a lord who should have known better.

Then he was surrounded by noise, like waves lapping at his knees. He was tugged toward the end of the table, directly opposite his wife, by a warm little hand that fit like his memories into his own, tugging with such insistent, undaunted strength that he had to follow.

"Come, Sir Graystone. We missed you. Will you help us fix the bakehouse? See, I told you he wasn't a mean ghost, Nellamore."

"You were right, sweet. But his name is Master Nicholas." The woman's voice was gently beguiling, but her gaze was bright with the enormous challenge she'd brought upon herself, flushed with an invitation that staggered him speechless. "Will you give him some of Hannah's bread, Pippa?"

"Oh, yes!"

He hadn't expected to be besieged so early

in the morning; would rather have had a moment alone with her, to devise a battle plan before her battalion appeared. But a moment later a thick slice of bread was being held up to him, as sweetly scented as his wife.

"Here, Sir Gargoyle." The bread sagged and then tore through its fragile middle, opening a window to three cherry-stained fingers, and then a pair of blue, grinning eyes. "Ooops!"

His wife sent a nudge his way with one of her quick frowns, as though he were shunning some sacred morning ritual and would cause an outrage if he didn't cooperate.

"Hannah made the bread this morning, Sir Gargoyle." The still-steaming slice tore through to the hard crust just as he rescued it.

"Thank you," he said, feeling like a trained bear in the market square, with everyone watching him as he put a corner of the crust into his mouth and bit down.

Hannah chewed in tandem with him, the artist steeling herself against her patron's critical opinion, when in truth it was the greatest pleasure he'd had in a very long time: the civilizing taste of the bread, the scent, the texture, the embracing warmth of the kitchen.

"Faulkhurst's first loaf, Master Nicholas," his wife said, taking the last of it for herself: a steaming part of his own. "It pleases me—all of us—to have you here to share in it."

A woman who made ceremonies of the everyday, who stood at the head of his scarred kitchen table in her plain, russet green chemise and work-worn kirtle like a queen presiding over her motley ministers, as though she believed they could bring about miracles.

Not that he had imagined a queen would ever kiss cheeks and brows, or console her ministers as they sat round her council table, nor would she fondly ruffle their hair with a touch that he craved.

"My compliments to your baker, madam." He turned from his wife's steady gaze and gave the elderly woman a nod.

"Oh, thank you, sir." Hannah blushed as pink as a young woman and he couldn't help but smile back at her as she gathered Pippa's hand. "Come along with me, Pippa, Lisabet. We've mint and thyme to gather out of all those weeds."

They left his wife smiling after them, until she turned it on him and sent his heart spinning, branding his cheek again with the memory of that unaccountable kiss.

"You'll never know how blessed we are to have Hannah with us, Master Nicholas. I'm an utter calamity in the kitchen."

Hardly a calamity, he wanted to say. Damp

and dewy as she'd been last night among the
kettles, and brimming with all the scents of a
spice cabinet as she was just now.

"And to that end, sir, very near the top of
my long list is the bakehouse. It's fallen down.
Did you know that? The roof caved in, at
least."

"Aye, I'm aware of the state of the ovens
and the bakehouse." He'd seen it collapse in
an elegant shower of glassy, red sparks that
he'd doused to keep his bailey from catching
on fire while the earth pitched and swayed.
The village hadn't been as fortunate.

"The kitchen oven is large enough for the
few of us, but scarcely big enough for the hundreds of loaves we'll soon need every day."

Hundreds, indeed. The arrival of Fergus and
Hannah had been a divine jest.

"We need a mason, Master Nicholas."

"I'll fix your bakehouse, madam."

"Can you truly?" She looked equally
pleased and skeptical when he nodded, and
retrieved the sheaf of paper she'd been working on last eve.

"I've had some practice." A whole chapel,
nearly finished.

"Practice enough to shore up an undercroft
vault, I hope."

"Why do you ask?"

THE MAIDEN BRIDE

"I don't know much about the ways of buildings, Master Nicholas, but the arch beneath the west curtain wall doesn't look quite plumb. And the passage beneath it—"

"Beneath the west wall?" Damnation. He knew the extent of the damage all too well, and suffered a horrific image of his wife lost to the cave-in. "Don't tell me you've been tromping around down there? I barricaded that passage last night against just that sort of trespassing."

"I'm not a fool, and I wasn't tromping or trespassing, or treading on your barricades. I was looking for my husband's food stores. With all due caution, I assure you."

"I don't care if you were looking for Bayard's massive treasure of gold and silver—"

"Oh? Do you think he might truly have a treasury, Nicholas? We could surely use one."

"I don't know, madam—but the west curtain wall is dangerous and out of bounds from now on. Do you understand?"

She drew herself up, queenly again in her squared shoulders and glare. "Aye, steward, it is dangerous. At least until it can be fixed— which I hope is very soon. Which is another matter high on my list."

"Add *defense* to that list of yours, madam. I

125

want a guard posted in the barbican at all times."

"At night only." She added something to her list with a flick of her quill. "I can't spare anyone."

"It's not a matter of sparing—"

"That be *my* job, my lady," Dickon sputtered suddenly. "Guarding the castle. You said so." He'd been hovering behind her, as though he thought she was in imminent danger of being accosted. Now the lad stepped bravely between her and Nicholas, his hand on his dagger. "I'm milady's constable."

"You?" Nicholas looked between Eleanor and the lad.

"Me!"

Christ. A green-willow boy—a highwayman—for a constable. He held back his protest, though; the boy was, in truth, the only option at the moment. Trainable, perhaps. He'd raised up many a squire to knighthood; it might be possible to raise a thief to a constable.

Huh—easier to raise the dead.

"Then get yourself and that dagger of yours to the gate, lad, and take your watch."

The boy bristled. "Milady wants the armory put to rights first. Don't you, milady?"

"I do. Perhaps, steward, since the barbican

and the armory are nearly in the same place,
Dickon may keep his post and make sense of
the chaos there at the same time." She was
wearing a fiercely motherly frown now, ready
to pounce on him if he dared take another
swipe at her cub.

But he had a point to make here, a clarification of his power to streamline his efforts to
secure Faulkhurst for his wife all the sooner.

All the sooner to be gone.

"I doubt that, madam."

"I could." Dickon stamped his foot on the
stone floor. "I bloody well will. I've given my
word to my lady to do just as she orders."

Nicholas looked across the table at his wife,
feeling himself on trial, with more to lose than
he'd imagined. Her respect, for one, and her
trust—and that surprised him.

"As you should, boy, but would you give
your life in her defense?"

His wife charged in his direction. "Master
Nicholas, that's enough."

But the boy pushed past her and barred her
way. "I'd fall on my dagger right now, if I she
asked me to."

She nearly threw herself in front of the boy
and wagged a terrifying finger at him. "You'll
do nothing of the sort, Dickon." Then at Nich-

olas. "And you, Master Nicholas will end this."

He would indeed, just as he'd planned. "Aye, my lad, your lady has chosen well in you."

Dickon's mouth had been open to protest, but he was quick and managed instead a squawking, "Has she? I mean, aye! She has."

"That I have, steward. And you should re-member that the choice is mine to make." Eleanor was appalled, unable to understand this baiting Dickon. It was unfair, unseemly, and out of his character—or so she hoped. The boy looked to her with pleading eyes, as though he were defending his soul, not know-ing if his judge was devil or angel.

Nicholas was circling the pair of them, glar-ing first at Dickon, then challenging Eleanor with a gaze that heated her nape and drifted like silk across her lips and made her touch them with her tongue.

"You'll do well, lad, to remember that a cas-tle is a place of defense and constant danger."

"I know that, sir!"

"Doubly so, Dickon, because our lady seems bound to trust anyone at all without cause." The blackguard stopped and stepped closer to Dickon. "Have you noticed that?"

The boy, once her eager champion, was now

agreeing fiercely with Nicholas, his brows beetling and his head bobbing. "She won't listen to me. Never has."

"Nor to me. Not a word, lad. Dismisses entirely the idea that someone might wish her harm."

"I never said that, steward."

He cast her a negligent nod and put a confederate's arm around Dickon's shoulder, patting it companionably. "We've trouble on our hands, Master Dickon."

"Aye, we do, sir. Big trouble." The boy had caught up Nicholas's gravity completely and mirrored it gesture for gesture, even shaking his head in masculine sympathy for their entire gender.

"If you mean that I am trouble, gentlemen, you haven't seen the sort of trouble I can be." Oh, but why bother with the pair of them. Next they'd be marking out their territories and telling daring stories of their greatest battles.

"As our lady's seneschal, lad, I am her deputy in all the matters of her estate." Nicholas groaned broadly, as though all his teeth hurt him. "Do pity me for that."

The bloody lout.

"Oh, I do, sir," Dickon said, his loyalty now shifted entirely to her steward. "A pissy chore.

I've held it myself for more than a year."

"Aye, Dickon. You've done an admirable job getting her this far safely—considering."

"Considering nothing, steward."

But the man only lifted his wily gaze to hers and spoke to her solely, making her wonder if he knew just how badly she wanted to thump him. " 'Tis my responsibility to guard and defend her rights and her person from here on. But I can't be everywhere, Dickon."

"No, sir?" The lad was in total thrall.

With sudden clarity, Eleanor saw Nicholas's purpose. How artful this steward of hers could be, so expertly politic when it suited him. She'd seen Edward do the same many times, patch over an outrage that he had caused himself through his ruthlessness, merely by changing sides to that of his opponent and becoming an accomplice.

A worthy skill and a highly treacherous one, to be guarded against at all times.

Thank God the man was so transparent.

"As constable, Dickon, you are my eyes and ears when I can't be there to watch over the lady Eleanor."

Dickon's cheeks glowed in the light of Nicholas's praise. "I'll be your nose too, sir, if you need me to be." He was nearly singing.

"Indeed." The man had a gregarious smile

locked down tightly in his eyes, one that drifted to her briefly and made her wonder how often and how deeply she would fall for his cunning herself.

"What about me, sir?" Fergus had been watching with wariness, and now struggled to his feet like an old soldier. "I'm a carpenter, you know."

"A carpenter, Fergus?" Eleanor could hardly believe their good fortune. "There you see, Master Nicholas? I prayed for a carpenter last night, and here he is. Have you done any smithing, Fergus? We need a blacksmith as much as we need a carpenter."

Fergus's brows knitted as he frowned and chewed on the end of his moustache. "Well, my lady—actually, I never actually been a carpenter. Though it's always been my wish to take up the trade."

"Ah."

Oh, blast. Eleanor hid her disappointment behind a huge smile that she was trying desperately to feel. "Good then, Fergus."

Nicholas asked evenly, "What *was* your trade, Fergus?"

Eleanor hoped for some craft that had required at least some knowledge of a hammer: a cobbler, a wainwright, an apprentice to either. *Please, God.*

"I was a nightman, sir. All my life." Fergus
scratched at his chin, then braved the stony
severity of Nicholas's jaw, some foot and a
half above him. "A cleaner of privies and cesspits."

Eleanor caught the wholly out of proportion
laughter in her throat, amazed at her steward's
outward patience and grateful that he didn't
crush Fergus with the derision that was so
plainly in his thoughts.

"Then you are well ahead of your wishes,
Fergus," he said, "as my lady needs a carpenter just now." He turned all of that dark-eyed
irony on her, lifted a brow and her spirits all
in that single gesture. A partnership. "And if
she has no objection, you and I and Dickon
here will see to inspecting her castle for creak-
ing timbers and precarious walls. If my lady
so orders."

The mutinous blackguard, using her own
words against her. Yet an odd feeling engulfed
her, warm and embracing, of being wholly
and steadfastly protected.

"Aye, go then, sir."

"As you wish, milady." He bowed only
slightly, but with all the courtly nuances of
any lord at Westminster.

Aye, and more lordly than most.

"Oh, and we are in sore need of a blacksmith, Nicholas. Do let me know when one comes though the gate."

She felt altogether tousled by his scowl, by the fierceness of it that seemed to lift her hair and brush at her neck and the ties on the front of her chemise.

"And you, madam, stay out of passages beneath the west curtain wall."

That made her smile, way down deep in her heart.

He was a mystery, someone else's wandering knight, to be sure. But hers to tame now, however briefly.

However magically.

Chapter 9

Eleanor began an accounting of the contents of all the storage rooms that she'd opened so far. But the clutter was so widespread and haphazard, with sacks of dried peas stored next to threshing forks, and those on top of fine linens, the only way to ensure a thorough accounting was to put everything in one room and sort through it.

And the only room that would begin to hold the contents of Faulkhurst was the great hall.

"A treasure hunt!" Lisabet's shouts and Pippa's squealing followed the pair of them into the undercrofts, and soon they were racing up and down the tower stairs, their arms filled with a mix of cups, shoes, and brooms.

Eleanor sectioned off the hall for kitchen goods, for linens, for furniture and chests, setting aside the odd hammer or harness for the stables. It would be a weeklong endeavor at the least to find everything, even if she could spare everyone in the castle for this single task.

"Please let me know immediately, Lisabet, if you find any books." Eleanor rescued the pail of candle bits out of the girl's arms and set it with the two jugs of lamp oil. "They'll be very large. Heavy, too.

"Books to read?"

"Only the estate records, sweet. Inventories and accountings, the harvest schedules."

Lisabet wrinkled up her dust-smudged nose. "What kind of reading is that?"

The most valuable kind of all: information. "Faulkhurst's best kept secrets, Lisabet."

"A real treasure! Pippa! There's a book somewhere with a secret inside!" Lisabet dashed up the tower stairs.

"Where did you hide your black heart, husband?" The records had to be in the castle somewhere, and with any luck she'd find the estate office at the same time, behind one of Bayard's hundreds of locked doors.

She hurried down the stairs to the undercroft beneath the great hall, armed with her lamp, her faithful picklock, and a sledgehammer for good measure.

She hung the lamp on a peg and fit the pick into a rusted lock, certain that God completely understood why she'd learned to pick locks

135

with such ease: to open the herbalist's cabinet at the deserted Priory of St. Oswald, to free Dickon and Lisabet from that horrid jail at Bristol. The skill was an uproarious source of humor for Dickon.

She did her level best with the small picklock, but still the rusted hasp just hung there.

Like so many of her husband's locks, it was impregnable. An overlarge hunk of rusted iron, corroded by the salted air of the sea, encrusted with his villainy. But hopefully, no match for a simple sledgehammer and a chisel.

She hoisted the long-handled thing over her shoulder, fit the chisel blade against the hasp, raised the hammer above her head, inhaled a breath of suddenly familiar, altogether intoxicating coolness, then put every ounce of her weight into a downward swing.

But the hammer went nowhere. At all. It hung with a magical weightlessness in the air just above her head.

"What—"

"Are you trying to take your fingers off at the wrist, madam?"

"Nicholas!" Furious that he could so easily thwart her—that he could sneak up on her like a shadow, as though he owned every passage, she kept a firm grip on the handle and turned beneath his arm, only to come face to chest with his frozen-frowned fury. "Let go this instant. I order you."

Nicholas decided then and there that the only way to save the woman from herself was to lock her up and toss away the key. "And I refuse, madam." He plucked the sledgehammer out of her hand and tossed it aside, well out of her reach.

"On what grounds, sir?"

"On the grounds that you are being careless with your well-being."

"I'm perfectly capable of breaking a few locks. I've been doing it this way all morning." She rapped on the panel with the heel of her hand, then leaned back against the door.

"This way?" Holy hell. "Wild swings with a sledgehammer and a chisel?" He took the chisel out of her hand.

"Lacking a set of keys to my husband's castle, I have no choice. You haven't seen any, have you, Nicholas? Keys to any of the doors?"

He nearly laughed. There was a whole ring of them rusting beneath the waves where he'd tossed them over a year ago. But she didn't need to know that. He would open the damned locks himself.

He'd never in his life had to lie about anything. He'd never needed to—he'd always taken what he wanted by force or coercion, had spoken his own brand of truth and to hell with the opposition, royal or otherwise. Now, speaking one falsehood after another to his wife didn't set at all well.

"I've seen no keys, my lady," he said, adding to his tenancy in hell. He wanted to press her up against the door and make love to her mouth, because she'd caught up her glistening lower lip with her teeth in her exasperation at him—and at her husband, that ghost that was forever hanging about.

"How about gunpowder? Is there any?"

She was utterly mad, and beautiful, the ends of her hair scented with cinnamon at the moment.

"*Gunpowder*, madam?"

"Never mind; I suppose a sledgehammer will have to do me. Now stand aside; I have loads of work to do, and you're in my way." The woman picked up the hammer again, nearly clubbing his knee with it before he caught the handle and took it from her.

"Allow me, before you damage one of us." He took a swing and the lock popped easily and clattered to the ground. She made an approving little noise in her throat that made his heart swell like a knavish fool's.

"Thank you, Nicholas."

She flipped the remains of the latch off the hasp, swung the door wide, and carried her lamp into the blackness. He followed her uneasily, not remembering what he'd left in here or in any of the other storage rooms when he'd locked the doors so long ago.

He'd prepared well for a long siege, at the beginning. He'd kept rigorous accounts in the estate records until it hadn't mattered anymore, until everyone had just slipped away.

"Nothing," she said, glaring into the single barrel that stood lidless in the center of the small and otherwise empty room. "I wish my husband were here beside me just now."

"Do you?" He was standing as near to her as he dared, close enough to see more than he ought to of the small, rounded ripeness of her breasts, their peaks hidden completely from all but his imagination, from the delight they would be to hold, to nuzzle.

His heart skipped along his ribs and his mouth was dry when he finally asked, "Why do you say that?"

"Because then, sir, I could curse him to his face, just as I constantly do under my breath for leaving me such a mess of his stores."

The urge to defend himself shoved at his pride, nudged him to say, "Your opinion of your late husband seems overly strong, considering that you never met him."

"I didn't have to meet him to know that he was a wicked man. Great heavens, his legends told me so, long before I was wed to him—even if only half of them were true."

True as it was, her indictment struck hard. It made him want to demand a list of all of his flaws in detail, so that he could at least dismiss the falsehoods and repair some of himself in her eyes. "Bayard was wicked in what way?"

"In every way imaginable. You must have known his reputation—the worst being that he was too cowardly to care that his tenants were dying by the score, too busy raiding and debauching or tallying his plunder, or outright hiding from the calamity, instead of sending help to Faulkhurst or coming himself."

Cowardly. He didn't want her to believe that of him, not cowardice. It hadn't happened that way at all and he wanted her to know, somehow. "You're sure that your husband abandoned Faulkhurst so heartlessly?"

"If not him, then his steward did so on his behalf and then locked the gates."

"Perhaps it was a mercy, my lady, to send them all away. To someplace better."

"Ballocks! William Bayard never did a merciful thing in his life—except for his neglect of me. I've never known a man so practiced at abandoning his obligations at the first hint of trouble. Whether castle or village ... or wife."

He hated that she could believe that of him. He hadn't abandoned her; he had believed absolutely that she was dead with the rest of her family.

Aye, but not in those first months of their marriage. He could have sent for her then, but he had been too busy sacking churches and razing farmers' crops, overrunning villages for their plunder. No time for a wife while he was despoiling his soul. Damnation. If he could just explain that she had been better off without him—that she still was.

She was just picking up the lamp when he realized with a stinging shock to his pride that her fingers were entirely barren of rings.

Even his.

A battering surge of possession threatened to swamp him, and he took her left hand and turned her palm upward in the cradle of his own, threading her fingers lightly between his own.

"He gave you no ring?" he managed.

He'd sent one to her at the time of the wedding, some little nothing, though he'd never even seen it himself. It was chosen by his ambassador to put a seal on the marriage con-

tract. John Sorrel—a bastard soul himself—
had stood for him as groom while he'd tended
to his other interests. He'd never spared the
ring or the wedding or even the woman he'd
married a single thought.

Yet now it angered him to the marrow that
she wasn't wearing his ring, alleged widow or
no. Worse—that he had allowed some other
man to place it on her finger.

"Do you mean my husband?"

He swallowed hard, cleared his throat.
"Who else would I mean? He must have given
you a ring."

"Yes, but it's gone."

"Gone how? Did you lose it?" He could easily imagine what it must have meant to her by
the sound of her derision: little enough to
make her toss it into the nearest gutter on
principle alone.

"I sold my wedding band in Doncaster a
year ago, to buy boots for Dickon and a new
kirtle for Lisabet; she'd outgrown hers. I also
bought three loaves of bread with the pro-
ceeds, I believe. Yes, and carrots. And an on-
ion."

A negligible amount for what the band of
gold and garnets must have cost his treasury,
and what it cost her pride. "Your wedding
ring fetched all that?"

Her eyes narrowed. "It was fashioned of alchemist's gold, Nicholas."

"I doubt that." He bit the edges of his tongue, sorry that he'd ever mentioned the damned ring, sorry that it made his gut ache to think of it placed on her hand in his absence.

"I never wore the horrid band after that travesty of a wedding ceremony." *Travesty?* Sorrel had said nothing of any problems. "It gained value in my heart only when I used it to buy food and shelter for the people I love. I don't miss it at all."

A belly-kick would have winded him less. "Well, good then. Fine."

"Did you need me for anything, Nicholas?"

Damnation. He couldn't very well tell her that he'd come because he didn't trust her to stay out of trouble for more than an hour, that he planned to keep a closer eye because he was terrified of her coming to harm. "Merely to report the progress on the armory."

"Why the armory?" She crossed her arms below her breasts and tapped her booted foot. "I told you specifically to start with the bakehouse. We need bread, Nicholas."

"Not until the forge is running again, which can't happen until the armory roof is secure.

One step before the next, in their proper order."

She looked wary but willing to listen. "How long do you think?"

"Two days, no more than three." When she frowned at that very reasonable estimate, he added, "Hannah can bake for the few of us in the kitchen ovens till then."

"There'll be many more than a few of us by then, Nicholas." He would have scoffed aloud at her moon-eyed fantasies, but she stalked out of the chamber with her lamp, only to turn back to him in the doorway, the light of her escapades dancing in her eyes. "Which reminds me, Nicholas. I'm looking for my husband's estate office. Have you seen it?"

A great, cold weight landed hard in his gut. His office. "Why?"

"Because I expect to find the manorial records there. Bayard's steward must have kept them somewhere central to the daily activities, in an office or the tithe barn, maybe the gatehouse."

In my private solar, wife, high in the keep. Every word of the last two years written distinctly in his own hand. "I suppose he must have."

"Yes, but where? I found a store of blank paper, ink and quills and sealing wax, but nothing that looked to be the accounting rolls.

Have you ever come across a chamber that might be such an office?"

"I'm sorry, my lady. I can't help you there." Not until he secured the records from the solar and hid them far from her sphere. There were too many of his secrets to be plundered among the lines and numbers. "Come, madam. I'll crack open a few more locks for you."

"You don't need to."

"Indulge my peace of mind, my lady."

He led her far away from the keep tower, breaking every lock they came across until she was too busy with her discoveries to follow him with her mischief.

Then he slipped away to the keep tower, where memories slowed his tread to a stop.

The last few steps up the stairs to the shuttered solar were a daunting distance, rife with the recollection of locking the door against that careful accounting of his sins, and his failure to protect the innocent.

He couldn't let Eleanor see the most recent records of the estate; she was far too observant. He was her steward now, and she would soon know his handwriting as well as she knew her own. A cataclysmic error, if she ever made the connection between Bayard and himself.

So he climbed the stairs, just as he had done

a thousand times before, dreading the buffeting memories.

Of racing Liam and his laughter up the steps, of catching him halfway and swinging him over his shoulder to gallop into the tower. *Again, Papa!* And so they had made their adventures each night, until the stars winked out.

This had been their refuge—his and his son's. Where the boy had played and learned his Latin and his numbers, where Nicholas had labored over accounts that he'd never paid attention to before, where he'd watched his son sleeping—terrified of the boundlessness of love that seemed to gather strength with every day. His son, tucked away safely against everything but God's confounding will.

Now the chamber smelled of dust and regrets and should-have-beens.

He closed his heart and gathered all his account books and his journals, everything that he'd ever been, and then escaped with them back into the comfortable shadows.

Chapter 10

 "A plow harness stored in the silk-
chest." Eleanor wheeled another
barrow of goods out of the door of the east
tower and thumped down the stairs into the
bailey, wishing she had a chamberlain, when
she noticed an odd little man come swaggering through the gate into the sunshine of the
inner ward.

He was every inch a bandy-legged fighting
cock, with a ragged green band tied across his
right eye and a rucksack towering two heads
taller than his stout shoulders. He was trailed
by an exceedingly pregnant sow.

The man stopped dead when he saw her,
preened a bit, hitched up his jangling pack,
and then deepened his swagger in her direction.

An outlaw. Oh, yes. She knew it for certain,
even before he opened his mouth to ask,

"Does this be Faulkhurst castle, missy?"

A housebreaker, without a doubt. A pig stealer, for certain. Arrogant, light-footed, and wearing a whole peddler's cart of things that didn't belong to him.

"Aye, sir, it—"

"Beggar me bald, I should ha' known better than to trust the bastard." The man threw his leather cap to the ground and stomped on it.

"Trust who?"

"Never you mind yourself, missy girl. Here I come all this way 'cause I heard that 'er ladyship was paying folks to live here."

Another wayward soul—and Nicholas wouldn't like this one a bit. "I know for a fact that she is doing just that, sir. You've found the right place. A tithe and a cottage and a—"

"A cottage, too? Here, you say?" He stalked around her on his short legs, his one eye as sharp as two. "Well, it damned well better not be one of those heaps of wattle and daub I just passed in that piss-pot excuse for a village."

Discriminating as well as enterprising.

"Who are you, sir?"

"The name's Mullock." He cocked his head sharply and looked Eleanor up and down with a smile that lacked a tooth at each of its corners. "And who do you be, mistress, when you're at home roosting on your lovely lark's nest?"

An *insolent* outlaw. "See here, Master Mullock, I don't care to know how you found—"

She would have finished setting the man straight about who was in charge here, but an enormous, sun-blotting shadow fell across the space between them and then Mullock was suddenly dangling above her, squirming and croaking like a frog on a fish line, held aloft by the scruff of his tunic by Nicholas's lethal fist.

"Master Nicholas, put him down."

But her steward was striding toward the gatehouse, or toward the jagged teeth of the seacliffs, by the cold fury in his eyes.

"No, Nicholas!" She chased after him, after those rippling shoulders, that broad back. She managed to grab hold of his dagger belt and dig her heels into the rocky ground. Pointless, as she sailed along behind him, a broken rudder to his momentum. "What do you think you're doing, sir?"

He stopped, a solid wall of leather to her colliding motion. He swung around to face her, still dangling Mullock like a spitting cat.

"I'm taking out the refuse, madam."

He started away again. But she was ready this time as she blocked his way with both hands extended, though his chest loomed. "Master Mullock isn't refuse."

" 'At's right, I'm—" His protest ended in a gacking sound and more struggling.

"Madam, he insulted you."

Mullock played fisticuffs with the breeze three feet above the ground, while Nicholas ignored him entirely.

"They were words only, sir. It takes a lot more than Master Mullock's coarse little insults to threaten me. I took no offense."

He spoke through his teeth. "Well, I *did*."

Mother Mary, she could fall hopelessly in love with all that nostril-flaring outrage. He was defending her as her husband never had, as her father never thought to.

Immense and protective, her shade in the hot sun. What a dear man.

And what a danger to her authority.

"I'm grateful for your concern, Nicholas. But it isn't necessary."

Nicholas couldn't recall a blacker rage, not even in the thickness of battle. Mullock wasn't fit to sweep the sand off the cobbles, yet he knew where his wife was going with her philosophies, and he loathed it with every part of him.

"He's a thief, madam. And a worse villain than that, I'll wager."

"Nicholas. Please. Let's at least hear what Master Mullock has to say for himself."

Not bloody much at the moment. But she was tugging at his belt again, a wife's familiar insistence, a gentle pleading for the life of this cur.

He brought the man closer and gave him this one and only chance. "If you want to live long enough to take another breath, Mullock, you'll speak to the lady Eleanor with the greatest respect."

"I wi—"

"The slightest slip, Mullock, and I'll cut your tongue right out of your fool head and feed it to the crabs. Do you understand me?"

Mullock nodded and flailed. "Down."

Nicholas let go gladly and Mullock splatted onto the cobbles, hacking and coughing as he struggled to his hands and knees. "Didn't know she was yours, milord."

Aye, she was that, and his pulse roared through his ears, leaving a ringing sound that deafened him to all but the whisper: she's *mine*.

"I'm not anyone's, Master Mullock. I am Eleanor Bayard, the lady here at Faulkhurst."

"You? The lady—"

"Master Nicholas here is my steward." She bent down to help the man, to dust him or

151

coddle him, but Nicholas yanked him upright by the scruff, leaving him wide-stanced and staggering.

He had every intention of locking the miscreant in the gatehouse cellar until midnight, then setting him out to sea in a leaky boat at high tide.

"I do apologize, Master Mullock," she said, brushing at the man's elbow, glaring at Nicholas. "We've gotten off to a bad start. But I assure you that you're quite welcome here." She'd sent that as a challenge to him, as though he still couldn't comprehend her logic—total reformation of souls, all because she wished it so.

She gave a gentle push against the center of Nicholas's chest to set him away a step, her palm and soft, cool fingers on the place above his heart, for the space of a breath. He nearly covered her hand to keep it there, but she had already moved past him to apply her balm elsewhere.

"Where do you come from, Master Mullock?"

Exactly Nicholas's question, but for an entirely different reason. Three people happening upon an abandoned castle in the course of a day wasn't a coincidence. It was the work of deliberate calculation.

Or the devil.

Or his very devious wife.

"I come here direct from Greenwich town." Mullock's eye darted from his wife upward to Nicholas, where he stood guard behind her, a place that felt all too fitting. In the full light of the cloudless day her hair gleamed a fiery copper, strewn liberally with gold, barely captured in a plait.

"Greenwich?" She retrieved the man's hat, brushed it off, and gave it back to him. He crushed it like a callow boy suddenly shy with his favorite lass. "What did you do there to get a living wage?"

"I was a—" he glanced at Nicholas, as though he might sense some uncomfortable truth, scoundrel to scoundrel "—well, I was a merchant."

And I am a monk. "Have you been praying for merchants, my lady?"

"Truly, Master Mullock?" She ignored Nicholas but for that hand again, reaching backward to touch his chest. He captured and held it bundled in his, because he could, and she couldn't do much about it, but tug and then relax. "What kind of merchant?"

Beads of sweat sprang up on Mullock's half brow, dampening the filthy green band. A brigand, about to confess his venal sins in his wife's court of charity toward even the lowest.

"Bought and sold a bit of everything, milady. Ship's cargo, private cartage, movable chattel, the like."

"I can guess whose chattel, Mullock." Nicholas knew exactly what kind of business the man was in. A land pirate, a dealer in stolen goods.

" 'Twas mine, sir. Whatever anyone wanted to buy, I was ready to sell."

"Or steal." Nicholas received a pair of scowls for that and a light poke from his wife, too near his tarse for her own good, for his. He let go of her hand and hoped to hell she hadn't noticed more than she should.

"Then you must be very good at knowing the worth of things, Master Mullock."

Mullock stalled, his eye roving between her and Nicholas. He obviously wanted insight into this illogical inquisition before he answered. "Aye. I did a fair lot of business in Greenwich and London."

"If your business was doing fairly, Master Mullock, whatever made you leave?"

"My bloody storehouse burned down a few months back, and everything in it. There was nothing left to me but these clothes."

"Then where did you get all this, Mullock?" Nicholas upended the rucksack onto the ground, disgorging plateware, a harness, a distaff, shoes, and an orange that had hardened to brick.

"Hey! That's mine." Mullock fell onto the pile, just long enough for Nicholas to pick him up again, for Eleanor to shoulder him aside and level a finger at Mullock.

"Is that how you came by your treasures?" The question was so piercing and unexpected it made the little man shift his weight. "Well, did you?"

He stubbed his heel into the ground and mumbled, "I collected the stuff as I come here."

"I think you stole it," she said, and Mullock's shoulders sagged.

"Of course he did, madam."

"Aye. I suppose I did."

"Because . . . ?" she asked in her perverse inquisition that could lead nowhere.

"Because it were there for me to take."

She glanced up at Nicholas, as though she'd proved her point once again. "Well, then, Master Mullock, you'll be glad to know that you'll never have to steal again. That is, if you choose to stay with us."

"What d'ya mean?"

Bloody hell, she was going to keep him, to cosset a housebreaker. In *his* castle!

"You'll find the work here backbreaking, but well worth it, a chance to be an honest merchant—for there *are* such creatures in the world. You'll have a tidy cottage in that piss-poor village, land to till, and your pride to cultivate. There's no reason to be looking over your shoulder for the law anymore. It all comes down to freedom, sir. I find it the most satisfying thing in the world. Yours for the asking."

Nicholas never would have credited it, but Mullock had the grace to blush a stark crimson, leaving him stammering.

"If it's all as you say, lady—" Nicholas had never seen such doubt strangled by hope "—I'll count myself lucky for having come here after all."

"Well, then, Master Mullock," she said, kneeling to pat the sow and to help the startled man stuff his rucksack with the stolen goods, "I've got just the job for you. And you start right now."

Nicholas knelt as well and tipped her chin toward him so that she'd listen clearly for once, so that she would understand that he forbade her ever being alone with Mullock.

"If he stays, madam, he'll work for *me*. At my side, never out of my sight for an instant. Do you understand? For me alone."

156

He'd never seen a pair of eyebrows that could so quickly change aspects; from softly soaring to a deadly, hawk-winged dive that would end in bloodied feathers and a whole flock of squawking.

"No," she whispered—only out of deference to the bastard's sensibilities, as though they were perishable and his were not.

"He works with me, my lady."

"I appreciate your advice, steward. But I've an important task for Mullock. If I can spare him next week, you can have him."

You'll stay clear of him, wife, because I'm lord here, and I say so, because I can't have you risking yourself.

"What task, madam?" Whatever it was, he'd take care of it later.

"He shall be the keeper of the wardrobe."

"Him?" Confounded, Nicholas glared at the man, who looked equally astounded. Spooked, and ready to run.

"Me?"

"Exactly you, Master Mullock." She stood up between them, set the stuffed rucksack upright against her knee, and tied it off at the neck. "I need someone to make sense of the mess that my husband and his steward left behind for me. The storage rooms and the undercrofts are a jumble. And have you thought,

Nicholas, of how we'll sort through all the chattel that will come out of the village? Someone needs to do something with it all. I can't spare the time. Do you read, Mullock?"

The thief's mouth gaped still. "No, milady."

"Then I'll find you a clerk. Somehow." She handed the man his rucksack.

"And you want me to manage this wardrobe?"

"If you please." She waited patiently for Mullock's assent, while the man twitched his eye and ran his filthy finger along the neck of his tunic.

"I do please, my lady," Mullock finally whispered, as though he feared being drummed out of the thief's guild if they ever learned he'd gone honest on them. "Very much so."

Damnation.

"Good. Come then—I'll settle you in and put you to work immediately." She started off toward the keep with the man and his sow, her hands sketching out her dreams against the sky.

In a single edict, she had appropriated Mullock's thieving and knighted him with her trust. He looked suddenly sainted, transcendent. Not that it would last. Men like Mullock crossed every class, from princes to peasants.

They lived entirely for themselves. She needed to understand this.

He would set her straight about unreclaimable brigands and impoverished hearts.

About a God who jousted with unarmed innocents.

Chapter 11

~ ᴏᴄ ~

"**A** solar? Way up here?" Eleanor hadn't seen the tower room on her first foray. Odd, because it hadn't a lock, though it was tightly closed up, smelling of dust and in dire need of the crisp sunlight that filled it when she slid aside the heavy drapes and opened the tall shutters onto the shimmering blue ocean that seemed to stretch out forever.

Bright and sublimely homey, with a small connected chamber through another set of drapes, with another tall casement window.

There were three barrel chairs and a small hearth, four braziers, a scarred worktable and benches, stout candles with dust-covered wax pooled in their tallow catches, pots of ink, coffers full of paper, upright pigeonholes stuffed with counting sticks, shelves of large books—

"Books! This isn't just a solar, it's the steward's office!"

Feeling wildly triumphant, she hefted an ancient-looking book off the shelf, spread it across the table and opened to the first page. It was, indeed, everything that she'd been searching for.

" 'Faulkhurst Castle. Household accounts: Michaelmas, 1301.' " Fifty years old, but there were many more books here, dozens of them. The record of every minute of the manor's years, its pulse and its livelihood: from how many chickens were used for supper on the octave of Easter, to the number of candles burned during Twelfth Night.

The newer books were thicker, but stopped abruptly, tellingly, four years ago—1347. The year before the plague had come.

The front page of the book was signed by a Rudolphus—whether merely a clerk or William Bayard's well-educated steward, his daily paragraphs were neatly scribed and set apart.

" '25 March, 1347. 'Delivered from the East Tower wardrobe to the armory, 17 ells of canvas, 4d.' for banners." The East Tower—exactly where she and Hannah had discovered the spinning room.

" 'To the kitchen: one-quarter ox, from castle stores, and one barrel salt. Three peahens, 1d.' "

She sat at the table and read on through a

hard, wintry year, with plowing and planting
and reaping schedules that clearly revealed—
as she had suspected they would—her husband's meanness of spirit: driving his tenants
to produce more than they could bear, driving
them off their land when they failed, collecting
harsh fees and taxes, showing no mercy toward those who needed it most.

All of his sins, recorded in the tidy quill
strokes of his dispassionate steward.

She scanned the lines quickly, chiding herself to stop with each turn of the page. But
toward the end of November of that year, a
single item in a single paragraph made her
heart lurch.

" 'One band of gold from Faulkhurst Treasury, 10s. To John Sorrel for the lord's bride.' "

The lord's bride.

"*Me.*" The brevity of the notation numbed
the tips of her fingers, heated smudges across
her cheeks. "I was an item on Bayard's accounting sheet. Not even a name."

Of course, not surprising at all. Yet it was
difficult to explain the hollowness that came
with seeing it inked with such casual perma-
nence.

The lord's bride—but never his wife. There was
no line for that.

An unwanted, unexpected grief washed

over her, thoroughly wasted on a regret that she shouldn't feel.

Because he didn't matter anymore.

Because, according to the common laws and those of God, he'd never been her husband at all.

Unconsummated. Incomplete.

Still a virgin—dangerously so, if Edward or his barons ever discovered that she and William had never met. How simply that could happen: a casual mention of timing, a little investigation into William's travels, then into hers.

The consequences terrified her, were unthinkable: that Faulkhurst might one day be taken from her by lack of a marital formality. No one need ever know that it hadn't happened, the ceremonial rending of her maidenhead.

No one but her next husband, if there ever was such a man—right in the middle of their wedding night when he would discover her intact and trembling, her home, her heart, completely at his mercy.

And there *would* be another husband someday—Edward would see to that.

Unless she found a remedy for her highly inconvenient chastity—some willing gentleman who wouldn't mind deflowering a virgin.

Someone like Nicholas.

Deflower you, madam? Certainly. Would you prefer before or after I finish the bakehouse?

Now.

But it would be never. Oh, God. Here she was daydreaming again—still—flushed and glowing to the tips of her breasts, breathless with imagining that Nicholas might kiss her there someday. His lips had been wondrously warm and questing last night, and he'd only kissed her fingers, their tips, and that stunning, stirring place in the middle of her palm.

But he was the absolutely wrong man for the task—should she ever decide to undertake such a rash act. He was her laborer and she the master: she'd made that decisively clear. It wouldn't be fair to him. He'd surely consider her request an order and feel obligated. She wouldn't take advantage of her position—no matter her desire for his kiss, or those appealing eyes of his, when they filled up with his passion. Or when he smiled from inside them.

No, a perfect stranger would be best of all. Unattached, unable to tell tales afterward.

Sneaking around with a stranger? This whole ridiculous scheme felt like an unforgivable betrayal. Not of her husband, oddly, but of Nicholas.

'Twill be my pleasure, madam. As it will be yours.

Blast it all. She took three long, deep breaths and righted her focus, forcing herself to scan the short lines of her husband's book once again, looking for more than had been there before.

The lord's bride. But there she was still, wedged between 'the expenses of the hounds in taking one fallow deer' and '250 salted herring from stores.'

"A pox on your soul, Bayard. An itchy, burning one."

She slammed the book closed and scavenged through the chamber for the most recent records, opening chests and trunks and wardrobes of male clothing. But the last book ended abruptly in 1347.

"You couldn't even leave me a few measly words about your castle, a few numbers, a few hints at how to dig my way out of your midden, could you, husband?"

Selfish to the end.

Not that she was going to give up her search, even though Rudolphus might have escaped with the records to one of Bayard's Burgundian estates when the pestilence arrived. If so, Edward had doubtlessly used them to eviscerate her husband's holdings after his death.

Another scavenger always waiting to pick at the bones. She'd be damned if she'd stand still long enough to let anyone pick at hers. The sound of Pippa and her pounding tread came chasing up the stairwell.

"Nellamore! Nellamore, look! Look what we found." Pippa flew into the room, slid to a stop, and grinned as Eleanor knelt to catch her. "See!"

Pippa laid a small toy horse—or some such beast—into Eleanor's palm; a sweet thing, crudely made of leather-jointed twigs, a sleek body, and a frayed rope tail. It was one-eared, begrimed around its middle, and smoothed to silk by a child's adventures.

It had been so well and deeply loved that when Eleanor brushed it across her cheek, she felt the soft breath of the boy who had left it behind. Her eyes pooled with sudden, unexpected tears, and her chest became stuffed and aching with a sob for him and all the children in the world.

Sad-faced in sympathy, Pippa crawled into her lap. "Why does the little horse make you cry, Nellamore?"

Ghosts, Pippa. Sudden, sad ones.

"He's just that sweet, Pippa. Don't you think

so?" The twiggy legs dangled from their tethered joints. A fine, neglected destrier, made by someone who had loved deeply, enduringly.

"Crying-sweet, he is, Nellamore." Pippa gave the poor beast a kiss on its nose, then tucked it into her bulging belt pouch. "Sweeter even than that 'normous block of sugar you found this morning."

"Much sweeter."

"Pippa! Lady Eleanor! Look!" Lisabet flung herself onto the landing and then into the chamber, lushly swathed in green-and-gold damask and spinning around in abandon.

"Lisabet! What happened to your face?" Eleanor's heart flew into her throat until she realized the girl wasn't bruised and battered, merely rouged crimson to her temples, her eyebrows kohl-black nearly to her hairline.

"I'm a lady, milady."

More like a misguided London tart, and far too innocent to be let loose on the world anytime soon. Lisabet wobbled, curtsied, stepped on the twisted fabric and then pitched forward into Eleanor's arms.

"What have you gotten into?" Eleanor set her upright, trying not to laugh at Lisabet, who was trying to be so grown up.

"Lady's things, I think. Aren't I lovely?"

Terrifying. And dear.

"Too lovely for words, Lisabet." She shooed both girls toward the door, leaving the books and ledgers behind until she could corner her steward and study them alongside him. "Come show me where you found the pony and these lady's things."

There was a whole wardrobe of fine lady's things as it turned out, from tissue-thin chemises and broidered kirtles to silken stockings and doe-hide slippers. Men's garments as well, splendid worsteds and camlets trimmed in sable and fox, and even a goodly amount of sturdy children's clothes that would fit Pippa and any other children who might come through the gates.

Lovely things indeed, delicate, extravagant. Booty from her husband's sacking and pillaging, no doubt, hoarded with care and camphor. The lady's robes and gowns had been her size exactly, richly cut and newly styled. Yet they hadn't been fashioned for her at all. For her husband's courtesans, or a mistress, perhaps.

Certainly not for his forgotten, virginal wife.

"You've done all this, Mullock?" Not two hours in his new position and the great hall looked like a London market. "It's astounding."

The man shied as easily as Dickon. "Thank you, ma'am. Sorry that it's not His Lordship's opinion, my lady."

"His lordship?" Ah, Nicholas. The man did have that lordly breeze about him, as though he'd never been subject to the whims of anyone. Not even as a soldier. A man used to giving orders and seeing them done. One mystery after the next, to be solved and sorted.

"What did Master Nicholas say to you?"

"Didn't have to say anthing, did he, ma'am? I can feel him watching me from clear across the bailey. Like a great flying beast, he is, ready to pounce on my back and tear me to a skeleton."

"I assure you, Mullock, he'll not harm you." But it would be good to reiterate that fact to "His Lordship," to find him at the armory. "He's only looking out after my interests."

"Can't blame him there, my lady. You've quite a cache to lose, if a fellow had a mind to steal. Which, o'course, I don't. But look at this here chest of silks, for one."

Mullock might have been a wily merchant thief, liable to steal her blind, but he did seem to know his goods—or else he spun a palatable tale of the value of Faulkhurst's potential.

A man well worth nurturing.

It was late afternoon by the time Eleanor

could spare a moment to speak with Nicholas—a double errand to also draw water from the gatehouse well, to test its taste against the kitchen cistern and the well in the keep. She had dipped a ewer's worth and was just rounding the picket wall of the stables—to speak to Nicholas about Mullock, when she was struck by a sight that rocked her to her bones and that changed the direction of her pulse.

Nicholas—standing high up on the ridge beam of the armory, his legs braced astride two rafters at the gable end a full three stories above the bailey, as beautiful and glistening and as near to naked as a man could be while still wearing his boots and long breeches.

Bedazzling, he was—gold-sinewed and sun-struck indigo, his too-long, wildly thick hair lashed by the wind, his broadly muscled shoulders braced by nothing but the blue sky as a backdrop. His effortless movements at guiding the huge windlass and the crane were as fluid as the pull of the sea, a part of the shifting sunlight and the wheeling gulls.

Everything that had made her the very opposite sex to the man gave her a tremendous surge forward, toward him and his enticingly flat belly and the compelling shapes and shadows just below that.

He straightened suddenly, leaving her helpless against the sight of him as he swabbed his forehead with his arm, then scanned the bailey for an instant.

She ducked behind the roof post, because he was utterly magnificent and she wanted to unabashedly stare. More, to reach up and touch him, to shape her hands over his corded muscles, to follow that darkly sleek tapering of hair that plunged from his stomach into the narrow waist of his breeches and beyond, toward all that wondrous male equipage that would be crowded in there by the handful.

Great heavens! Where was she getting these thoughts? From her plan—that ridiculous worry over the status of her marriage, her pesky virginity. She blinked hard, but the full, virile image of him was as clear as ever, as though she held him in her hands.

That part of him.

Christ, Eleanor, what are you doing?

It was *his* voice inside her head, Nicholas's. Dark and whispering, as though he knew the course of her thoughts and was as astounded at them as she. As pleased, as intoxicated.

She sat down hard on a stump, consumed with him, exhilarated, her skin on fire, thinking of counterpanes and Nicholas and wedding nights not yet begun—

"Oh, my!" She closed her eyes and stuck both hands into the ewer of well water. She splashed her face and throat with its coolness, trying to remember why she had wanted to speak with him—Mullock, yes, and Nicholas's lordly ways. Finally she dared a look at the man and his labors, but only through her lashes.

"There, Dickon," he shouted. "Slowly, lad. Lower it a foot now."

"Aye, sir!" Dickon stood below him in the armory yard, as red-faced and straining at keeping the tension on the rope between the windlass and the tie down at his feet, as Nicholas was at ease supporting the entire weight of the crane arm and the battered ashlar block that dangled from it.

"Steady, lad." Nicholas's great arms glistened as they flexed and shifted, guiding the block onto a bed of mortar with the ease of a master mason. "There, Dickon."

He released the claw clamp and the block seated itself beside its twin. A perfect fit.

Amazing. She had watched the architects and masons expand the nave of the abbey church at St. Catherine's, a fascinating work of precision and science, employing dozens of tradesmen and a tangle of large, quaking machines. Nicholas's methods were more simple, but his lines were every bit as clean, and completely unexpected.

But then, she would never have expected him to be so skilled at carving eccentric little bears out of oak, or taming Dickon's loyalty.

"Milady will be pleased, sir. Won't she?"

Pleased wasn't nearly the right word. Toppled was closer. Enchanted. Dickon shaded his squinting eyes with his hands, his enthusiasm for his new mentor obviously having grown in the last few hours.

"Ask her yourself, lad. She's sitting there by the picket."

Found out! Eleanor's heart took a shameless tumble. She looked up and directly into the naked interest of Nicholas's gaze. Though she should have blushed to the roots of her hair for spying on him, she felt altogether wanton under all that sizzling heat.

"Well, madam? What do you think?"

That you are magnificent, sir. That he was light and dark, that he was wooden bears and iron locks. That he would deflower her grandly and with great passion.

Aye, and that he was waiting patiently for her to answer him.

"You were right, Nicholas." She went to stand beneath the gable.

"Was I?" He flicked a brow, his amazement

a complete charade, and utterly charming. She would give him this victory; she had no intention of bridling his ingenuity or his skill. Just that unacceptable possessiveness of his.

"Aye, Nicholas. You were right to begin with the armory as you did."

"Milady!" Dickon shouted. "Do you see the roof? Isn't it fine?" The boy was part of the machinery now, his weight and brawn keeping the next block aloft until Nicholas swung the arm into its place.

"It is that, Dickon." And so much more. Success seemed so possible, so fragile. She'd be a fool not to recognize how much she would have to depend upon Nicholas in the coming days, the years. His knowledge and his rippling strength.

"Lower the block now, lad." The lordly voice that could surely bellow across a battlefield also guided and cajoled. "Slowly, to the left."

Dickon grunted and steamed as he lowered the block an inch at a time, an encouragement at a time. When at last it settled into the mortar, he let go of the rope and collapsed spread-eagled and panting on the cobbles.

"Here, Dickon." Eleanor, waiting happily with the ewer, helped him sit up and held back his hair. "Drink."

He gulped until he fell back again, still gasping. "Thank you, my lady."

All the while she was aware of Nicholas on the roof above her, watching carefully, making his stern assessments. Her hair must look like a badger's nest. And here she was, mooning after the man—making impossible bargains with him in her mind—her apron green-stained and askew, her kirtle and linen sleeves littered with bits of straw and cobwebs.

Chiding herself for letting the mere sight of the man stop her in her tracks again, in the midst of a very busy day, she turned warily toward him. Still, her heart leaped and skittered when she found his eyes glittering, and knew that she must sound completely dull-witted when she asked, "Are you thirsty, steward?"

Parched for you, wife. Nicholas had seen her long before he'd spoken, keeping careful watch over the bailey, over his wife and Mullock while he wrestled with the armory. She was a fascination of shapes and sounds and sunlight, grace in her movements and in the lyric of her voice. She had extended her arms skyward toward him, lifting the ewer; irresistible, because he was dusty and parched, and she was the shady coolness that he craved.

"Aye, madam, if you please."

She met him at the bottom of the ladder. He took the pitcher and drank deeply, letting some of the rock-borne chill stream down his chest, dousing his hair and the back of his neck with the last of it.

"There's plenty more in the well, sir, if you should need a bath."

"I'll remember that, my lady." He ought to tell her about the grotto of steaming water in the catacombs, the place he bathed in peace each night, simmering away the knots and the tightness. But she was smiling too softly at him as he scrubbed at his hair, her unblushing gaze following the rivulets down his chest and, bolder still, curious as hell, toward his waist and his dagger belt, until she inhaled in a light, sharp gasp, then raised her wide, un-wary eyes to his.

"I approve, Nicholas."

"Of?" He held his breath, hoping for . . . he didn't know what he was hoping for.

"Of . . . of—" she swallowed, blinked twice, and then waggled her hand toward the sky. "Of all this industry. You and Dickon. And Fergus?"

"He's in the carpenter's shed, oiling the saws, counting nails. That's far safer than letting him loose with a hammer."

"Thank you, Nicholas." She ducked inside

the dimness of the armory, then started up the
ladder to the ridge beam, allowing him an
unobstructed view of her trim ankles, of lean
calves of golden honey, that must have somehow seen sunlight in her travels. Lying
spread-limbed in a high meadow, perhaps, her
skirts hiked to her thighs, or higher, or bare
entirely.

Sweet, holy hell. His wild imaginings caught
him soundly in the groin and raised a sudden
sweat that had nothing to do with the labors of
a mason.

"We were fortunate, my lady. It lacked but
a half dozen large stones to repair the gable."
He cleared his throat the way he'd very much
like to clear the molten desire from his veins,
but she was there inside him like his pulse.
"There, you see—where the ridge beam had
been shaken off the peak."

She ran her hand along the nearest rafter,
climbed a few more rungs, then looked down
at him as he held both stiles of the ladder. He
tried not to make too much of her smile, or
listen to the nuances of meanings in everything she said to him. Madness came of that
way of thinking.

"Are you sure it will all fit back together
again?"

Every piece but you and I, wife. His heart emp-

177

tied of the fullness she'd become. "Like a child's wooden puzzle, madam. It will soon be sound enough to carry the full weight of the roof and the rafters."

"Then we'll need a source of rushes soon."

"There are plenty to be found on the banks along the millrace, madam."

"I should have guessed that you'd know exactly where to find the reed beds." She started down the jouncing rungs, too quickly for him to step away from the ladder before she was caught up inside the cocoon of his arms. She turned her round, ripe bosom and the fullness of her dazzling smile on him. Her mouth was only that far from his, and damp from her tongue.

"I don't suppose that you thatch too, steward?"

Bits of lightning splintered inside his head. *Oh, my lady wife, would your thatch be scented as your plait is? Shaded with cinnamon and damson, hiding your treasures from me while I sought them attentively? Would you moan and writhe and call my name gladly if I kissed you there?*

And here. He could so easily brush his mouth lightly across her temple, against the damp little curls there. He wanted her. Wanted his wife.

And all her trappings.

"Do you," she asked, "thatch?"

"I—" He managed a deep, steadying breath to clear his fevered mind of her sheltered delights. But she was still here, inside his arms, creating bright images of sunlight on her honeyed thighs, of glistening auburn, of sniffing where she would be most fragrant.

He was drowning in his lust for her, and the woman hadn't even been in his care a full day. If she had any idea that he was burning for her like a summer wildfire crossing the Steppes, she would turn him out of her life—wisely.

"Perhaps, Lady Eleanor, you should pray fiercely tonight for a better thatcher than I."

She tilted her head like a robin disappointed in the spring. "Well then, sir. If you think you can't—"

"I'm sure I can't." Won't. Shouldn't. Christ!

Her disbelief was obvious, and made him ache with willful pride that she had gifted him with such extraordinary powers to provide. "Then I shall pray, sir."

As will I. Desperately.

"Good," he said roughly, ready to send her safely on her way.

"Nicholas?" She set her cool fingertips into the center of his bare chest, then the flat of her palm, and every thought he'd ever had sizzled

179

out of his brain. His erection strained against his sword belt where her thigh rested against the length of his.

"Yes?"

"Uhm . . ." She rocked on one foot, then the other, shyly, wholly out of her nature. "I just wanted to say . . . to assure you . . ."

"About?" She flushed, the high color on her cheeks, in the rose of her lips, hinting at secrets.

"About . . . well, the kiss I gave you. Last night."

His stomach lurched, shoved a noisy breath out of him. "What about it?"

"I just wanted you to know that I meant nothing by it."

"Nothing?" His heart plummeted, splintered as it hit bottom. "Nothing at all?"

She caught her lower lip with her teeth, watching his eyes, his mouth. "Barely anything."

Crushed. Stepped upon—that's what he felt. Staggered that she could flatten him, when he'd taken her boldness for so much more. "What the devil does 'barely' mean?"

"Barely means that it was . . . a kiss of peace between us. There." She shrugged, flipped her wrist. "That's all. I promise it won't happen again."

"Well, I can't, madam." He cupped her chin like the sinner he was, and with every ounce of will banked inside him, he brushed the very edge of her damp mouth with his—only there. And then her soft cheek. But lightly, chastely, because there would be no turning back from the pleasure if he stayed longer.

It would be dangerous if he let her little sigh mean too much. If he dwelt upon the thumping in his chest, the rush of ecstasy when she brushed at his nape with her hot little fingers, at the rim of his ear.

"You missed, Nicholas." She'd kept her eyes open the whole time, seeming astonished.

What the hell did she mean, that he'd *missed*?

Don't ask. Don't. He only clicked his tongue and shook his head.

And he would have been just fine if he hadn't lifted her gently off the last rung of the ladder, if his fingers hadn't fit so perfectly around her small waist, if his thumbs hadn't met so perfectly just beneath her breasts to make tender cups of his hands.

If her eyes hadn't flared, if her request hadn't been so privately made against his cheek, so thoroughly sultry as he stood her on her feet.

"Will you meet with me tonight, Nicholas?

After supper, after everyone is abed?"

"What, madam?" He roared like an injured lion, set her squarely down and stepped back, shaking off the dangerous scent of her, purposely conjuring images of walking barefooted across a bed of shimmering embers. "What the devil are you asking me?"

Her soft brows winged deeply, and she looked at him openmouthed, as though he'd just taken leave of his senses—not that he had any left to leave. "I thought you were interested in hearing all of my plans for the castle."

"I am. But you can't expect me to—"

"Only last night, Nicholas, you demanded that I include you in my every last thought on any subject regarding the castle. Aren't you still?"

"Interested?" What a driveling, besotted fool he was—for not keeping her at arm's length, for kissing her, for Christ's sake. For *missing*—whatever the hell she meant by that.

He said evenly, so that he wouldn't growl, "Yes, of course."

"Then you'll come tonight?"

"Yes." *God help me.* He felt stripped of his will, exhausted. Tested to his limits and beyond, when all he wanted was to serve her justly and then be gone as quickly as possible.

"After supper then, at my husband's office."

He caught himself before he answered. "Which is where?"

"In the tower keep, Nicholas. A solar, really, and my new bed chamber." She beamed at him, triumphant against her husband once again and nearly crowing in her pride. "I found the estate office."

"And the manor records, my lady—did you find them, too?"

Did I leave any damning evidence of myself for you to use to impeach me?

But she only harrumped at that other man in her life—the wicked-hearted one who'd died and left her all this misery.

"So far, I've found everything but the last four years. But I'm not going to give up. I'll find the other records, somewhere. And then you and I can study them before we decide on which crops to plant and where to plant them."

Christ, he'd forgotten that she'd need forecasts to grow a sturdy crop that would feed her tenants. Which fields had been marled, which had lain fallow.

"And I did wonder, Nicholas—do you read?"

He nodded at the worry in her eyes, disgusted at himself for putting it there. "And I write as well."

183

She sagged happily back against the ladder, her whole face brightening. "I was hoping that you could, though I am surprised." Not surprised at all, if he read her rightly, but damned suspicious, cocking a doubtful brow at him. "You were a foot soldier; how did you come by such learning?"

It had been knocked into his head at Balliol and then at Merton, when he wasn't carousing in the taverns or bedding some willing wench. "A soldier gets bored when the battling is done."

He didn't deserve her smiling approval. "You're a marvelously fine man, Nicholas."

He'd never in his life been called fine or marvelous, and wanted desperately to know why she thought so. "In what possible way do you mean, madam?" he asked as cooly as he could manage.

"Soldiers usually hie themselves off to the nearest village and find themselves a barrel of ale and a . . . well—" she touched the tip of her tongue to the arc of her lips, left them glistening, inviting him "—you know what I mean. So I applaud your dedication."

God, she was beautiful and blushing. And absolutely *his*. "I'm not a saint, madam."

Her eyes widened, and then she smiled, fanned at the bright spots on her cheeks, and picked up the forgotten ewer. "Neither am I, Nicholas. Neither am I."

She left him with that enigmatic call to arms.

Not a saint? What the devil did she mean by that? She'd damn well *better* be a saint.

His saint, his virginal wife. From head to toe—and every sultry place between.

Chapter 12

~~~oo~~~

Supper seemed more like the opening day of a market faire than the simple feast in her new home that Eleanor had imagined.

Chests and barrels and furniture were piled around, and Pippa and Lisabet were drawn to them like friendly little bees to a forest of hives. Dickon took his meal in the gatehouse; Fergus and Mullock at the trestle, eating as though they had never eaten before. Hannah managed her bites between the hall and the kitchen, and Eleanor not at all.

Nicholas had snagged a loaf of rye and some cheese and then apparently disappeared to work on the armory, because she soon heard his hammer against stone.

Even through all the chaos—*his* chaos. Deep inside her chest, flittering around like a bird wanting the sky.

He kissed me.

But he hadn't really kissed her; it only seemed that way. Just tit for tat, that sort of thing.

Then why had his mouth been the most delicious, the most stirring thing she'd ever felt against her cheek or any part of her? Why had time stopped; why had the armory floor started spinning? And why had he lingered two heartbeats longer than she had the night before?

All of it nonsense—not to be repeated.

Addled and distracted, she finally—as he had predicted—whacked her shin with the sledgehammer.

"Oh, blast it!" The pain shot everywhere at once, splintered into her shoulder and out her toes. She stifled the pitiful howl that would bring Nicholas running and chiding, but she hobbled and hopped around the great hall, now the center of attention.

"Oh, Nellamore! Owwwww for you!"

"I'm all right, dear."

But Pippa kissed her hand and Mullock dragged over a bench for her to sit on, and Hannah brought cold rags, and Fergus a sturdy walking stick.

Eleanor burst out in an unseemly bout of laughing, hugging them all. Because though her leg burned like fire, she loved her new home and family dearly, so much that her heart seemed too big for her chest.

It all overflowed in streaming tears and more laughter—almost the hysterical kind. Especially when Mullock regaled them with his amazing skill at a hurdy-gurdy he'd found in the undercroft. When the dancing began, she forced herself to dismiss her injury.

An hour after sundown everyone was asleep, the hall peaceful and quiet save for Fergus and Mullock, who snored in antiphonal chorus.

Thoroughly exhausted and suddenly reluctant about meeting with Nicholas to study her plans for the next week, Eleanor hobbled up the stairs toward the solar, grateful for the walking stick.

Just as she hoped that she could hide her accident from Nicholas by sitting down before their meeting, she heard him on the stairs below—that solid footfall and a resonant accusation that rippled up her legs and melted the knot in her stomach.

"Are you limping?"

"Well, of course, I'm *limping*." *And it's your fault*, she wanted to say. *For being so distracting*.

Blast the man, she resented having to turn and face his scowling, but he was already burning holes in the back of her skirts with his glaring, and pointing at her leg when she finally hobbled around to confront him.

"It's nothing."

"It's *everything* to me, madam." A breathless sentiment to throw to a woman he'd just kissed. He charged up the few steps between them two at a time, then pointed to her legs. "Show me."

Ha! As though she'd just lift her skirts for him and obey. "That isn't necessary—"

"You'll sit." A single sweeping gesture from that great paw of his had her sitting on the step. He knelt in front of her and shoved her skirts up past her knee, like an insistent bridegroom.

A bridegroom.

Oh, yes—the man was perfect. Strong and raven-haired and tossing off his orders as though he had a husbandly right to her. But that sort of daydreaming was too much for this very long day, too close to her thoughts be borne.

"What the devil are you doing, Nicholas?" She tried to shove her chemise back down, and to shove away the fluttering butterfly in her chest that told her it was just fine that he was so interested in her legs—more than fine, that his hands were hot and imperious.

He grabbed her ankle and stretched out her

stockinged leg. "Good Christ, madam." She'd never seen him so angry, and she tried to get away, but yanking her foot proved fruitless; it might as well have been anchored into mortar and stone. "How did you do this? And when? Why didn't you tell me?"

Her shin had become an angry lump, bulging her stocking, looking far more dramatic than it had an hour past when she'd been dancing with Pippa and Fergus, and far worse than it actually felt.

"Really, Nicholas. A bit of foolishness is all. I was only—"

"Sledging away at another of those damnable locks? I'm right, aren't I?" She would have lied, but everyone in the hall knew the truth and would tell him when he asked.

"Yes."

"Bloody hell. I told you to come find me."

"It wasn't a very big lock."

A moment later he and his expert fingers were all the way up her dress, had her garter points free, and her stocking slumped round her ankle as though he were planning to bed her there on the steps to the solar.

And that suddenly didn't seem like such a disagreeable idea. Her troublesome maidenhead gone in an instant, taken by this very strapping man. And the idea would have

come from Nicholas himself, not from her—
not a request by his lady or a demand for his
labors, which might impinge upon his morals.

"Bloody hell, woman, I warned you to take
care." He was rumbling curses under his
breath, wincing as he examined the bruise as
though he had been wounded himself. "You
might have broken a bone."

"I didn't break anything—except the lock."

He cradled her calf in his hands—his very
large, very capable hands—raised her leg, and
slowly, delicately inspected the profile of her
shin against the lamplight. "Look at this."

She was looking, but not at her leg. At his
face and his fury and all his fineness. Another
wholly inappropriate thought lodged itself
like a wicked whisper inside her belly and
warmed her there: that he might be planning
to nibble where he was looking so intently,
right there behind her knee where he glided
his finger; and then trailing those marvelous
lips all the way down to her ankle and back
again, higher, perhaps, to that warm and
quickening place which seemed to be shamelessly calling to his fingers as they moved
along her calf.

Dear God. And here she was, lounging like
a strumpet across the steps and his leg, with

her kirtle and chemise rucked up to her bare thighs.

"You were damned lucky this time, madam."

I am still, sir.

"It's only a bruise." But still he turned her leg this way and that, as clinically distant as a battlefield surgeon. Hopefully—please, God—he was unaware that her heart was thrumming, that he'd completely unstrung her.

For she was trembling on the verge of asking him to take care of her little virginity problem.

"Let me see your hands." He took them before she could object and raised her ragged palms for her to see. "Just as I expected: blisters. Why aren't you wearing your gloves?"

"One's missing. I've never been able to keep a pair together." Now he had her boot off, and then her stocking. "Nicholas!" *Not in the stairwell,* she nearly said.

"Blisters here, too." He was frowning at her toes, tugging at each of them until she was squirming against a giggle. "And here and here, inviting poisons and fever."

"You're quite free with my limbs, steward." She tried to sit up, but that only exposed more of her thigh and heaven knew what else.

"All this because your boots don't fit you.

THE MAIDEN BRIDE

How long have you had these?" Off came the other boot, to thunk its way down the stairs to the landing.

"Dickon found them on a deserted cobbler's bench. It's the best I can do at the moment."

"Your stockings are riddled with holes." Now her legs and feet were entirely bare, and his hands were so warm, so thorough.

"I have only that pair."

"And a great hall filled to bursting with chests of clothing and shoes."

"You're so sure of that?"

"You'll have boots and stocking in the morning, if I have to tear through the goods myself. Have you suffered any other injuries in my castle that you haven't told me about?"

His castle, still. His arrogant claim rolled off his tongue as though it had belonged there. So, apparently these were not *her* feet, or her blisters.

"I'm perfectly capable of taking care of myself, finding my own linens and boots."

He made one of his heated, head-to-foot studies of her, then stood abruptly. "You're coming with me, madam."

"Where?" But she was already in his arms, caught up against his chest, and he was starting down the steps with her. "I'll go peaceably, Nicholas. I can walk."

"Not without your shoes."

"Must I point out that you just stole them off me?" And her stockings—with those large, fine hands of his. "Where are we going?"

"Did you ever wonder where the hot water that pours into the kitchen comes from?"

"You're taking me to the kitchen?" But he was heading the wrong way for that, toward the cellar and then into the darkness at the bottom of the stairs, into that odd, sulfurous smell that she'd often noticed along this corridor.

"Not to the kitchen, madam," he said with a rumble of dark amusement that thrilled her.

He shouldered open a door that she hadn't known existed, then bolted it again—more of his secrets. Like a quick summer fog off the river, the cold, damp air of the passage was chased away by the heated air of boiled minerals.

The very same smell as the kitchen, only stronger.

"Sister Hypathia."

"Who?"

"The herbalist at St. Catherine's. It smells like her cauldron did at summer's end: herbs and minerals. Sulfur and dragon mint."

This scent was similar, though not as greenly floral, and grew stronger, damper as Nicholas carried her deeper and downward into the undulating passage, until the walls were no longer made of castle stone, but of twisting fissures in the bedrock.

The last fissure opened onto a wide staircase and an even wider chamber, lit by three oil lamps that must burn and flicker all the time.

The devil's grotto.

"My dear sir, what have you found here?"

Soaring stone-carved ribs, vaulting high up to a center point, and beneath that at the grotto's center was a large, steaming pool of water, a dozen feet across and twice that wide. It was bounded on the near side by ancient, square-hewn stones, on the far side by a low, rocky outcropping, and was fed from a fall of water that came tumbling out of the wall and then exited over a ledge at the foot of the pool into a sieve of fissures in the damp floor.

"For your well-being, madam." He stood her on her feet and shucked her of her woollen kirtle, down to her chemise, then lifted her over the side to dangle her legs. "Sit here."

But the moment she felt the heat against her flesh, felt it hiss deeply into her calves, she slid off the edge of the pool into the wondrously warm water that reached all the way to her waist.

"Oh, my, Nicholas." She cooed as her knees melted with the pleasure, then she let herself

float free on her back in all that caressing water. "You found me a bit of heaven."

*Aye, wife—but it makes me ache like the devil
for you.*

Chapter 13

⟨◦—◦◦◦—◦⟩

Nicholas knew he was in dire trouble the moment his wife's hem hit the steam. He'd meant her only to sit on the ledge and dangle her legs and hands, but now she looked like a lounging selkie, waiting for a wave to come slip her back into the sea.

His exquisitely beautiful wife.

"So you fancy yourself a doctor, Nicholas, as well as a soldier and a mason and a diplomat." She smiled blissfully as she floated, her eyes closed, her hair playing loosely in the constant current, dancing with his senses.

"I am merely your steward, milady."

"Much more than that, Nicholas. What other secrets are you holding back from me? That you are an alchemist? Or a wizard—for there is no other explanation for a place like this."

He stood at the edge of the pool, hardly able to breathe, to think beyond her chemise floating in the lapping waves, the bobbing of her breasts and her dark nipples visible in the lamplight. He wanted to join her there. To join *with* her.

He turned away instead and tormented himself with the sound of her splashing and torrid thoughts of her toes and his tongue.

Christ.

"I give you but a few moments longer, my lady, then I want to see your blisters and that bruise of yours." *And every other part of you.*

"You're right; we really should be in the office, planning the harvest campaign. But, ah, Nicholas, this is marvelous. And to think that I might have come to Faulkhurst as Bayard's bought-and-paid-for bride."

A safe enough conversation, if one that ate at his pride. "You find that so unthinkable?"

"Now, more than ever." *Splash. Sloosh.* A long, wispy sigh that he felt against his ear. "As entirely unimaginable as the marriage was itself. I was perfectly happy cloistered with the Sisters of Mercy."

What? He shook his head of the buzzing. "You were what, madam? Cloistered?"

"Yes."

He spun around against his better judgment, certain that he heard thunder all the way down here, a bolt of holy scorn. "Cloistered, as in a nunnery?"

"At St. Catherine's. This is far too nice, Nicholas."

Bloody hell, he'd stolen a nun. This *ravishing* nun, from a very jealous God.

He stomped into the pool to his thighs—his boots be damned—and straddled her legs to tip her to her knees, then bent over all that sultry, steaming bliss.

"Tell me that again, madam. You were a nun when Bayard married you? A holy sister?"

She knelt like a coy mermaid peering up at him, one pink shoulder completely bare and tantalizing, the front of her gown drooping dangerously, just covering the maddeningly dark point of her breast.

"I wasn't anywhere near holy, Nicholas." She raked her fingers through the curtain of hair that was streaming out around her. "And I certainly wasn't a nun."

His heart climbing into his throat, he knelt too and made her look at him directly with those eyes of dark amber. "You weren't even . . . what is it called—betrothed?" Promised to God, or whatever the devil they—"

"A novitiate?" The water defined her rising brows more clearly against her fairness and starred her lashes. "Good heavens, no. Why would you think so?"

He couldn't answer. She'd taken his breath away again, left him sputtering again. And relieved—because he hadn't been certain what he could have done, if he'd actually stolen her from a nunnery.

"I'm just curious about the lady I serve." Sopping wet to his breastbone, Nicholas leaned back against the edge of the low wall, crossed his arms against his chest, and stuck his heels into the stone paving of the pool.

"I wasn't well suited to the life. Not at all." She smiled brightly at some secret facet of her past, then pushed backward in a swirl of skirts and a pale bare foot, only to come swimming back toward him, smiling, beguiling him again. "I loved my beds of hollyhocks and my daffodils too much for that. I dearly wanted to stay there forever, but I wasn't interested in vows."

"None beyond your marriage vows then."

"Not even them." She shook her head fiercely, as though he'd suggested she take up witchcraft. "Especially not marriage vows."

But we are married, wife, well and truly, until I take care of the matter. He'd never actually considered her desires; she had merely been his bride. She needed only to show up and be married to him. He might have been a beastly scourge to her at the time, but he'd been a damned eligible one.

"Isn't that every woman's hope, my lady: marriage to a prosperous and powerful baron?"

Her laughter echoed off the vaulting. "How very like a man to think that a woman wishes to be handed from father to husband like a sack of turnips, forced to keep his household, to wait contentedly for him to come home from his warring and whoring, then to suffer his embrace—at his pleasure, and only long enough to beget him sons and sons and more sons—before he scurries off to his mistress's bed."

Here he was again, unjustly accused of deeds he'd never had the chance to commit against her. Not that he would have strayed a heartbeat from this woman—not if he'd known her as he did now.

"Sorry to have offended your sensibilities, madam. Now, let me see your hand." He stuck out his own and she paddled toward him.

"Oh, but you don't offend me, Nicholas. You're pigheaded and arrogant, and you try to negate my authority at every turn—"

"I've been more than patient with you—"

Her laughter ended in a delicate snort of disbelief. "But in all that, you've never offended me."

201

"That's good to know."

"I speak of my father's treatment of my poor mother, and as I'm sure my life would have gone with my husband." She stood up in her sopping, translucent chemise and gave her hand to him, already prunish around the blisters. He studied her palm with a pinpoint focus because to look up would be to see too much through her gown. A glance, and he would surely be blinded for his sins.

"He wouldn't have beaten you, my lady. He wasn't that kind of man."

She looked up from where their fingers entwined, dragging his gaze along with her, because he was nearly beyond resisting her. "How can you know for certain that William Bayard didn't beat his women?"

Hell's teeth; he set his own traps, then stepped right into them. "I would have heard of it, if he had. That sort of reputation precedes a man."

She pursed her lips, thwarted in her beliefs. "Well, whether he would have beat me or not, my wedding night to William Bayard was as abrupt and as quickly done as my wedding to him was."

He snorted. "Your wedding night? Madam, you haven't had a wedding night with your husband."

"I—But, I. . . ." She paled to chalk and took in a small breath of terror. "What the devil do you mean by that, Nicholas?"

Christ, what *did* he mean? Damn, he hated this lopsided cat-and-mouse game. He scanned her face for clues, trying to recall what he'd just said, where he'd gone wrong. But he found only stark apprehension. What the hell would she *think* he meant? "That . . . well, my lady . . . that you couldn't possibly have—"

"Slept with my husband?" She stuck her fists into her hips. "Is that what you're accusing me of?"

Hardly an accusation. "If it seemed that way, it was only because you never met your husband."

"And?" She was a lunatic. Or he was.

He took a few steps closer, walking on thin and crackling ice here. "Then you couldn't possibly have slept with him, could you?"

"Damn you, William Bayard!" She turned away in her fury, sputtering curses.

Nicholas froze. His identity discovered, just like that. He couldn't move.

She whirled back on him and leveled an accusing finger. "Do you see, Nicholas, the position he's put me into? A marriage by proxy, and then he dies before he sends for me."

He. Not *you.* He sagged with relief. She hadn't guessed his identity. He recovered enough to say, "Unfortunate."

"*Unconsummated*, Nicholas." She threw out her arms. "Do you realize what that means?"

Yes, painfully so. The linen of her gown clung like window glass. "Well, my lady . . . that you are—"

"Not completely married."

Untried, he'd been about to say.

"I am in legal limbo, Nicholas, if anyone ever wanted to make an issue of who has the right to Faulkhurst. Our dear king, for one. I can't have that threat hanging over me."

Christ, she was right.

"It doesn't take a great Oxford scholar to realize that if William and I never met, then we never shared a bed. An unconsummated marriage isn't necessarily binding and has all sorts of dangling ends."

"Yes, it has." Another mark against his care, another pledge he must keep to her. That somehow she wouldn't lose her home. "I'm sorry, Eleanor. I wish that—"

"Eleanor." Her smile filled her entire face, lit her eyes, and sent his heart spinning out of control. "You said my name."

Because it felt so right. "Did I? I am sorry for the liberty."

"No, please. Whenever you wish to." Her hair swayed in time with her hips as she settled again into the water. "And I'm sorry about my ranting. I'll take care of it in my own way. It's just that . . . well, you startled me. And the subject of my marriage makes my blood boil."

He encouraged her to ramble while he gathered up his resolve. "It wasn't exactly the marriage celebration that you had imagined?"

A decisive business transaction on his part, because de Lacey had offered him the bridge at Laberre and an overlook of the whole Tampangne Valley.

"I wasn't given any time to imagine a celebration of any kind."

He remembered the swiftness of his decision; timing had been critical—and now it counted for nothing at all. She was the only thing that mattered now. And his pledge. "But at least there was a ceremony to consecrate the bargain between you and Bayard."

"Ha. It might just as well have been a bargain between me and my groom's ambassador. John Sorrel, if I remember his name rightly. Baron of something or other."

"Arrone." One of his fee knights, infamous for his skill at squeezing the opposition of its last objection. The very reason Nicholas had sent him to do the deed.

"Do you know John Sorrel, Nicholas?"

Blazing hell—that again. "I knew *of* the man only."

"When?" She narrowed that studying frown at him, her legs paddling behind her inside the billowing of her skirts.

"A soldier sees dozens of battlefields, my lady. Thousands of soldiers."

She stood and came toward him again, wearing her suspicions in her eyes, in the tilt of her head. "Aye, but you weren't just a foot soldier, were you, Nicholas?"

This was exhausting. As exhausting as watching her breasts sway in her clinging chemise, beautifully formed, and wholly forbidden to him.

He swallowed roughly. "How do you mean, my lady?"

"You speak as a knight and hold yourself as one, without an ounce of subservience to your nature. You read and you write." She came to stand directly in front of him, investigating his face. "You seem to know the innermost workings of a castle and the court, and have more than a passing acquaintance with men like my husband and my father and the Baron Arrone.

I'd like to know who you are exactly, steward.
Beyond your name."

He'd been working on this part of his fic-
tional past, and it was an exceedingly clever
story. Poignant, too, which she would appreciate. He shook his head wearily as he had
practiced in the gatehouse, cast his gaze to the
water, and even added a clicking noise with
his tongue.

"Alas, my lady, the youngest of four broth-
ers receives none of his father's titles, nor a
teaspoon of his lands, and must find his own
way in the world."

"The fourth son of a lord?"

"Langridge."

She clapped her hands together. "Just as I
suspected: a landless knight errant."

Nicholas sighed—for a deeper-hued effect,
at the success of his tale, and because she
seemed so very pleased. "I am that, alas."

Her sympathy was plain. "Penniless?"

"Aye, completely." He stepped out of the
water and sat on the ledge to wring out his
boots.

"Left to wander?"

"Interminably." This was finally going as
he'd planned.

"How then did you escape the Church?"

"I—" *haven't*. The heat in the room rose pre-

207

cipitously, from the guilty flush of a deceitful monk who hadn't yet taken his vows, who didn't know the first thing about observing them, who could only quake and stammer whenever his wife came within a hairbreadth of him—as she was standing behind him right now. "Just as you have escaped marriage to William Bayard, milady. Fortune, I suppose."

She sat beside him, facing in the other direction, her feet still in the water. "You may have escaped a monk's habit, Nicholas, but I haven't escaped marriage at all."

The woman was always racing leagues ahead of him. He turned to face her and straddled the ledge, his stockinged foot in the water again. "What do you mean? Have you gotten yourself betrothed? To whom?"

"To no one at the moment. But if I'm successful in rebuilding Faulkhurst, Edward will want it held by one of his barons, won't he?"

Nicholas felt all of his tomorrows spinning darkly, airlessly out in front of him. "He will, my lady, without a doubt."

"I plan to be even farther-sighted than he is. I will be the one to decide who my next husband will be."

Her next. His stomach flipped, his chest suddenly molten with a burst of black jealousy.

"Do you?" He imagined his wife and Robert

Marston sharing an overripe pear in a sultry summer orchard, the man following a glistening trail of sweet nectar down her throat ... and between her breasts.

Which belong to him at the moment— shaped perfectly for his hands, his mouth, waiting there for him with their rosy peaks, not a foot away.

Aye, and he could well imagine that bloody bastard Hugh le Clare reaching for them while he danced with her, salivating over her with a dozen other miscreants as though she were a prime game hen.

"And to that end, Nicholas, I've determined to begin a discreet search for the right man."

A doubled surge of anger and a lastingly inconceivable loss hit him. He wanted to be far away from her by then, while other men courted her, kissed her. He couldn't take that.

"And when will you begin this discreet search?"

She smiled shyly and said quietly, "I've already started."

Another blow that struck the air from his chest. Now she was expecting some randy swain to come striding through his gates, searching out her bed, her kiss, that fragrant, unsullied place between her thighs that belonged to him.

"How, madam? Where?" Improbable woman. "Are you making midnight raids into Ravensglass?"

"Aye, Nicholas, running all the way there and home. How else do you suppose I came by the blisters on my toes? But they feel much better already." She laughed lightly and raised a foot to him out of the water, shook off the drips, and then stuck it into his lap, already crowded with his erection.

She was all ankle and calf and wiggling toes, and sighed when he ran his finger down her instep.

"You'll soak here tomorrow, too," he commanded.

"Yes, steward. And the following tomorrow."

He stood before he could drag her into the pool and make love to her.

"And in case you're concerned, you'll have no trouble finding yourself a husband of your choice. They'll come running."

And I will pick them out myself, by God. Sort the chaff from the grain. Suffer that affliction as well, chosing a worthy man for her. If such a creature lived.

She stood up in her dripping gown, that one seductive shoulder tormenting him with the weighty roundness just beneath. "Why do you say that?"

He was shaking with desire for her. "It's the truth, madam. You are that beautiful. More than that."

"I am?" she said, catching her breath and beaming, tugging at the end of her splendid hair. "Nicholas, you're very kind to say such a thing."

"I'm far from kind, my lady. I'm very much a male. Very much—" he swallowed, trying to make rules between them, even while he broke them "—affected by you, as any man would be when you go looking for a husband. Your castle and your estate notwithstanding."

"Are you?" She looked straight into his eyes, ready for whatever answer he gave, ready to do battle or concede or just listen.

"In every possible way that you could imagine. You need to know that of me." There was too much honesty, and not nearly enough cool air between them. Though a thousand leagues wouldn't be far enough.

"I think I do know, Nicholas." She was flushed above her gown, and staggered him with her slow gaze, innocent wisdom, and powerful instincts. "Some of it, at least."

"Then you know that I didn't miss, earlier. I didn't dare go further."

He stood fast as she rose onto her toes and lifted her fingers toward his temple, intent on

211

some mischief of her own. "Didn't miss what, Nicholas?"

"At the armory. When I kissed you."

And he really ought to kiss her again. Briefly. Just to satisfy his curiosity that her mouth wasn't nearly as succulent, as sweet, as it appeared to be.

"You did miss." She caught her lip between her teeth, holding in a pleased smile or a teasing giggle, feathering her fingers through his hair, making it difficult to breathe, difficult not to smooth his hands up her waist, to cup her breasts, to nuzzle there.

"My aim was precise." He would ask for another simple, unadorned kiss. To take the edge off his desire to bed her every time he saw her, heard her laughter. To clear her scent from his brain and allow him to think again.

"But you kissed me here." She pointed to the corner of her mouth.

"Too close?" he asked, wondering when he'd combed his fingers through the hair at her nape, when he'd cupped her chin and tilted it to him.

"Not accurate, Nicholas. A courtly kiss of peace is more on the cheek. And less . . ."

"On the mouth?" Great God, he was playing with fire, foolish for letting himself believe this would blunt the edge of his need for her. She was honeyed wine, and he feared he would drink too deeply before he could let her go.

"Exactly, Nicholas." Eleanor's pulse was singing; his words brushed her mouth like a steamy kiss, but he still hadn't yet. And she was waiting shamelessly for it, her skin on fire when he touched her mouth with his finger.

"Exactly not here, madam?"

"No. I mean, yes." He drew his thumb across her lower lip, his eyes smoldering, his mouth so close that her breath mingled with his, his hand spanning the column of her throat, from her jaw to the path between her breasts.

There, too, Nicholas. I want you to kiss me there.

"God, I shouldn't, Eleanor."

But then he did, a wondrously gentle brush of his lips against hers, a ragged sigh that seemed to come from somewhere deep inside him.

"Beautiful, Eleanor." Then he bent and closed his warm mouth over hers, captured it fully, deeply.

"Oh, Nicholas." His kiss possessed her like the sunlight, shooting sparks right down to her toes. She clung to him, gripped his sleeves, and then slid her hands behind him to bring him and his stunning hardness closer; an exquisite shape against her belly that made her squirm and sigh.

It was the very worst thing she could have done apparently, for Nicholas raised up like a bear, backed away from her, and swabbed her kiss right off his mouth with one hand and the other.

"Holy God, Eleanor."

"Oh?" She righted her gown and her dignity. "My kiss was that horrifying, was it?"

"Ah, no, love. It was that . . . intoxicating."

Her heart leaped. "Well, then—"

"Then, nothing, my lady." He scooped her over his shoulder as he would a sack of flour, then stomped off toward her chamber, ignoring her questions all the way, then left her in her standing in the middle of the room, her heart in complete disarray.

Chapter 14

"**N**icholas?" Eleanor awoke to a growling rumble, dreaming that she was snuggled beside Nicholas beneath a warm counterpane.

She sat up in the dimness of her new chamber and remembered, blushing, that he'd carried her here to the steward's office from the grotto.

After their kiss—more than a kiss. It was an extraordinary dividing line in her life: now there was before Nicholas had kissed her and called her "love" and every day that came afterward.

The sound came again, rumbling across the floor from the other side of the doorway drape, up through her soft felt and feather pallet, as regular as a forge bellows, and as deep as the call of a buck in full rut.

"Nicholas?" She slipped out of bed, parted

the drapes, and would have stepped on him if the moon hadn't been peering in the casement window.

He lay stretched out on a pallet that seemed only the size of a pillow in contrast to his hugeness, bare-chested and wearing only breeches.

And he was snoring, deeply, peacefully—as though he hadn't rested in years.

Shavings from his carving were scattered across his chest. A merry little bear lay finished inside the palm of his hand, looking altogether contented there.

An enviable nest, to be sure. A shameless urge to lie down beside him washed over her—to snuggle herself into that welcoming space beneath his shoulder and fall asleep to his breathing.

But why the devil was he sleeping in her chamber?

"Nicholas?" She knelt beside him and hadn't even touched his shoulder before he bolted to his feet, armed with the small wooden bear.

"What?" He swabbed his hand across his face and shoved her behind him, her breasts to his broad back, protecting her from something he saw in the shadows. "Has the siege lifted?"

216

He was dreaming. "No, Nicholas." She came around from behind him and took hold of his hand. "You were snoring."

He peered down at her, more bleary-eyed than she had first realized. "What?"

He was obviously exhausted and should be sleeping in a better place than this. "What are you doing here?"

He glanced down at his hand and found the bear there, and frowned. "Protecting you— this is as near as I can get without actually sharing your bedchamber. Which I can't very well do because we're not—" He seemed to stop breathing entirely, stumped for the very simple word.

"Because we're not married."

He let out his captured breath in a rush. "Yes. There, you see—"

"And you're protecting me because . . . ?"

He snorted and tucked the bear head first into his dagger sheath, then advanced on her until she stepped backward into the curtains that divided the two rooms. "Because Mullock is a thief and Dickon was a highwayman, and God knows what other brigands you'll let walk through your gate, my dear."

"So you plan to sleep in my chamber every night to protect me?"

"Yes." He was staring sloe-eyed at her

217

mouth and dampened his lips as he had before he'd kissed her, sending those rampant shivers through her, anticipating whatever he had in mind.

"Thank you for your concern, Nicholas, but it isn't necessary."

"It is until I say that it isn't, my lady." He gathered her against him with his arm, his body warm and thrilling—the largeness of his chest, the strong male part of him awake and pressing against her belly, his mouth moving against her temple so that she barely heard his whisper for the clanging riot of her heart. "Though I don't know, my dear, who the hell's going to protect you from me."

A silly thought. She would have told him so, but for the sudden footfalls and hammering on the door that was as frantic as Lisabet's voice.

"My lady? Come!" Eleanor leaped past Nicholas and slid the bar, her heart paralyzed with terror as she threw open the door.

"What is it, Lisabet? Who—" But Lisabet was already yanking on her arm.

"Come quick! There's a lady here in the great hall, and she's in an awful hurry. Hannah said for you to come."

"A lady? In a hurry?" But Lisabet scurried down the steps, and Eleanor after her, Nicholas on her heels and then a dozen steps ahead of her as they reached the great hall.

"Holy hell." Nicholas stopped dead in his stride, was a thick wall that she had to move aside before she saw what he did: a woman standing in the glow of the coming dawn, her arms hooked under her bulging belly, balancing her weight backward, as pregnant as any woman Eleanor had ever seen.

Hannah, completely transported with joy, paced alongside the woman and the stick-thin boy who must have found his way here, too.

"Cora's babe is coming, my lady. Very soon."

A birthing! Dumbstruck with joy, Eleanor hurried to them, blinking away her tears, but they welled and then fell anyway.

"Mullock, have you seen a birthing stool anywhere in all this mess?"

The man looked stunned. "What be that, ma'am?"

"A chair with the front removed from the seat."

"Never heard of such a thing."

Eleanor quickly found one, and sent everyone on errands. She spared a glance at Nicholas, who stood apart from the comings and goings, a giant, leaning silhouette against the hearth, watching Eleanor and then Cora as

219

though he believed the woman was contagious, and that Eleanor herself was the mastermind of still another folly.

She put her hand on his, absorbed his scowl and his heat. "Go find yourself some sleep, Nicholas. We'll be eleven when you wake."

Bloody hell. Now he was running a nursery.

The whole birthing affair set the kitchen out of bounds to Nicholas and the other men for the entire day and well into the night, an impenetrable enclave of women and their mysteries.

When night came again, Nicholas took up residence at the dais table in the middle of the great hall, all the better to keep Mullock's calculating greed in his sights. The boy, Toddy, had eaten as if he hadn't in weeks, then had fallen asleep on a hearth pallet hours ago.

"Soon, Nicholas," Eleanor said a dozen times. He saw her only in hurried streaks of shimmering white skirts as she raced through the great hall on her befuddling missions.

And each time she passed him, tossing him a smile or a sigh, he regretted every moment of his life before her. Every moment but Liam.

He could easily imagine his wife's belly growing large with his sons and his daughters. And all her generous, consuming happiness smiling down on him every morning.

Sometime in the small hours after midnight, after prowling the castle for doors left open and gaping gates, and checking that Dickon was at his post, Nicholas returned to the great hall to wait out the babe.

Eleanor was sitting at the long table, one hand propping her chin, fast asleep. It was no doubt meant to be a brief nap, but she was breathing soundly and sagging to the left.

"To bed with you, madam." When she only wiggled her nose, he lifted her into his arms, and she snuggled under his chin as he carried her up the stairs and into the solar.

Nicholas had hoped his heart would behave more wisely tonight, but it was battering him again—for more reasons than he cared to count. Because she spoke in unknowing allusions, and he listened too carefully for every one of them.

Because this had once been his office and his bedchamber, and had lacked only a wife to make it whole then. This wife, this beguiling one who snuggled against him, her dazzling hair piled on top of her head—a loosely knotted, wildly red crown, adorned just above her left ear with a sprig of wilted violets.

The familiar breeze off the ocean tumbled from the high windows, scented with her cinnamon and saffron, and Hannah's rye bread.

Hardly the same room he'd skulked around in the afternoon before, looking for his journals. She'd scrubbed it clean of the darkness and the aching in his stomach. Something warm was pouring into his heart, yearnings for the impossible.

She stirred. "Cora had a healthy little girl, Nicholas."

"Good." That made eleven souls for him to watch over.

"I'd like one, too."

"One what?"

"A babe, someday. When I find a husband."

He slipped her onto her pallet, a sorry thing that needed a frame, and covered her with the counterpane, knowing there were warmer blankets somewhere. He hadn't burned them all.

"Good night, my lady." *My wife.*

He might not be able to kiss her or to sleep beside her, but he damned well wasn't going to risk anyone doing her mischief.

They'd have to go through him to get at her.

Plink.

There was that sound again; the ringing of hammer against stone. Eleanor bounded from the table to the office window, and tried to

catch the sound as it came again from the evening darkness.

Plink.

She'd noticed its melody twice while she was settling Pippa into bed, and many other times in the last few days. Nicholas would know the reason, but he was never around when it came—and she never thought of it except when she heard it.

Plink.

The sound took her back to the masons who came every morning to work on the abbey church. A sound so familiar at the time that it had become a comfortable breeze, like the regular bells of the convent's daily offices as she went about her garden chores.

Only this wasn't a bell, it was a mason's hammer. Nicholas's. And it wasn't coming from anywhere inside the castle or the bailey or the bakehouse. It drew her to lean over the window casement into the darkness, where it seemed to be rising up from the cliffs below.

Or from the foaming sea that tossed and misted the pale blue light of the full moon against the rocks. An old piece of iron chain, banging with the ebb and flow of the tides?

Plink.

"Hello!" She shouted her loudest, but the lonely word came back to her on the breeze.

She was sure that Nicholas was at the center of it—sure she would find him out there on the cliffs somewhere, building a ship or fixing the wharf, the bright moon silvering his broad, bare shoulders just as the sun turned them to gold.

But working at night—and so near the cliffs? What was the man thinking? She raced down the tower steps, out onto the curtain wall, and into the enduring wind, to look for him over the side.

"Nicholas?" If the plinking was his, he'd become invisible down there where she'd yet to explore, because there was no safe path around the base of the castle. But there was nothing below the ramparts but those hungry-looking rocks and the sea.

But the plinking was closer now, and freed of its echo.

She hurried up the external stairs that led onto the flat roof of the next tower, where the night had grown to enormous proportions and the wispy clouds skiffed past her nose.

Plink.

She scrabbled out across the thick embrasure, lying on her stomach and clutching the rough edge of the stone with her fingers, and peered over the side.

Good heavens, there was a chapel. A tiny

one—or a very large one; the soaring height of the tower and cliffs and the vast proportions of the boiling sea muddled her judgment.

But it was a chapel. Hiding there below the castle footing, where the great cliff divided into two; one part sliding away toward the restless waves into a rocky shelf of starkly limned shadows; the other lifting skyward, offering up the chapel on a dark promontory, standing fast against the constant wind, its crippled tower in full view of the sea yet masked entirely from the castle.

A tattered thing, roofless and ringed by moonlit rubble, so utterly beautiful in its loneliness. It was embraced in shadowy, meticulous scaffolding, rigged with pulleys and a great, freewheeling windlass, like the skeleton of a giant bird no longer able to fly.

The whole of it made her heart ache.

And made her think of Nicholas.

She watched the stars for a long time, waiting for the sound to come again, but it never did.

Chapter 15

A chaos of blessings. That was the only way Eleanor could describe the next morning at Faulkhurst.

Her wayfarers seemed to be dropping out of the wide blue sky like angels from an overcrowded heaven.

She and Hannah had only just fed the children when Nicholas strode into the kitchen, looking like a storm about to lay waste to a shoreline. She could only imagine that his truce with Mullock had fouled completely.

"What's happened, Nicholas?"

"I would see you now. In the great hall." He lowered that rock-rumbling voice, his gaze piercing. "Immediately." He left then, obviously expecting her to follow him.

"Come see what Master Nicholas found in the village, Nellamore." Pippa hurdled after the man, his little shadow.

He was standing in the center of the room, taller than ever, and he and his blazing, impatient temper were flanked by a trio of the most hairy-limbed, stouthearted, good-humored characters she'd ever seen.

"Lady Eleanor Bayard," he said through his stark white teeth, like a truculent court herald forced into service at sword point. He made one of his irreverently mocking quarter bows. "Your new *tenants*, madam."

"M' name is Skelly, m' lady," the largest of them said. "An' these two blighters beside me be Volney and Samuel."

They all bowed excessively and with a good deal of ornament, and had barely straightened when Samuel asked, "Might we have a bit of something to eat, milady? We've come a far distance."

That made her terribly happy. "From where?" she asked as she hurried them to the table. She could feel Nicholas narrowing his gaze at her, no doubt suspecting her of some nefarious deed to have gained seven new people in the last two days.

And he would be nearly right, if the truth be known. Not nefarious, exactly—but with a certain amount of risk.

"We're from out the Fens way, milady."

"That far away?" Then her unorthodox plan

227

was working fine, marvelously in fact. Nicholas was watching her more closely than she'd like, though, because she felt a bit guilty for her secret. But it was hers to make and hers to keep, whatever the man's opinion.

"I'll expect two of them at the armory, madam," he said. "In a half hour's time."

He left abruptly, but came storming back into the hall not ten minutes later, having collared an unruly teenage boy in each of his broad fists.

"These must be yours, my lady." He gave the newcomers a shake to stop the wide-eyed squabbling between them. "I found them outside the gate."

"Thank you, Nicholas."

He glared and rumbled at her, then at the growing accumulation of crates and tables and chairs that Mullock and his crew had carried in from the four corners of the keep.

Then he stalked out again into the blazing sunlight, taking a huge amount of her breath along with him.

He wouldn't approve of the reason for her success, but they were coming. Not in wispy drifts, but by the handful.

Heaven-sent, each one of them.

Faulkhurst had a grand total of sixteen residents now. The castle was alive with people, who were running efficiently hither and yon. Things were going well. Maybe too well.

Rumors would soon spread beyond those she had planted, of her success, of her widowhood.

And then it would begin.

Edward's machinations, another husband she didn't love.

And Nicholas. . . . but there her imagination ended. Because it all seemed so clear, yet so impossible.

Nicholas shucked his clothes and his boots, and steamed off the stone dust and sweat and the chill of the sea air in his underground grotto pool. The deep and ancient place was the only remaining refuge where he could reorder his thoughts after his wife had scrambled them.

As she had today with her parade of opportunists.

Miracles, Nicholas, she would say if she were here in the pool with him, swimming her eddying circles round him like the selkie she probably was. If he ever dared invite her again.

But this migration was no fluke; she had concocted something that stunk of shadiness, something that would come back soon to harm her.

And tonight he would know the source of all her hand-fashioned miracles, or else he would—What? Explain himself fully and then annul her on the spot?

He'd have been bloody all right, if she hadn't been so . . . perfect. So wifely.

But then what sort of blistering punishment would that have been, eh? Ah, no. He had to fall madly in love with the woman—a folly that he meant to cancel immediately. He simply wouldn't look into her eyes, wouldn't listen to her laughter, or let her share her sugared plums with him.

He had to practice to leave her.

He dressed in a clean tunic and leather hauberk, locked the door behind him, and climbed out of the catacombs to the foot of her tower. The sound of a battering ram somewhere above him sent his heart into his throat.

Surely a squad of Edward's bowmen or a band of Mullock's cutthroats was clamoring up the stairs ahead of him, toward his unsuspecting wife.

"Christ." He drew his dagger and took the steps three at a time, steeling himself for a battle to the death if need be.

"Stand away!" Her chamber door was gaping wide and the candlelight dancing against the dark walls as he charged into the room, through a cloud of her floral fragrance, and right into her trap.

"What's the matter, Nicholas?" She was kneeling in her night shift in the middle of the room, wrestling with two badly jointed timbered pieces, poised to strike a mending peg with a mallet. "What are you doing with that dagger? Has something happened?"

"I thought we were under attack, madam." He sagged against the table and sheathed his dagger.

"Not that I know of. Why didn't you tell me about the chapel, Nicholas?"

"The what?"

"The chapel out there on the seacliffs. I saw it last night." She was clad to her ankles and wrists in her plain, unadorned night shift, hair newly washed and tousled every which way. When she stood, she might as well have been wearing cobwebs, for the brightness of the candles lining the edge of the table behind her created a tantalizing silhouette.

He ought to leave immediately, ought to save his inquest for a greater distance, a safer time—when her defenses were down, and his were in better repair. "The chapel isn't safe, madam. It hasn't a roof."

"I could see that well enough. But it should be listed with the other buildings that need mending. Have you been working on it for long?"

He hadn't been working on the chapel at all lately, but on Liam's little headstone. Every night, for the few minutes that he could manage until his memories crept upon him and made his hands quake until the chisel was useless. A few letters more and he would be done. That much closer to being able to leave here.

"I do what I can, madam, when I can. But the chapel is beside the point. I want a brief but comprehensive explanation from you."

"As I do of you. Is the chapel on your list?"

This wasn't going to be easy; he could smell the blue lightning in the air between them, hated the falsehoods he told with such increasing ease.

"Yes, it is."

"Good, sir. Because we do need one, and a priest. Even a monk would do nicely." She gave the peg a smack and the two pieces went together with her smile.

Nicholas broadened his stance, crossed his arms against his chest, and looked straight down his nose at her. "Where the bloody hell are they all coming from?"

She blinked innocently. "What do you mean?"

"Well, let's take Skelly for a start." He stepped squarely in front of her, because she was as slippery as one of her merry thieves when she had a mind to be, then took the mallet and the peg out of her hand and set them on the table.

"He's from the Fens, didn't he say?" He wasn't in the least surprised when she put her hands on her hips. "I'll take my mallet back."

That only made it easier for him to lift the woman off her feet and set her on the tabletop, the better to keep her in place for once and watch her eyes for her riddling.

Because she was practiced at that, and he'd become vastly susceptible to her since he'd lost his mind and kissed her.

"I want to know exactly how you are conjuring your minions, madam—the sixteen of them who've stumbled across my—my path since you arrived here."

"Actually, Nicholas, it's seventeen as of this evening." She was gazing up at him with such unwavering innocence that he didn't notice, until his pulse thickened to honey, that she was running her beguiling fingers lightly through his hair, idly tucking it back behind the ridge of his ear. Her explanation dashed

233

around inside his head like eiderdown.

"Seventeen." He had heard that much.

"Aye, Nicholas, Wallace arrived just after supper. He says that he's a blacksmith!"

"Bloody hell, madam." He caught her hand before he lost himself completely and did something idiotic—like spanning the scant inches between them and capturing her mouth with his. "Another man arrives out of the mist, which bears out my point exactly. Is it your sorcery that brings them here?"

"Don't be absurd." She laughed too easily and looked guiltily away, then tried to slip down from her perch. But he held her there with his hands on either side of her hips, the length of his thumbs sizzling from the warmth of her nearly bare thighs.

"Have you posted a sign on the crossroads at Penrith and Furness?"

"No." She shook her head, but captured her plait and began to fidget with its tail.

"Nay, of course you didn't. Mullock surely didn't come that way, and I doubt any of the rest would know their own name if they saw it writ in large blocks. I want to know how Skelly and Cora and John and all the rest of them knew to come to Faulkhurst."

"I can't say exactly how they came."

He bent as close as he dared, said with

bared teeth, "I think you can, Lady Eleanor. We are out on God's last outpost. Did you leave a trail of coins for them to follow?"

"Of course not." Then her eyes lit brightly and she ducked beneath his arm and was off the table, to pluck a quill and knife from the holder. She began to shape a hasty nib. "But that's a fine idea, Nicholas. Brilliant!"

He was at her shoulder in the next moment, lifting the quill out of her hand. "Don't even think it, madam."

She turned toward him and opened her mouth to speak, but he put a finger across her lips to stop her. A damnably stupid thing to do, for they glistened in the candlelight, soft, warm, and much too near.

Too much his wife.

Arousal now seemed a constant state for him, a radiant rush of pure lust that made him feel callow and brutish. And he had once again trapped her hips between his thighs and the table.

"Tell me where they come from so I can still repair the damage. These are grave matters, and grave times. I am your steward, am I not?"

"A very good one, Nicholas. Quite miraculous, really." Her gaze was smoky and, Christ in heaven, she moved her hips—slightly, experimentally. He stood away before he could read the meaning of the wondering in her eyes.

"As your steward, madam—" he cleared his throat "—I cannot, I will not, haphazardly accept a parade of strangers streaming through the gates at all hours without question. Tell me how and why they are coming."

Another denial perched lushly on her lips, worried there by her teeth and her so rarely downcast eyes. He thought for an implausible moment that he had truly cowed her, but the eyes that found him sparkled with the mischief of success.

"Rumors," she whispered finally.

Not the answer he was expecting. In fact, it was no answer at all. "What do you mean 'rumors'?"

"I believe that's the reason so many people are coming." She clapped her hands together between her breasts, suddenly eager to confess. "You see, Nicholas, when I left Westminster, I knew that I was on my way to a castle that was entirely deserted."

"You told me that."

"I had no money, no prospects. So I planted the only crop available to me: rumors. In every town and village and crossroads we came to."

"What the devil kind of rumor has the

236

power to send people on a pilgrimage to the ends of the earth?" He leveled a finger at her when she would have opened her mouth. "And don't tell me that Faulkhurst has suddenly become fashionable because you've offered a cottage to each man. Good God, woman, there are thousands of abandoned cottages in villages all over this kingdom. *Real* cottages, complete with roofs and working hearths, standing upright. Unlike the village here at Faulkhurst, which looks like it slid down a mountain and landed in a heap. What possible rumor did you spread about?"

"That's exactly the challenge I had to meet, Nicholas. The rumor had to be something splendid and bold—beyond the offer of a cottage, as you said. Or a guild craft. It had to be . . . simply astounding."

Dear God. He'd commanded the most dreaded soldiers in all of Europe, had overrun seemingly impregnable castles, razed cathedrals to their undercrofts, flattened villages and pirated merchant vessels under full sail. And yet the woman terrified him as thoroughly as his son had with his lopsided, toothy grin.

Because he'd loved them—would have died for them.

"Go on." Although he wasn't sure he wanted to hear another word.

"All of this idle talk had to be as utterly unbelievable to the timid as it was to the lordly, but tantalizingly possible to anyone with dreams enough. To Cora and Mullock and Fergus and Hannah. Do you see?"

Oh, he saw the lure of her quite well, felt it as the tide feels the shore. He'd once had dreams of his own—great, spinning ones that were clouding his head just now. Impossible ones, because now they were perfumed by this woman whose eyelashes were tipped in the same gold as the sun.

"You've told me exactly nothing, madam."

"Well, sir, as I traveled through towns and villages, I stopped in alehouses and inns." Blushing beautifully, she slanted her smile at him, and then tugged at the front of his tunic, drawing him close enough for him to feel her breath against his mouth. "And then I merely gossiped."

"About?"

"Most anything for a short while. And then I'd offer up something like this—" She rose up on her toes, and whispered into his ear. "I understand, Master Potter, that the Lady of Faulkhurst Castle . . . Do you know where that is, sir? The castle?"

"I do, milady." He found himself nodding, stealing a sniff at her nape, deeply jealous of every potter and innkeeper along the Great Northern road.

"The lady, I'm told," she continued in her private charade, whispering very close to his mouth, brushing his beard with her mad tales, "is paying a tithe to each of her tenants for the next five years."

"Is she indeed?" Nicholas was still nodding blithely, still marveling at her scent, close to kissing her, to driving her backward against the table, when he finally heard her words. "A tithe! Did you say a tithe, for God's sake?"

" 'Yes, indeed, my good potter. I heard this from the butcher, and he from the reeve's nephew. It must be true. A tithe to her tenants, so they say, instead of the other way round.' And so I went on and on."

Nicholas lifted her chin sharply. "Tell me that you didn't."

"But I did—and to great success. Word spread so quickly that the rumors I lit as I came through a town's east gate met me in a bonfire as we were passing out the west."

"Why the hell wouldn't they? You're lining the streets of Faulkhurst with gold."

"And I'll wager that's why they're all coming. Along with the cottage I'm offering, and the guild craft and the virgate of land."

"God save you, woman, are you completely mad? Tithing to your tenants?" Leaving chaff for Edward's coffers? He couldn't let it happen, had to keep her out of Edward's hellish dungeons.

I am your lord and husband, woman, and you will stop this madness. It boiled like a fountain inside him, but he capped it tightly. Nay, logic would have to suit.

"You can't afford to keep that kind of promise, Lady Eleanor." He hoped he hadn't bellowed.

"I can't afford not to." Obviously angry, she stormed away from him, back to her noisy project. "If you haven't noticed, winter's on its way. I've a castle to run and a village to rebuild as soon as I can. You don't understand."

She whacked the peg into place, and he realized that she was putting a piece of furniture together.

"I understand that your tenants will fall to rebellion and throw you into the sea when you can't pay this tithe to them." He grabbed a handful of pegs and her mallet and had the rest of the holes filled a minute later.

"Thank you, Nicholas," she said from her knees. "I'll pay them as I promised."

"With what? Seashells? Tax money? If you

haven't already noticed, Edward covets far more than his share, and he *must* be paid. If he discovers that you have succeeded in your commerce without giving him his due—and he will—you'll find yourself languishing in a dank and forgotten dungeon at Westminster, at the very least."

A bed. She was putting together a bed, dragging the foot rail across the room and into place now.

"Edward won't be looking to Faulkhurst for years, Nicholas."

He couldn't stay that long—only until the harvest came in. Damnation, he'd never met anyone so hell-bent upon her own destruction. He couldn't allow it.

"Edward will find you out, madam." She held the rail upright and poised to strike the top of it with the mallet, to better seat the joint that was as stubborn as she was. "Rumors travel even faster at court than they do along the snickleways of town. And their repercussions are far more costly."

"Dammit, Nicholas! Then how do I feed them all? How do I keep them from starving?" She gave the bed frame a whack. "I'll pay my taxes, my tithe to the church, and the same to my tenants."

"They're not *your* tenants, madam. Any

more than if they were golden bangles and Dickon had stolen them off a lord's baggage train. You have enticed serfs from their masters, and that is patently illegal."

"You can't have it both ways, steward. A few nights ago they were outlaws, skulking through the king's forests, planning to attack my home with cudgels. Today they are someone else's highly valued tenants."

"A few nights ago, I wasn't aware that you were planning to flout the king's authority so blatantly."

"I'm certain that Edward doesn't care a whit about the people who come to Faulkhurst."

"He bloody well does. You are breaching his Ordinance of Laborers."

She had a spectacular way of pouting when she was stymied, a lithe hip tilted toward him and a wildly raking eyebrow. "His what?"

She was finally listening. Here was hope that he could deter her without revealing too much of his identity. " 'Tis an ordinance enacted by Edward and his barons three years ago—during the worst of the pestilence in the south—against asking for or paying excessive wages, willful idleness, and luring laborers away from their rightful lords."

She narrowed her eyes and their thick, feathery lashes, then made a harrumphing sound in her throat that seemed to dismiss dangerous kings and their conceits.

"Well, wouldn't he *just*. God help the common man who desires to be paid his worth when his labor is suddenly found to be extremely valuable."

Madwoman. "That isn't the point."

She went back to her malleting, squaring up the three-sided box she'd just made of the rails and the footboard. "Nevertheless, Nicholas, I will tithe to my tenants as I've promised them—in credits or in kind, if need be, and we will prosper together."

"By deliberately breaking the king's peace. I'd search closely through your husband's papers if I were you, madam. The edict will be among them somewhere. Read it with care and memorize it."

He'd make sure she did, even if he had to rifle his own office and put it in front of her obstinate nose.

She frowned. "It's probably hidden away somewhere with my husband's estate records."

Bloody hell, that's exactly where it was. But beside the point.

"In the end, madam, your tenants will be punished and you'll pay thrice the fine to their masters. Your castle will be forfeit, and you, my dear, will be jailed. And frankly, I don't want to be around to see that happen."

She blinked at him with those wide eyes of hers, as though he'd injured her to the quick and she hadn't expected him to have the power.

"Then I think it's best for you to leave, Nicholas."

His heart gave a single hollow thump and then stopped. Leave? Not while she courted danger with her deluded schemes. Not while he had breath. Though his heart was beating wildly, he lowered his gaze. Looking humbled would have to serve.

"Perhaps I spoke out of turn, madam."

"You did. And *I* am determined." He only imagined her stubborn foot stomping firmly on the plank floor.

"Yes, my lady."

He risked a glance at her and found her eyes reddened, looking worried.

"I hope that means you'll stay."

Long enough to save you from yourself, wife. And from me. "It does."

"Good." She caught her breath, then touched her lips. "Because, whether you believe it or not, I would miss you sorely."

And I— But it wasn't safe for him to finish

that sentiment. Simple regret would have to serve when he finally left her to her life; not emptiness or grieving. He couldn't afford to miss her—though he already felt tethered by her threads of silk, tugged tightly by the way she launched herself headfirst into every new thought.

Like this massive bed.

There was something sharply familiar about the intricate turning of the bedpost, about the finials and its floral profusion. He lifted the headboard and knew for certain.

"Where did you find this?"

She sat back on her heels and blew out a breath. "In the wardrobe. It was in pieces and covered with dust, but I finally realized it was a bed. I love the carving."

But of course, this wasn't just any bed.

It was their marriage bed. A wedding gift from a wine merchant in Calais. He'd had it sent home to Faulkhurst, expecting to some-day consummate their marriage upon it.

And here she was—his stunning bride—struggling to put it together herself, stopping to run her finger along the trailing tendrils and smile at him.

"It's fine handiwork, isn't it, Nicholas?"

Cherry wood, burnished to nearly the same

shade as her hair, though not as vibrant or lustrous. Not nearly as silken.

It's our bed, wife.

He wanted to say that. More, he wanted to take her in it. "It is, madam."

"Will you help me finish it, Nicholas?"

"It would be the greatest pleasure of my life." His hands shaking badly, he took the mallet from her and drove the peg into the hole with one stroke.

When the frame was together, the rope strung and crosshatched, and the feather mattress and soft linens in place, she stood beside their marriage bed, looking nervous as a cat.

"Nicholas?"

"Yes." He unhitched his sword belt and tossed it onto his pallet, more casually than he felt because he didn't trust her—or himself—when she took on that softness around her mouth, when she tracked his eyes with such care.

"Are you going to bed now?" She had a hank of her gown at her thigh and was twisting it up around her finger, measuring him with her wide eyes.

"I am. It's midnight. Well past it. You should be to bed as well."

"Yes, and, well . . . along those lines—" She bit at her lips, drawing a soft rosiness to them.

"I was wondering if you would mind very much if we ... I mean ... if you—"

"What is it, my lady?" He'd never seen her like this. "Would I mind what?"

She cleared her throat, took a large, worried breath as if she would speak a long court defense, and started to pace, just out of his reach.

"It's just that I've been thinking about the other night—in the grotto. The night we ..." The flush blossomed, spread down the front of her night shift, into that place he dreamed about. "The night ... you remember."

"I'm not likely to forget." Not the night, nor the yearnings she roused in him; the taste of her, the feel of her skin in those sweet places he never should have explored.

"I haven't, either. Won't ever forget. So that brings me to the subject that we discussed that night."

He fumbled through his memory, not recalling much more than that she had tasted of sugared plums, and herself, and he'd nearly claimed her. "What subject was that?"

"That I'm still a virgin."

"Ah, that." Nicholas turned away, sure she could see his raging need for her through his breeches. It wouldn't do to frighten her. She was nervous enough as it was about the matter.

247

Since he wasn't looking at her when she spoke, her next statement made no more sense than a pack of chittering squirrels.

"Make love with me, Nicholas."

The woman had finally driven him out of his mind completely. He'd started to hear things. He turned back to her and watched her mouth this time, those plump, rosy lips that tasted too much of forever.

"Will you, Nicholas?"

Aye, the madness was indeed the starry-eyed woman he'd married in such arbitrary haste. All his regrets and all his expectations, his longing and dreams tangled together in one astonishing temptation to believe in her miracles, in the redemption of the damned.

"Will I . . ." *Make love with my wife?* Is that what she'd said?

She held out her hand to him as she had done so often, staggering him with possibilities. "Please, Nicholas."

He shook his head, trying to rid his ears of the ringing. "What did you say?" Because he wasn't quite sure. This could very well be one of his dreams.

"I want you to make love with me."

He found breath enough to whisper, "Do you know what you're asking me, Eleanor?"

She nodded, emphatic and eager, blushing

248

as though she knew all the places he could take her. "Aye, Nicholas, I do know."

"I'm sorry. I can't." He couldn't move. Dared not, for any momentum at all would send him into her arms.

She looked highly affronted, fisted her hands into her hips. "Why can't you?"

"Because, Eleanor—" *I'd want to stay.*

"Because we're not married, isn't that it?" She turned away, cupped her hand over her mouth, and then both against her cheeks. "You and your honor."

He had little enough of that, and more than enough confusion. "Eleanor, why are you asking me this?"

She sighed so deeply that he ached to hold her in his arms. "Because William forgot to bed me."

"He didn't forget." *He burns for you, my love.*

"Well, he didn't get around to it, did he?"

"No." He was breathing as roughly as she.

"So I want you to do it in his stead." She made it all sound so simple, so right.

"Why me?" Though, Christ knew, he couldn't imagine another man with her.

"My husband can't possibly object."

He'd be a damned fool not to. "Eleanor, please."

"He appointed John Sorrel to marry me. So

249

I'm appointing you, Nicholas, to bed me. It's only fair."

And marvelous and head-spinning.

And impossible. "I'm flattered by—"

"Don't be, Nicholas." She wagged a finger at him. " 'Tis estate business of the highest priority."

"Estate business?" He wanted to smile at her dramatics, but she seemed deadly serious and bewitching, and he was paralyzed by his adoration.

"How else do I protect Faulkhurst from Edward? I need you to ravish me as soon as possible."

Christ, her logic made him ache for all the years they would be apart. "Why?"

"Because my second husband will undoubtedly be surprised to discover his wife a virgin. Wouldn't you be, Nicholas?"

"Indeed, but that's a private matter between you and—" Nicholas paced away, trying to outrace the image of his wife with another man "—and your next husband."

"But I can't risk that."

"It shouldn't be me, Eleanor."

"It shouldn't be anyone else. I trust you with my life. I trust you to be fair and understanding. I couldn't trust a husband more. I didn't choose my husband, but I'm free to choose the man who deflowers me now. And you do find me attractive." She smoothed her hands over her night shift, exposing his favorite lines, the darkness and the light of her. "I've noticed that about you."

"Noticed?" She must have heard his gulp.

"Quite clearly. That very male part of you grows hard and exceptional when you kiss me. Like it did in the grotto."

Wonderful. "You're right, Eleanor. It does. I do."

"I know what it's for." She was pointing now, heating him further.

He turned away. "You're not helping, Eleanor."

"What if I disrobed completely, stood naked before you? Would you be tempted?"

"Whether you're robed or not, I am tempted. Right here, right now, you intoxicate me."

"But you won't?"

"I can't."

She was a cloud of scented heat at his back, whispering to him of his own fantasies. "And if I came to you at night, Nicholas? If I slipped into your bed and kissed you—"

"I couldn't imagine a greater torment."

"But you still wouldn't?"

"No."

She threw up her arms, then backed away from him. "Of course not. You're a man of honor, Nicholas, and here I am trying my best to seduce you, when I promised myself that I wouldn't."

"That's not it."

"Well, then. I've made an utter fool of myself tonight."

"No, Eleanor; I am honored by your trust. And I've never been so tempted by anything in my life."

Eleanor had never seen him wear a more stricken look, never felt more confused as she watched the man she adored walk out of her chamber.

Her heart had stopped beating some time ago, and now it was just plain bleeding, making her fingers cold and hot and her legs shaky.

"Oh, my dear steward, what would you have said if you'd known what was really in my heart?"

Marry me, Nicholas.

Chapter 16

"We found the market cross in the village, milord, just where you said it would be."

"And the second well, Skelly?"

"Framed up, sir. You'll be drawing water from it by the end of the day."

"Excellent. I'll be there when I'm finished here."

Eleanor loved to work beside Nicholas as he wrestled with the castle reckonings and she made plans for the coming weeks; loved that he managed it all right in the middle of the great hall amid the clangorous comings and goings of the supper preparations.

Hannah seemed to love it, too. "Sugared apples for you, Nicholas," she would say, tucking a plate of it and dark slabs of bread near his elbow. Lisabet saw that his cup was perpetually filled with cider, and Pippa made sure that her Nicholas was never at a loss for a bouquet of dandelions.

He was by every measure the protective and proficient steward, sprawled with his elbows and arms taking up the whole of two trestles when he was scrawling in his rough script.

Or pacing off the stables or prowling the ramparts, wanting to see everything firsthand, as he ordered and interrogated and cajoled the nearly fifty tenants who'd found Faulkhurst in the course of the last ten miraculous days.

Fifty people—who ever could have imagined? The fields were being plowed and planted right on schedule, and Fergus and Wallace, the new smith, had repaired the mill wheel.

Fifty was a grand number, which gave her pause over Nicholas's warning about the Ordinance of Laborers. Because he was a wise man, and because he seemed to care so deeply for her dreams even though they weren't his own, which made her heart ache with an impossible kind of love for the man.

He'd never mentioned her rash request to deflower her, but slept each night wrapped in his blanket with his face to the wall. But the deed still needed doing, and he had not given a reason that satisfied her, so she would ask him again one day. Until then—

"Your laundry shed is finished, madam." Nicholas leaned over her chin-propped musings, his dark eyes luminous and nearly smiling.

He smelled of apples. And bedsheets. And happiness.

Marry me, Nicholas.

"Dear God!" She stood sharply and stared at him, her heart pounding, hoping that she hadn't really let that out between them.

"What, madam?"

"What did I just say, Nicholas?"

He blinked at her and tugged at his perfectly black, perfectly shaped beard. "I'm not sure I know, madam. I had just told you that Fergus had finished the laundry shed." He leaned close enough to hear the hammering of her heart, and whispered, "Granted, it's not exactly plumb, but I'll take care of that tonight after he's gone to bed."

You're the finest man I've ever known, Nicholas Langridge. And I'm afraid that I love you.

"I—That's . . . that's excellent, Nicholas. Especially since two laundresses arrived only yesterday."

He chewed on the inside of his cheek, dipped those dark brows, and whispered again, to her alone, "They are ladies of ill re-

pute. Out of London, I suspect. You do know
that, don't you, madam?"

"Aye, Nicholas, and isn't it a fine thing that
we've shown them a better way?"

It seemed an ordinary reply, but the man's
whole aspect softened. The indigo of his eyes
deepened, and right there, in the full chaos of
the great hall, he ran his thumb across her lips,
softly, intently, as stirring a kiss as she could
ever imagine.

"*You*, my lady, are a fine thing. The finest
I've ever known."

"Oh." Her heart soared and sang. And it
came to her to ask him again to make love
with her, for she had a terrible sense of fore-
boding about all their success.

But he was tugged away from the table to
sort out a raucous disagreement between Mullock and the clerk she'd assigned to him.

"I canna write as fast as the bloody man
speaks." McDowell poked at Mullock's chest.

"Cause ya listen like a deef old woman, Mc-
Dowell." Mullock belly-butted the man, who
belly-butted back.

"Enough, the pair of you."

In all disputes, Nicholas accomplished his
stewardship as he did everything—thoroughly and long into the night, as though he

was rushing to be finished before he could be overtaken by some calamity.

Last week he was master mason, overseeing the armory and the bakehouse and the crumbling passage in the west wall and dozens of other projects.

This week he was resurrecting the village, lane by lane, salvaging timber and tools and roofing slate—when he wasn't consulting with Dickon on the state of Faulkhurst's defenses, or advising Richard about the fish weirs and the mill.

Or walking the fields with her, platting the crop borders that still needed sowing sometime in the next two weeks. He was as opinionated about farming and husbandry as he was about pulleys and forges and millraces.

Not even the children seemed to confound or distract his efficiency.

Not even Pippa.

"Here, Master Nicholas." Pippa opened her hand and a fistful of acorns rolled all over the pantry accounts. "Is that enough, do you think?"

"How many have you there, Mistress Pippa?" He looked fiercely businesslike, glowering across the table at Pippa and Toddy and their three equally unscrubbed companions, who seemed awed to silence by the commerce between steward and child.

"Uhmmmm...Well..." Pippa and her golden curls disappeared under the table, only to turn up on the bench between Nicholas and Eleanor.

"As many as these." She held up five tremendously grimy fingers.

Nicholas seemed completely unfazed by the little hand in his face. "Which is what number?"

He also seemed altogether comfortable when Pippa crawled up onto his lap and made herself and her pointy elbows at home there. "Dunno, sir."

"Well, if you're going to be of any help to me, Mistress Pippa, you'll have to learn that this is five." He counted the tips of her fingers one at a time, making her recite each number along with him. Then he turned to the other children and made them recite the same. Still the stern teacher, still the vigilant steward who was looking after his accounts.

Still Pippa's very own and much adored gargoyle.

"And these are five again," she said, proudly holding out her other hand. "Do you see them, Nellamore?"

They were wiggling right under her nose. "I

do, sweet." She saw very much indeed.

Nicholas shared a wryly pleased smile with Eleanor, then held the girl's hands still.

"And how many fingers do you have on your two hands, Mistress Pippa?"

"Ten." But the answer had come from Toddy, who seem astonished that he'd spoken at all.

"Exactly right, Master Todd." Nicholas lifted Pippa off his lap and stood her on the bench between them. "Now, Mistress Pippa, off you go to find me as many feathers as each of you have fingers."

She squatted on her haunches and peered at him, nose to nose. "Each of us, Master Nicholas?"

"Ten each, Pippa. Start with the kitchen garden. Toddy will show how many ten is if you forget."

"I won't forget!" They scampered off in a noisy clump toward the kitchen, while Nicholas gathered up the acorns and put them in his steward's coffer.

"*What* did you tell Pippa to find, Nicholas?" She couldn't credit her hearing. First acorns and then—

"Feathers." He stood as he rolled up the planting map and tucked it under his arm.

259

"I'm off to the village, milady. We're raising the cobbler's roof today."

"What kind of feathers, Nicholas?" She followed his long strides out of the hall to the portico steps.

"Gull, robin. It doesn't matter."

"Yes, but why do you need them? Pillows? Feather beds? Every mattress in Faulkhurst is newly stuffed with fresh straw."

He stopped and smiled at her, as handsome and as able as any man she'd ever known, and clearly pleased at this secret he was hiding. "I thought you of all people would know, Lady Eleanor."

"I . . . don't." Eleanor was at a complete loss, but melted completely when he tucked his thumb beneath her chin to lift it, leaned down, and said, "Opportunity."

"How do you mean?"

"Feathers are ten a farthing if you know who's willing to buy them."

"Feathers are?" *Feathers?* Then it hit her squarely in the heart, taking her breath away with its sweetness.

He'd been playing with the children all along, sending them off on errands of their own to make them feel important, or to keep them safely out from under foot.

He was already heading for the village,

drawing a half dozen men alongside him as he crossed the bailey.

Twice that afternoon she caught sight of him in the village, as she and her crew were plowing and planting the bean strips in the hillside fields.

But watching him was an idle pursuit that brought on impossible fancies, and a crick in her neck besides. So she and Figgey concentrated on their plowing, the mare dazzled by the freedom of the open field, her unshod hoofs throwing up clods in every direction.

She'd forgotten her gloves again, and she'd just stopped Figgey in the midst of a furrow to wrap her hands in her apron when a stream of children crested the ridge and came running toward her.

As always, Pippa was in the lead, her muddy hem held up to her knees, her chubby little legs pumping across the furrows.

"Look what we found, Nellamore!"

"Did you find Master Nicholas's feathers for him?" They stopped and surrounded her.

"Lots! And these, too, Nellamore."

All their little hands opened to a menagerie of bears and badgers and rabbits, freshly carved and expectant of grand adventures.

Eleanor laughed and knelt to pick a napping fawn out of Molly's palm. "Where did you

261

find these?" Dear God, she hoped they hadn't raided Nicholas of some cache he'd been carving.

Toddy hopped his whimsical rabbit along the freshly plowed furrow. "I found my rabbit sleeping in the cabbages."

"And mine in the sage." Eamon leapfrogged his hedgehog over Toddy and the rabbit, and the pair of them raced along the next row.

Nicholas. He'd purposely sent the children to the garden for their feathers, after planting his offerings to be discovered and played with.

And loved.

She looked out over the village and found him immediately, spotting him by the stark midnight of his hair, by his stance.

He was clearly mourning a great loss, someone as dear to him as he was to her.

"I know where they came from, Nellamore. The animals."

She bent down to Pippa's beckoning. "Where?"

She cupped Eleanor's ear. "From Nicholas."

"You may be right."

"I think he needs my pony."

"Oh, Pippa!" Eleanor kissed her sweat-begrimed cheek. "I think he does, too. Run and take it to him."

*   *   *

Nicholas was two steps up the ladder against the tithe barn when he felt a tug at his shoe and heard a voice he'd come to cherish.

"We have a present for you, Master Nicholas."

There seemed to be dozens of children milling about below him, all of them carrying their carvings, Pippa with the largest smile. "A present, for me, Pippa? It can't be the feathers; I'm paying you for those."

"Come down."

Nicholas dropped from the ladder, knowing that his wife must have had something to do with this, and knelt beside Pippa.

"For you, Nicholas." Pippa upended her belt purse, and after a few shakes a shell fell out onto the ground.

"Well, that's the best present I've had all—"

"Not the shell."

Then something else dropped out of the bag—and with it a wave of memories that blackened the edges of his vision.

Liam's gangly-limbed, sad-tailed pony, clumsily carved of sticks, because it had been his first attempt at trying to win over his son. It had suffered Liam's love bravely, and had died with him.

"It's a pony, Nicholas. Do you like it?"

"Where did you get this, Pippa?" He had only breath enough to whisper, and his heart thudded against the hollow of his chest. He picked up the pony in hands that shook, remembering the tentative wonder in the boy's eyes when he'd presented it.

Do you mean the pony's for me, sir?

"I found it on our first day."

Aye, for you.

"Where?"

Why, my lord, for me? That question had hurt him most of all. That he had failed his own son in such unforgivable ways.

"In the kitchen."

Because, boy, I'm your father.

"He wants to be with you, Nicholas." Pippa leaned over his arm and moved the horse's dangling legs with her finger, setting them to gallop in the air.

"Well, I thank you for the pony." An offering to a son who had never known a father's love till then. From a father who had just learned what it meant to be truly afraid.

Pippa cupped his ear for one of her noisy secrets. "An' we thank you for the animals."

Toddy squatted in front of him. "We found this many feathers, too, sir."

Nicholas counted up all the fingers, and reveled in all the smiles. "Sixty, looks to me. How many farthings is that, Toddy?"

"Six?"

"Six exactly." Nicholas stood. "Come see me in the hall after supper and I'll pay out your farthings then."

They streamed away from him like little birds, headed toward his wife in the fields.

A school. A village school, and a cleric who didn't mind having his robes tugged on or his toes tromped.

Aye, a school would please his wife, would make her smile.

Nicholas had never let Mullock far out of his sight, still as surprised at the man's genius for organization as he was suspicious of it. He was a jumble of contradictions, alternately course-mouthed and then respectful; watchful with that piercing, single-eyed focus and then excessively gregarious.

But always insufferably congenial. All of which damned him for a charlatan.

So Nicholas wasn't in the least surprised when he discovered Mullock slipping out of the great hall late one moonless night, his wiry shoulders loaded down with the same towering rucksack that he'd arrived with. It rattled and clanked as Mullock dodged through the shadows, bulging with stolen plate and God knew what else.

"Go, with my blessing, Mullock," he said beneath his breath. *And welcome to everything you can carry, as long as it takes you far away from here. Away from my wife and her fragile dreams.* Eleanor would be disappointed in Mullock, but it couldn't be helped. A valuable lesson in treachery.

She would need to know this of men, when he was gone.

Still, Nicholas quietly followed the scurrying thief into the shadowy village, past the tidy mountains of lumber and piles of slate, past the new well house and the market cross. There Mullock finally slowed, staggered under his unwieldy load, then stopped.

At first Nicholas thought he'd been heard, so he hung back in the shadows. But Mullock was only muttering to himself.

"Past time, it is, be damned." He hitched up his pack again and barreled forward, but only got three steps before he stopped again. "Beggar me bald!"

He turned back this time and stared up at the castle. "Bloody, bleedin', beggarin' hell."

He yanked a sack of coins from out of his belt, shook it hard, then laughed fondly,

crowing-proud that he'd succeeded in outwit-
ting the Lady of Faulkhurst.

"On with it then." Mullock took three more
steps . . . then rounded back on the lane again
and stalked back toward the castle, muttering
as he passed by Nicholas's hiding place.

"Forget something, Mullock?"

"What the—" The man staggered backward
a step. "Ah, it's you, milord. Bit dark out, ain't
it?"

"Indeed. Your chance to leave, Mullock—
free and clear. I won't stop you. In fact, I'll
spare you a fine mount to be gone."

But Mullock slumped his shoulders. "Bleedin' cockles, Master Nicholas, I'd like nothing
better than to just leave."

"The road is wide-open and calling to you."

"You may think so, milord, just as I did. But
just you go and try to leave here yourself,
someday. You won't find it easy at all."

He didn't expect to, but for far different reasons than Mullock could imagine. "You've got
what you came for, made a tidy profit."

"A whole lot more'n tidy. But it's her bleedin' fault that I can't just up and leave." Mullock nodded up the castle road, his dark eye
glistening with resentment.

"Whose fault is that?" Good Lord, maybe
his wife had been right after all.

"Milady's. She's not a lady to disappoint and then expect to live a single day in peace afterward, is she?"

The man had the right of it.

"It was the saddest day of m'life when she trusted me, sir. Just—" he threw out his arms, jangling his pack "—just trusted me, 'at's all. With every bloody thing in her bloody castle. Beggar me, milord, what's an ordinary fool to do with that kind of weight pressing on him?"

What, indeed?

Make love with me, Nicholas.

"He'd leave, if he were wise."

"Aye. An' being the fool that I am, I guess I'm stayin' put."

Christ, I envy you, Mullock. For staying, for the freedom to love her without consequences.

Mullock started trudging back up the hill, weighed down by a scrap of woman whose only weapon was that she trusted too freely. "Here I thought I was feelin' so grand 'cause I was setting her up to steal her blind. But all along, 'twas just too bloody good to be bloody needed for once."

Bloody good indeed. He and Mullock were a pair: a couple of sinners finding that hell could be nearly impossible to distinguish from heaven.

When they reached the stable, Mullock

268

stopped and reached his hand out to Nicholas's shoulder.

"You won't tell her will you, sir?"

The poor man didn't know that his wife had a gift for knowing everything. "She won't hear it from me, Mullock. That I promise."

Eleanor had been gathering tally sticks from the new tithe barn in the castle forecourt when she saw Mullock sneak across the dark bailey with his pack. Too heartsick to follow and stop him, she could only stand and stare, then feared the very worst when Nicholas stealthily followed the man.

Not you, Mullock. Please. She hadn't wanted to believe it of him; hadn't wanted to imagine that he'd plotted his theft against her, against them all.

Disappointed to her soul that Mullock hadn't understood his own worth, she bundled the unnotched tallies and busied herself so that she didn't have to think any deeper than how much barley she would plant in the morning, because it hurt too much.

Then, weary to her bones, she climbed the stairs to her room, ready for a good long cry.

"Do you never sleep, woman?"

"Nicholas." He was the familiar darkness that made her heart slip. A long warbling sob shook her. "Mullock's gone, isn't he, Nicholas?"

"No."

She snuffled and pointed out the window toward the gatehouse. "But I saw him go. You did, too—with his pack full to bursting. What happened?"

"He changed his mind." Nicholas threw his dagger belt onto the clothes peg, looking like a husband come home to their bed after a long day's labor.

"Oh, good." She gathered up her cloak, wanting to find the man and thank him. But Nicholas stopped her at the door.

"Where are you going?"

"I want to welcome Mullock home."

"Christ, woman, leave the man a speck of pride. Don't ever tell him that you saw anything of it."

"I wouldn't think of hurting him. Nicholas! You didn't clobber him, did you?"

"Never laid a finger on the man. I even offered him a horse to be gone."

"Nicholas, you didn't!"

He shucked his boots and then his sword belt. "I never did trust the man."

"But he's staying?" She took another halting step, wanting to throw her arms around him for saving Mullock, for everything that he meant to her—all those things that were so difficult to put into words because they were such a part of every day, of who he was.

"He's staying—in spite of the fact that you've ruined him." Nicholas groaned as he lay back on his pallet, then turned his back on her.

"Me? I have?"

"Like you've ruined me." He sighed, and she could already hear the sleep in his voice.

"How have I done that?" He waved a weary hand at her, a dismissal. "Did you two share a barrel of ale while you were gone?" She stepped between Nicholas and the wall, sat down, and leaned back against him.

"Go to sleep, Eleanor."

"How have I ruined you?" When he didn't answer, she tucked herself into the crook of his arm, then fused her back to his chest, sure that she would draw an objection from him.

But he only slipped his arm around her waist and dragged her closer. "Because, my dear, you have stolen my will completely."

But Nicholas, you've stolen my heart, and I can't imagine a more remarkable thief.

It took long minutes before she heard Nicholas's heart settle against her back, until his breathing eased, until his marvelously steadfast erection finally rested.

Chapter 17

Your *chapel, for my son's life.*
It had seemed a damned fair bargain with God at the time, his guileless, guiltless son offered earnestly against the sad ruins of a church—neglected for as long as he could remember—to be rebuilt with all due reverence, by his own hand and reconsecrated in His name. For His almighty purpose.

One father's honest pledge to another, far more accomplished One.

The task of rebuilding had seemed monumental at the time, ultimately compensating because it did seem so very impossible. The bell tower had tumbled down sometime over the course of uncaring decades, had broken the slate roof into tiny pieces and scattered them, had crushed the rafters, and shattered most of the cornice on its descent into the sanctuary.

He'd spent months sorting through the rubble for usable pieces, clearing away the destruction. He had fashioned the scaffolding, the winches and windlasses, the work sheds, moving lime and cement supplies from the castle's stores, gathering tools—and learning how to use them.

Hard labor, which he was grateful for, for he had never allowed himself idle meditations over the meaning of the pestilence, or the fear that his bargain could go so very wrong. The days had felled him with exhaustion, and ensured that his sleep would be dreamless oblivion.

Only to wake and start again. Because he'd mistakenly thought he could overtake his sins.

In all his years of warring he'd never once spared a thought for his soul or for anyone else's. His had been a brutal commerce, best executed with expedience and a distant heart.

But in the midst of plundering a chapel so much like this one in a war-tattered village in some forgotten part of Brittany, he'd been brought to his knees by a boy.

One so like his own son that it had felled him.

Though no one would have blamed him, in the heady heat of a battle one body looked just like another, this one small and cowering in the nave of a chapel.

Out of habit, out of numbness borne of too much bloodletting, he'd raised his sword to strike a bloody blow for his king, for his own conceit.

"Please don't, sir."

It was a small, unsteady voice. A dark-haired boy daring to plead for his life, though a sword point dented the pliable flesh at his throat.

"Don't kill me, sir. I beg you. I'm all my mother has now. My father was just killed at the gate."

Nicholas had lowered his sword, feeling righteous in his code of honor—that he had never, would never, kill a child or a woman. Beyond that, it hadn't mattered to him.

"Your father knew the risk of resisting."

"He was only a cobbler, sir. Now I'll have to be so—for my mother."

Battle-brave, the boy had been. And as bone-thin as all the rest, because his town had been sacked three times that year alone.

"How old are you, lad?"

"Eight."

Eight. For some reason he'd never under-stand, he'd thought then of his own son, the peasant girl's bastard. The boy who had his eyes and his coloring, who'd been conceived on a winter's night, of a virgin he'd dallied with until she'd made her arrogant claim against him.

A son.

His flesh. His blood. His legacy.

He noticed the blood that had spattered him through the day's efforts, soaking through the mail to wet his tunic, and bile had risen in his throat, hot and bitter and tasting of metal.

This was his legacy? This bloody game, tearing down homes and slaying fathers, leaving children to starve?

"Go, boy. Now. Keep yourself to the shadows." He'd kept down his stomach until the boy was gone, and then he'd thrown off his helmet, dropped to his knees, and spilled his guts out onto the chapel floor.

He'd bawled like a baby when the priest held his forehead, and again when he'd poured out his confession on his knees until he was empty and aching.

Always thinking of his son, the one he'd denied.

The town had fallen an hour later, and the carnage in the streets had sickened him again and again, until there was nothing left inside to give.

He'd left the battle and then the camp, had

scoured himself in a hot spring to boil off the evil that clung to him, and he'd set sail for Faulkhurst.

Running from his past or walking into a dark abyss, it hadn't mattered. He'd given himself over to his God, and he'd found his son.

He had worked here in the stonecutter's shed at night after the boy was asleep, after tending the sick and burying the dead, working for hours by the light of a dozen cresset lamps, chiseling away at the oak timbers that would once again span the vault above the altar.

Sometimes still, when the moon was at its palest, he could see his son's dark eyes grinning shyly from behind the edge of the church wall.

Can I help you, Papa?

My boy. Nicholas swallowed hard against the sorrow and turned away from the surging flood of memories, fitting his chisel into the small channel in the stone marker.

Liam, it read—crudely, because he wasn't very good at the subtleties, and because his hands so often shook while he tried to work.

And beneath that: *Beloved Son.* Or so it would read when he left Faulkhurst, as soon as he finished those last two wholly inadequate words.

A simple, trembling tap with the hammer was all it would take to begin, one tap after another to mark the place he'd buried him. He'd grown expert with the mason's tools, but cutting heavy stone blocks hadn't the dreadful finality of carving this inadequate tribute to his son.

"It's beautiful out here, Nicholas."

For the briefest moment, he thought her voice had come from the sea. But she was standing in the rock-strewn pathway between the shed and the forlorn sanctuary, not a dozen feet from him, framed by glints of moonlight and the flinty cliffs.

Peace and simple adoration and the pale saffron of the last moments of the sun softened her brow and her smile, and every part of him quickened—his pulse and his breathing and his groin. He came off his workbench and stood like a statue, not at all certain how he felt.

Invaded. Grateful. Terrified. Wanting to confess.

"Aye, it is beautiful, madam." *You are.* "How did you come?"

She looked back toward the castle. "I took the path along the rocks."

His heart pounded in sudden, helpless fear. He should have known she would scrabble her way out here eventually, should have shown her the passage beneath the wall. He stumbled over the need to stop her where she stood, to keep her from wandering the cliffs and slipping into the waves.

"Christ, madam, a misstep and you might have killed yourself." He took her hands, looking for the scrapes that came from climbing over the rocks.

"Are you a goat then, Nicholas?" She was grinning patiently, allowing him his tirade as she always did. "How do you come every night?"

Her hands were softly callused but uninjured, so he let them go. "There's a passage. I'll show you."

"Ah." She seemed unconcerned, at home with the sea, closing her eyes and tilting her chin to the brunt of the everlasting gale.

"Which is no reason not to consider the place dangerous, madam. The chapel and the cliffs themselves are." He gestured toward the rubble and the rawboned rafters of the chapel, but she only shook her head at him, collecting the billowing sea spray on her cheeks and the ends of her hair, like fiery pearls.

"You haven't let me fall yet, Nicholas." She

looked down at the chisel in his belt, then to the workbench in the shed, to the rectangle of limestone sitting atop it and the mallet lying beside.

His heart took off like a rocket. He wanted to throw himself in front of the evidence as she went to the shed, to block her view from his shame.

She caught her hair with a sweep of her arm, held all of it fast against her chest and read simply.

"Liam." Sweetly whispered like a prayer. Then she looked up at him in her diabolically compassionate way.

"Who was he, Nicholas?" The sea came to life in the silence that she left riding the air. Thrashing tides and a whirling reel of spin-drift dared him to speak the truth.

All of it.

That he was William Nicholas Bayard, the husband she reviled. That she was his wife. That the boy whose grave lay beneath the wind-bent pine in the corner of the churchyard was his son.

His heir and namesake.

But he'd learned long ago that the truth had many colors; could be tinted in shame as well as in honor.

"Liam was my son."

279

She put her fingers to her mouth, and her eyes widened and sparkled with quick tears. "Ah, Nicholas, no."

She was grieving with him suddenly, for a boy she'd never known. In every way that counted, he'd been her son, too, though she could never know it. For she was the kind of woman who would have loved the boy beyond all measure.

Her warm, protective hand slipped over his, between his fingers to clasp tightly. Then she rose up on her toes and brushed her cheek against his, and whispered against his ear, "Be with your boy now, Nicholas. I'll find you later."

"No." He surprised himself when he held tightly to her hand, unable to let go when he ought to keep his distance from her gentle weeping, from this unexpected island in the middle of a churning sea. "It's ... fine. I was—"

But he couldn't finish, only gestured to the bench, hoping she'd understand.

"Your son." She touched the marker, ran her finger along the L and smiled with her generous heart, as though his clumsy asymmetry had made it more exquisite. "How old was he?"

It was a mother's voice that slipped from

her so easily, kindly and encouraging. Fashioned perfectly for a boy's scraped knees and loose teeth, for arms that would cuddle and care.

Yet he had to fill that space between them with more falsehoods, the next lie about Liam becoming a part of the first. Step by step, denying his son his rightful place in the world as he skirted the truth.

Which was no different than he'd done for years, and it sickened him to choose that path with Eleanor.

"Liam was about eight."

"Toddy's age."

"I think so."

She closed her eyes for a moment, and he felt the shaky sob that she was trying to mask. "What a lucky boy to have had a father like you."

He could at least counter *that* false impression. He turned from her to the workbench, and bundled up the chisel and then the hammer in a leather clout. "In truth, I wasn't a father to Liam at all, madam."

Any more than I was ever a husband to you, ever could be.

"I can't imagine that, Nicholas. I've seen you with the children."

"I was a soldier by trade, remember." He

tucked the tools into a chest and shoved it under the worktable, rocking the lamps and the long, flighty shadows.

"I've never known a boy who wasn't proud to have his father serve the king."

"Ah, but you see, this boy wasn't mine."

"Wasn't? Then why—"

"That's what I had always told myself." He calculated each word as he said it, keeping to the barest details. "I had no use at all for families or children—or wives, or anyone but myself. Though Liam was my blood and my flesh, I denied him my name, almost to the end."

"What of his mother? Did you—" She so rarely faltered in her course that he wondered at her hesitation. "Did you love her?"

She would want to think that he did. "She was an easy skirt to me—the woodward's daughter. As innocent as I was carnal and corrupt."

"Nicholas, you were never—"

He held up a hand to stop her. "Please, madam; I know my own history. You know nothing of me beyond your own goodness."

She sat on the bench, her hands in her lap. "What happened to her? Liam's mother?"

"She died. I don't know when, or why. The boy was left to himself on the streets. I found him there."

"On the streets—such a young boy."

"I came very late to fatherhood, my lady—and I had much to make up to my son." Brushing this close to the truth made him feel recklessly free. "But the boy didn't know me at all. He was terrified of me when I first came for him. Hid from me, even."

For some reason that made her smile. "And so you made toys for him, didn't you? Carved dancing bears and hedgehogs." Of course she would follow that trail; he'd led her there.

"My feeble campaign to win him. I was . . . resolved to be his father. And he was as reluctant at first."

"Oh, Nicholas, I suspect that your Liam came willingly to you in no time at all."

"It took weeks, madam. Long, wasted weeks. And much cajoling. But in the end, we had only six months together, my boy and I."

"Were they good ones? Good times for you and Liam?"

"They were—" He swallowed back his ragged grief, focused on the horizon, the sea, its margins now barely discernable from the evening sky. He took a breath and then another. "They were heaven to me. And undeserved."

Eleanor had tried not to weep, had tried to let Nicholas have his sorrow in his own way, but an ungovernable sob finally shook her.

No wonder he haunted Faulkhurst: His son had died here. No wonder he prowled the ramparts and protected its heart. He was so wrong in his opinion of himself.

"You were blessed as few men are, Nicholas. To know the true love of a son."

He turned away again and wrapped the boy's headstone in another leather pouch. "Ah, my lady, if you'd only known him. . . ."

She watched as he laid the pouch on a shelf below the workbench. His hands shaking, lingering overlong in the caress, this restless beast bested by a tiny boy's heart. It was so difficult to let go of unfinished sorrows, impossible to do it all alone.

"Was Liam dark-haired like you, Nicholas?" she whispered. "Dark-eyed?"

When he didn't move, or speak, she feared that she'd pressed too hard. But then he nodded. "Yes."

"And strapping, too. Strong. I mean, for all of his eight years?"

He turned away from the bench and met her eyes. "He was. And I—" But then his manner changed abruptly, her steward once more. "What is it you wanted of me, madam? What brought you out here in the middle of the night?"

It was a start. A place to begin with this man

who had such a tight hold around her heart.

"Because, Nicholas, you missed supper with us—much to Pippa's distress. So I thought I'd come let you know that you made the children very happy today with their lessons."

They were shyly delighted eyes that found hers. "Did I?"

"You know very well that you did."

The blackguard tried to shrug off his benevolence, but it was the essence of him. "Habit."

"One to nurture, Nicholas." For the children that he loved now and who loved him back—as she did. "I hope you're prepared with your deep sack of pennies from our treasury. Pippa has a bucket of feathers for you."

She felt ruffled again, focused upon as he straightened his shoulders. "What sort of name is Pippa? What does it mean?"

"I don't know. It's what she called herself when I found her in a peach orchard."

"That little thing?" Then the great man was frowning, outraged for the child who now lived in his circle of care. "By Christ, was she alone?"

"Aye, and she seemed an angel to me, too weary just then to climb to heaven. And so I kept her. I want to believe that she was left there lovingly when no one was able to take care of her. She was bundled up in a long, finely embroidered linen shift."

"And suffering the plague; I've seen the marks." That seemed to anger him, yet he sat on the edge of the workbench, caught her hand and drew her to stand between his knees. "What of Dickon? Was he infected?"

"He and Lisabet both. I found them among the dead in a Bristol jail."

"What were you doing in a Bristol jail?"

"Breaking into it."

"Into a *jail*?"

"Aye, I had to. The jailers had died and left the gates closed. Ah, Nicholas, I saw that everywhere. Just as I had to do at the hospital at St. Albans, and the asylum at Bath."

"You broke into all these places?"

"Brazenly. I wonder what Edward would think if he knew? I stopped where I was needed, where I thought I could do some good. And look what I found." She spread her hands wide, hoping that he would see that she meant him, as much as she meant anyone in the world.

"And you were spared completely."

"Aye."

"I know the signs too well myself." He threaded his fingers through her hair, lifting it off her nape. She drew in a staggering breath as he brushed his fingertips along her neck, sending sparks of fire sizzling across her breasts to the very tips.

"I don't expect ever to know why," she managed, wantonly tipping her head to give him better access.

"Because they needed you, madam." This was said so near to her mouth, she thought he would kiss her—hoped that he would, because he hadn't in so long.

"And you, Nicholas." His hair was softly clean and clinging when it brushed her hand.

"Please, madam." He gripped her hips in his wide hands and gritted his teeth as though she'd injured him.

"Someone must have needed you as well, Nicholas." Another whim of daring made her kiss him on the temple, where his hair curled slightly off his forehead. "I know that I do."

"You'd best stop that, my lady, else I'll be taking you up on your offer."

But she couldn't stop, didn't want to, because his brow tasted of the sea and his mouth of sweet fire when she brushed it with hers.

"Eleanor!" Then she was inside his embrace, held there by the fullness of his kiss, this wonderful man who loved his son with such sorrowful tribute, who would love her fiercely if he allowed himself.

Marry me, Nicholas. It was on her lips again, filling her heart with elation, more powerful than ever. But his face was buried in her hair, then trailing heat down her throat as he cupped her breasts through her kirtle and groaned in his marvelous way.

"Oh, yes—there, Nicholas." She sighed, clinging to him, to his hardness, to his mouth and its questing.

Aye, and to the first sparks of a wild, near-impossible idea: that he was the son of a titled lord, and he must have ties to the king—favors to be granted.

Not impossible at all.

Her proposal sang in her heart, made her ruck up her skirts like a wife, and straddle his lap and wiggled closer.

He reared up, his eyes flaming like the devil's, like a startled schoolboy's. "Eleanor, where are you going?"

"Right here, Nicholas. Can't you feel that?"

"Christ, woman!" He inhaled through his teeth as though she'd wounded him in her squirming, though he was making sounds of pleasure in his throat, holding her hips, pressing her down and his own hips against her. "I feel nothing but you, Eleanor. And you feel so good to me."

"So right, Nicholas—that's how you feel to

me. Like I belong here." In his arms and in his lap and in his heart, beside him in his sorrow, and in the wildness of his joy when he could finally celebrate his son.

And theirs.

He was wonderful and hot, his lovely tarse as hard as one of the stone blocks that held up the arches of Faulkhurst. It pressed thickly against the center of her, the place that ached for him, for his touch.

Aye and for his kiss, because she could imagine that, too. Could imagine getting to know all of him.

She reached for him, sliding her hand down his warm chest, pulling at his belt, his tunic.

"Eleanor!" Her name shot out of him as he stood with her, his eyes wide in wonder, his hands clasped round her bare backside, keeping her legs wrapped around his waist.

"Yes?"

He was breathing like a warhorse, his nostrils flaring. "I can't do this to you."

"Then—" *marry me*, she was going to say.

But he shifted his weight and stood her up on her very weak legs. He caught her hand and brushed his mouth against her palm, then tugged her away from the shed.

"Come, madam. I'll show you the safe route back to the keep."

He led her through the sanctuary, and its simple beauty stopped her: the unglazed windows, the rafters open to the sky and the stars.

"I think I won't like it as well when the roof is finally repaired, Nicholas."

He was standing behind her, a part of the sky as she craned her neck to see it all. "Why, madam?"

"Look at all we'll miss of the heavens."

Chapter 18

———— ⟋⟍ ————

"**T**oddy, what do you mean that Pippa's lost?" Trying not to panic the boy or herself, Eleanor lifted him onto the table with its ribbon streamers and smiled at him, then fluffed his hair.

"I haven't seen her for hours. Not since the music started for the faire."

Nicholas looked pale as he knelt in front of Toddy, his voice steady, but his eyes intense. "Think, boy, where did you see her last?"

Toddy squirmed and scratched at his ear. "Well, we were in the kitchen with Hannah, making cakes, and then Pippa 'membered a surprise she'd found."

"A surprise? Where?" Eleanor sat down beside him and laid her hand on Nicholas's, because she needed his comfort, needed the assuring squeeze he'd given her.

"Pippa wouldn't say. She wouldn't let me come."

"All right, boy," Nicholas said, chewing on the inside of his cheek as he scanned the ramparts for those golden curls. "We'll find her."

"I'll take the west towers, Nicholas."

He kissed her quickly, caressed her cheek with his hand, and then took off for the undercrofts.

Long minutes later, Eleanor entered the cliff tower calling Pippa's name, and nearly cried with relief when she recognized the little form all hunched up against the wall.

"Pippa! What have you gotten yourself into?"

"A very dark place, Nellamore." Half-in and half-out of a small opening between two slats in a stone niche, with her shoulders caught.

Eleanor dropped to her knees and ran her hands over the little limbs. "Where does it hurt, sweet?"

Pippa moaned a little. "My tummy."

Dear God, a stomach injury. "Did you fall on your tummy, Pippa?"

"No, I've got a terrible hunger, though."

"You're hungry? Just hungry?" Laughter bubbled up inside Eleanor's chest.

"Have you any sugar plums, Nellamore?"

"Oh, sweet—"

Nicholas came bursting through the door, his hair strewn every which way. "My God, Eleanor, is she—"

"No, Nicholas. She's just stuck."

The poor man was linen white, his eyes wild as he sank to his knees, felt the same limbs that Eleanor had, then stuck his head against the opening in the wall. "What in God's name are you doing, Pippa?"

"Finding a bag of treasure."

Without preamble, he threaded his fingers through Eleanor's hair and planted a kiss on her mouth, then went back to his gentle, relieved scolding.

"You'll ask me or Nellamore next time you go looking for treasure—or anything else. Do you promise me?"

"I do, Nicholas."

"Now hold still, Pippa. Duck your head." He struggled and strained against the slats, his hands so huge and careful as he tried not to hurt her. But Pippa's shoulders still wouldn't come.

"Keep her talking, Eleanor."

Eleanor rubbed the small back and watched Nicholas with her whole heart. "What kind of treasure were you looking for, Pippa?"

"I found it. A bag."

"Of what?"

"I don't know. But it jangles."

And it did. Nicholas turned a wry smile on Eleanor that made her want to have all his children.

"Are you by chance holding the bag in your hand, Pippa?" he asked calmly.

"Oh, yes. I won't let go."

"Well, I need you to." He was patience itself.

"But I found it."

"And I'll get it for you as soon as you come out." Cajoling and fierce.

"All right, Nicholas."

He freed her an instant later, caught her up with a whoop and held her tightly. "You scared us to death."

"I didn't mean to." Pippa fell into Eleanor's arms next and hugged her tightly.

"Here's your treasure bag." Nicholas held it out for the child.

Pippa reached inside the dusty bag and pulled out a carving of a rabbit. One of Nicholas's carvings.

What was it doing in a dusty old bag, let alone tucked away in a dangerous chink that was just the size to trap a little girl?

She hadn't the heart to warn him just now. Not when he was busy blowing raspberries against Pippa's neck, raising squeals from her.

"Was that your stomach I hear, Mistress Pippa? It's growling like a bear."

"I think it's time we feed it before it tries to escape."

Nicholas sailed with her down the stairs, waiting for Eleanor when she reached the bottom.

"She's a ferret, my lady."

"Aye, she is, Nicholas. I ought to send Pippa looking for my husband's records."

She expected a smile from him, but dark sorrow rolled across his brow, stunting her breathing. He took her hand firmly. "Come, my lady. There's a bakehouse that needs blessing."

"From the dust of your fields, Almighty God, to the mill, to the baker's hand, we—"

"He's not a priest, madam." Nicholas had only meant to lean down and whisper his suspicions about the stocky-limbed cleric into his wife's ear, but he was met with her distracting, heady scent of bay and mint, and then the glancing edge of her blushing cheek when she turned her head to level a frown at him.

"Father Edmund is a fully tonsured friar, Nicholas," she whispered back to him.

"A tonsure requires only a sharp razor, madam. He is a mountebank."

"Please, Nicholas." She touched her fingertip to her lips and then to his, apparently to quiet him. But she'd left her own dampness there, a taste of cinnamon and the spark of surprise that did nothing for his composure. "He is a simple mendicant who knows his scriptures."

He leaned closer to all that heady danger and whispered, "More like a jongleur, madam, who has only recently learned the worth of a priest's indulgences and now peddles them as he used to peddle headache potions."

Father Edmund's rounded pate glowed pink with a sunburn—clear signs of a recent shaving. His heavy black robes flapped in the wind as he stood with all due solemnness on the steps of the bakehouse, waving an untidy sign of the cross on the door.

Whether false or real, when he turned with the first loaf to come out of the new bakehouse, he was met by cheers and jostling.

Two dozen cottages had been completed in a month's time. A few months from now the harvest would begin, and his penance would be complete.

The thought was as satisfying as it was desolating, because every one of her successes brought him closer to leaving her.

The feasting moved from the market square

to the bailey, and his heart ached already for the loss that he would feel.

Eleanor and her miracles. She was the miracle, to him and to the others who danced and sang.

"Dance with me, Nicholas."

He turned to decline her invitation, but she tugged him into the carol ring, where he was lost entirely.

"Madam, I know nothing of dancing."

"Take Cora's hand and mine and then just follow along."

"But I—" Then he was circling with them, the whole village and his wife, changing directions twice before he realized there was indeed a pattern to the lunacy.

And then just the two of them were dancing, in an intimately suggestive circle. Her palm against his, rousing him to grab her out of the crowd and kiss her.

She turned away, and then back again to him. Great God, the flirting she was doing with him, as intentional as hell. It was dazzling, expanding his senses, trapping his gaze and his brain as they brushed and turned and brushed again.

"Now away, Nicholas." He did so reluctantly, saving a whiff of her to savor in case she didn't return.

"And now back to me."

Oh, yes. And back again, my lady wife. Others were dancing, but none of them mattered. Nothing mattered but the moment.

"Are you sure you've never danced before, Nicholas?" A gallant woman and kind, to ask that question of a man who was treading on her feet in perfect rhythm with the gittern and the tambour.

"Never." But he'd watched plenty, always dismissing the fools, always believing that the pleasure of a woman was in the bedding. Lifting the lightest skirts of the local beauties had been his game and his goal. Hell, he couldn't recall even kissing a woman longer than it took to get to the good stuff. Straight for that crest, the release of the battle that had always raged within him.

What a fool he'd been, not to have realized. He'd never been so roundly aroused, so drunk on a woman, so like a liquid that flowed and eddied, that sought her peaks and her valleys, the center of her heart. He'd heard erotic tales of coupling for hours, titillating to be sure, but clearly fantastical and a seeming waste of time.

Making slow, dancing love with his wife in a crowded, torchlit bailey was the headiest of intoxications, barely touching, skimming glances, and storing up the scent of her so that he'd never forget her.

The lovely woman was cupping his chin now as she passed him in her sinuous measures, brushing her cheek against his on the next pass, now toying with the hair at his nape.

And when she brushed past his mouth with hers, it was the simplest thing to catch her up into his arms, and then but a single step behind the arching pillar to stand with her in the near dark as the music played.

"Oh, Nicholas, come."

Christ, yes. She was waiting with her kiss, waiting for him to close his mouth over hers, her hips tilted to meet his erection as though she'd expected it to be there. And why the hell wouldn't she? Just to breathe her air was to harden him to steel.

"I could dance with you forever, Nicholas." She was dancing still, her eyes closed, humming low in her throat, her hips having learned too much of him.

"For now, Eleanor. Just for now will have to do."

Chapter 19

"**A** message for you, my lady," Dickon called.

Eleanor looked up from shoveling and slogged out of the millrace, drenched with mud and water weed. Dickon was running headlong down the village lane, waving a packet over his head, dodging a cart of lime and two men shouldering a rafter piece.

He'd put on weight and brawn, and now looked masterful and old for his years in his studded hauberk. Her highwayman turned marshal, who still blushed at every kind word sent his way.

"A message from where?" It was the very first she'd received at Faulkhurst, and it worried her for no nameable reason. She took the packet and turned it in her hands before popping the seal.

"From some place called Torryhill Manor. Dernbrook is 'is name."

The missive was sealed with a green-waxed impression of a sneering fox. "His? The messenger? Does he wait for an answer?"

"No. He's here himself—Dernbrook is. And a fellow with him called Arndell or something."

"What? The Earl of Arundel? Oh, damnation." This stank of Edward and his machinations. "Where did you put them?"

"Coolin' their heels at the gatehouse."

"You jailed the earl?"

"Didn't lock 'em up, if that's what you mean." Dickon waggled his finger at her, an exact replica of the way Nicholas waggled one at her so often. "But you can't go trustin' just anyone, milady. 'Specially when six of 'em come riding up on real horses."

Real horses, carrying real earls. Blazes.

"Then go escort them to the keep, Dickon, quickly. Tell Hannah to feed them. I'll be up in a moment."

Torryhill Manor. She popped the little green fox off the missive, knowing that whatever the message, it meant gallons of trouble.

" 'Sir David Dernbrook to the lady Eleanor of Faulkhurst, greetings. Let it be known in warning of writ of summons to the king's assize in Newcastle that you have covenanted unlawfully with seven villeins of my own manor at Torryhill—' I've done *what*?"

"What have you there, madam?" Nicholas looked fierce as he strode up to her, tearing off his gloves, the whole of him dusty with rubble and streaks of dampened daub. Enchanting and utterly feral, his dark eyes fueled by a radiance that never failed to startle her heart and tie up her breathing.

"We have visitors, Nicholas."

He swiped most of the grime off his face with his sleeve. "More of your outlaws?"

He wasn't going to like this at all. "Edward's, I fear."

"Edward's? What has he sent you?"

She held up the message as he came to read from over her shoulder. "Have you ever heard of a Sir David Dernbrook?"

"Dernbrook—never heard the name before. Probably new to a recently vacated holding; there are too many these days. Upstarts, to a man, and not to be trusted. What has he got to do with the king?"

He sounded as lordly as any baron she'd ever known, tossing off biting opinions of politics with the ease of a king's minister. This supposedly penniless, wandering, fourth-born son of a minor lord.

"From all I can gather, Nicholas, this Dernbrook seems to think that I've stolen seven of his tenants from him."

Nicholas snorted and took the missive out of her hand. "You probably have, madam."

"Ballocks, Nicholas. He's obviously a madman. Read there." Feeling more outraged with every passing moment, she jabbed at the next line of ridiculousness. "He says, 'the unjust damage comes at the cost to me of one saddler, two smiths, a carpenter, and three reapers—' "

"By God, it has happened, madam." Nicholas scrubbed at his hair as he always did when he was riled. "You and your rumors have been found out."

"It's merely jealousy, Nicholas, because we have people at Faulkhurst who are willing to plant and reap, and he doesn't."

"I agree with you on one point, madam: This sort of jealousy makes for a deadly enemy."

"You know as well as I that we harbor none of Dernbrook's tenants here. Has Fergus ever been his carpenter? Or Cora his alewife? An elderly nightman and a woman who until recently had made her living on the back streets of York? No and no."

"It matters not what the truth is."

"It does to me. Blast the man! Three years ago, he'd never have wanted someone like Skelly or Mullock under his roof."

"A great many things were different three years ago."

"Not the strength of a man's honor."

"Nevertheless, my dear, you'll have to prove his claim false in court."

"This is nonsense. I will not pay ludicrous fees to the king and then damage to Dernbrook for his imaginary villeins. I'll have to straighten out this matter for good." She started up the castle hill, detesting the feeling that she'd lost control of her own home.

"Where are you going?" He had a marvelously thorough way of gaining her attention, of putting himself between her and the sky.

"To disabuse Dernbrook of his ridiculous suit against me before it grows out of hand."

"It already has. It's scheduled to be heard at the next assize."

"That's not nearly soon enough."

"It has to be so. I'll present the case myself. And in the meantime, you will bide your time and your temper and leave well enough alone.

I'll send a message to Dernbrook's man of law—"

"Actually, Nicholas, he's here."

He always grew quiet as his face darkened. "Dernbrook is here? Now? At Faulkhurst?"

"Aye. Probably because he thinks that he can intimidate me because I'm a woman, and alone."

"You're not bloody alone."

"I know that—but the man has gall. Read what else he says there: that I'm to cease and desist immediately, and to give his seven supposed tenants back to him. They're *my* tenants, not his. I've promised to care for them at all costs, and I refuse to do what he demands."

"Sweet bloody hell." He read the document more closely, his jaw clenched and working, eyeing her when he was finished. "You may not have a choice, madam. The law is clear."

"Oh? And just who do I sacrifice to this clarity of law? Dickon? Skelly? Do I take Lisabet from her home, from her goats and that rangy long-horn cow?"

"Don't be absurd."

"Who then, if you're choosing? Because the man is waiting in the keep to steal them away."

"I'll take care of it."

"No. I will—I *need* to, as a point of honor.

305

Otherwise, I'll look weak, like I have to rely on a man to fight my battles for me."

"That's what a steward is for."

"Blast it all. Dernbrook wouldn't dare bring this suit if my husband still held Faulkhurst instead of me."

Nicholas lifted her chin with his thumb, his eyes clear and his smile steady. "Your husband would never have put himself into this vulnerable position, madam."

Oh, and that was a kiss he set against her mouth, to stall and confuse her. "Then we'd still be waiting for a baker and a horse to come riding through the gates." She backed safely away from him. "No, Nicholas. The real reason that Dernbrook is bringing this suit against me, rumors or no, is because he's too miserly to pay a reasonable wage to his tenants. And now he thinks he can just steal mine. He'll be sorry he arrived at my door, Nicholas. My case is excellent."

"Have you ever answered a writ, madam?"

"Not a writ of my own, but I'm not wholly inexperienced. I did have a hand in the outcome of a suit, between the abbess at St. Catherine's and the pig butcher."

"For . . . ?"

"Menacing the countryside. The pig butcher, of course; not the abbess. Too many flies in the

306

summer, too near the abbey close with its horrible stench. The turning point for us came when I suggested to Mother Abbess that she take the judges and the jurymen on a tour of the offending yard, which happened to be on a particularly warm day. . . . Needless to say, we won."

"A quarrel between a pig butcher and an abbess is not in the same league as yours with Dernbrook. He is holding up the king's own ordinance against you—which you have clearly and deliberately violated."

"And that's where Dernbrook will lose on all counts. He hasn't a mote of evidence to back up his claim against me. He couldn't possibly—because he's mistaken. He needs to know that I am in the right and that I plan to fight for myself. And he needs to know this immediately."

"My lady, this is not the way between two lords."

"Then what is, Nicholas? Shall we hold the man hostage? Or gather troops to ride out and besiege him at his manor? Is that what my husband would have done in my place?"

Nicholas shoved his fingers through his hair again. "He would have—Bloody hell."

"Exactly. I'm going to do this my way."

"If you're so damned set on scuttling your

307

whole defense, madam, I'll present your griev-
ances to this Dernbrook myself. Today." He
rolled up the writ in his brawny fist and
started past her toward the castle.

"Hold there, Nicholas." She chased after
him, caught him at the well house. "How do
you mean that I'll be scuttling my defenses?"

He rounded on her, caught up her nape in
the wide span of his hand. "If you present
your case to Dernbrook here and he stands patiently by and listens without comment to
your clever testimony, he'll doubtless be very
glad that he did so."

"Aye, because of the trouble I shall save him
in the long run."

"Nay, madam; because when you meet him
again at the autumn assizes, he'll go before the
judges knowing exactly what evidence you
will use against him, and you will have given
his lawyers three months to decide the best
way to refute and discredit you. So he will win
because you allowed it."

"I—"

"You what, madam?"

"I—I think we'll never have a better chance
than this very moment, with our own evidence
right to hand. And with the Earl of Arundel
to stand as witness."

"Arundel? I'm not going to let you drag the matter all the way to Arundel."

"I don't have to go anywhere." She glanced at him and then up at the castle. "He's here, too."

"The Earl of Arundel?" He looked sharply to the castle with a blazing frown that should have blown the roof off the keep. "What the hell is he doing here?"

"My question exactly, Nicholas. I suspect that Edward has had a sneaky hand in this suit. Checking up on my progress, his barons circling me, poking at my flanks."

"More than your flanks, madam." He frowned, paced away, and looked again to the castle. "Damnation."

"I can't just leave them waiting, Nicholas. I have to go meet with them before Hannah puts them to scrubbing pots in the scullery. I'll do this myself, but I would welcome you standing in support of me."

Uncharacteristically, he hesitated. "I'll see to these weirs and then I'll be up." He caught the loops of ribbon that secured the scoop of her chemise and held her fast. "Behave, madam. You're on the scarring edge of the law here. I don't want you to slip."

Mother Mary, the man made her feel warm

and malleable all over. And slightly guilty for bringing the trouble upon them.

But only slightly.

"You were just a little right, Nicholas."

"Yes, I know." She wanted him to kiss her again, to give her courage, to lighten her heart and make her pulse sing. But he was already stalking off toward the millpond and the clump of men working the damaged race.

Arundel. Damn the man.

Nicholas's heart stood-stock still as he watched his wife hurrying up the road toward the castle, gone off in her headlong stride to where he couldn't reach her, couldn't help her out of this entanglement, or call her back— because he was still and always would be William Bayard.

Because he and Arundel had fought too many battles together, shared too many women, had too many tankards of ale together. Had even sat at counsel with Edward on occasion.

Not even a beard, his overlong hair, or a far different heart would be an adequate disguise.

He was trapped, unable to help the woman he loved when she needed him most.

Chapter 20

E leanor knew that she hardly looked the lady of the castle at the moment, with mud and water weeds stuck to her kirtle and in the sopping ends of her hair, but that couldn't be helped.

She'd barely gotten through the portico and into the deserted great hall when she heard from the hearth a rudely growled, "You there, girl."

Girl? Oh, bloody fine. There were three men in a clump: Arundel to be sure, stocky and graying and frowning; a younger man of light good looks; and a swaggering fellow. Dernbrook—the churl who had called her "girl," and was now looking down his lumpy nose at her.

"Yes, milord?" she said, dipping a chambermaid's curtsy. Let him think he was leading a stealthy raid against an unprotected widow. "Can I help you?"

"Name's Dernbrook. Sir David Dernbrook. Torryhill Manor, as I've told at least three people in the last ten minutes. Where is your lady?" He was gruff, disdainful, and as sneering as his little green fox.

Hmmmm. . . . Where, indeed? "Which lady would you be meaning, Sir David Dernbrook, Torryhill Manor?"

He cleared his throat, spat the leavings into the fire, and then raised his volume considerably, as if a peasant was obviously deaf to a civil tone. "Eleanor Bayard, the Lady of Faulkhurst. She was supposed to be coming in from her fields to meet with us."

"Oh! Well, sir, she's been busy at the fish weirs. That storm came on suddenly. I'm surprised you weren't drenched by it." This was a marvelously sweet place to be sitting just now—this crumb-on-the-table proximity to the man who sought to cheat her because she was a woman.

She crossed the remaining distance to the hearth, stopped directly in front of Dernbrook with her hands posed as she'd once seen Edward's queen do when she meant to flatten her opposition with a single glance, then said in her very finest "milady" voice, "Welcome to

Faulkhurst, Sir David. And you as well, my lord Arundel. I am Eleanor Bayard."

"You?" Dernbrook wrinkled his nose, sputtered. "Are who?"

"Lady Eleanor. Lord William's widow. I'm sorry for the chaos, but I do welcome you all." She put out her hand to him as any lady ought, but Dernbrook made a caustic face and drew himself up.

"What is this trickery?" He looked to his fellows. "Arundel?"

But the earl was already nodding a respectful bow in her direction. "Good day to you, Lady Eleanor," he said, a hand to the shoulder of the young man standing beside him. "This is my nephew, Percy."

"My lady." The young man was good-looking and gallant as he bowed over her hand. A few years her senior, but wholly unpracticed at hiding his dismay at the sight of a lady with grime edging her fingernails. Still, he had tried.

Arundel's civility only seemed to make Dernbrook bluster even louder, no doubt scandalized that his current archnemesis should be so mud-drenched, so peasant-filthy.

"I've never heard of such a greeting!"

"I do apologize for my appearance, my lords, but we're dreadfully short of hands here for all the work that needs doing. None of us at Faulkhurst escapes the blisters or the mud or the backaches that come with hard work. I'm sure you find the same to be true at Torryhill Manor, Sir David. Especially these days."

"I—I—I—By God's teeth, Lady Eleanor. This was damn unsporting of you. Letting me believe—"

"I understand, sir." She picked a large chunk of sedge off the point of her elbow. "I often believe only my eyes and not my common sense. I'm sorry that I wasn't here in the keep to receive you."

"And well you should have been. Your constable detained us like we were criminals. Damned impertinence! I'd have that boy whipped if I were you."

And you would be eternally sorry for that, Dernbrook. A cold, assessing resolve slipped through Eleanor's veins. "But you're not me, Sir David, are you? I'm afraid my constable is new at his post and overeager to protect me."

"That's no—"

"Ah, my lady, you've been out in the fields plowing again, haven't you?" Hannah came scolding out of nowhere to set a tray of cups and a ewer of new wine on a nearby table, and handed Eleanor a warm towel. "You look a fright."

"We nearly lost the lower fish weir, Hannah. But we rescued it." Eleanor scrubbed her face with the towel, ignoring Dernbrook and his harrumphing, uncertain how to judge Arundel's quiet observation.

Hannah nudged her and nodded toward Dernbrook. "Any of these fellows be a pantler, my lady? Could use one, you know. And a good sauce man, too."

"Ah, no. Gentlemen, this is our cook, Hannah. Will you be staying the night with us? You're certainly welcome to."

"That depends, Lady Eleanor," Dernbrook said over the rise of his crossed arms and his barrel chest, "upon your cooperation."

"I pride myself on cooperating, sir. That's the only way we can get things done at Faulkhurst. Hannah, be a dear and bring a loaf of your sweet nutbread for our guests." She handed Hannah the dirt-streaked towel and the woman scurried off. "Now, sir, if you'll tell me how I can help you—"

"You know damned well how, Lady Eleanor. Unless you haven't read my—"

"Your writ?" Eleanor wished that Nicholas would hurry along, wished most of all that he was standing by her side, grumbling his opinions into her ear. "Oh, yes, I have read it, sir. But it made no sense to me at all."

"Well, of course it didn't, my lassie." The man seemed to take her admission as some kind of validation of his cause. His eyes rounded in fatherly kindliness. He smiled crookedly and laughed as though he'd been holding in the goodness of his nature. "There, you see, Arundel? I told you the girl was out of her league. At least she knows it. Now then, my lady, hurry along and send me your steward, then. I'll deal with him."

Eleanor felt the tips of her ears go steamy hot as Dernbrook calmly shucked his gloves and sat down in her barrel chair, poured himself a cup of her wine, and made himself excessively comfortable in her great hall.

You thin-witted, insufferable little toad.

"You'll deal with me, my lord. I am the mistress here, responsible to the last grain of barley that is ground to meal. I insist upon attending to the affairs of my household without any man's counsel, unless I seek it."

Dernbrook laughed still. "You'd best seek it now, lassie. Come, come. We haven't got all day."

Her blood near to boiling, Eleanor planted herself firmly on the table edge as she'd often seen Nicholas do, and clasped her hands together in her lap to keep them from shaking in outrage. "I think, Sir David, that I'll do nothing at all until you tell me exactly why you believe I have stolen away your tenants."

He blustered and waved a finger in the air. "Because seven of mine have disappeared."

"Did you perhaps eat them?"

He thumped his fist on the table and stood. "How dare you make light of this!"

Behave yourself, madam. Though Nicholas's warning was only inside her head, she felt him close by, watching from somewhere.

"I make light of it, sir, because your claim against me is unfounded and ridiculous—as I shall prove it to you and to His Lordship."

"Those tenants are mine, lass. And there are probably more hiding somewhere on your estate." The man stood and hitched his thumbs into his belt, then strutted to the screens and peered into the hallway as though she'd hidden them from him. "I'll have them back, or you'll be in mercy to the court and to me for more than you can bear."

"What do you think I did with your people? Kidnapped them? Do I hold them for ransom?"

"As good as. I've heard of your tales of gold-paved streets and freeman's wages." He

317

strode back toward her, throwing the silent Arundel a conspiratorial nod.

"And how many buckets of gold did you pick up on your way through the village?"

"There, you see, Arundel? Not the least bit aware of the trouble she's in. I know for a fact that until six weeks ago, Faulkhurst was an abandoned ruin. And now it's—" He fluttered his hand in the direction of the bailey.

"Flourishing," was Arundel's imperturbable reply.

"Thank you, my lord." Eleanor dipped the man a curtsy, surprised at his support. "But we flourish only because we've been blessed with one miracle after another, Sir David. And because we've worked each day until our fingers bled."

"Ballocks, Lady Eleanor. You've defied the king and stolen laborers from me."

"Mind your tongue to the lady, Dernbrook." The earl's nephew looked suddenly fierce and red-faced. His uncle caught up the young man's elbow as if to restrain him from entering the fray.

Dernbrook sank in on himself for a moment, turtlelike. "Yes, yes, of course, my lord Percy. But her untruths will catch her up—which is the very reason that I brought along not only records from Torryhill to prove my claim absolutely, but also, my lady Eleanor, the earl to stand surety for me."

"To warrant your debate only, Dernbrook," the earl said evenly.

Eleanor nodded her gratitude for that clarification, still unsure what was going on between the earl and his sulky, excitable vassal. "I'm very pleased that we can take care of the matter out of court. Frankly, I dislike the idea of the king taking his fees every time two of his subjects have a dispute."

Dernbrook snorted, obviously surprised that a mere lass would have such a logical opinion on a matter of law and commerce. "At least we are in agreement on that point, Lady Eleanor."

"And on others, I hope." Her account books were sitting on the side table, as they always did in the midst of a busy day, ready to be consulted or added to at a moment's notice. She carried one of them to the large hearth table. "How large is Torryhill Manor, Sir David?"

Dernbrook looked as though she had accused him of lacking the full allotment of male rigging. "At three thousand acres, Lady Eleanor, Torryhill is my least substantial manor. I have seven in total. Torryhill is well fortified, and held by me directly from my cousin here."

A cousin to the earl? Oh, blast.

"Then you must have hundreds of tenants to keep track of. I have not nearly as many. But here is my accounting, as current as the rains of two hours ago. Now, shall we get down to the matter of your missing 'one saddler, two smiths, a carpenter, and three reapers—' "

"Damned right."

"Then let's compare my records against yours, Dernbrook. Name for name, craft for craft." She opened to the roster of tenants, grown so long and so broad that it made her smile in spite of her outrage. "Where do you wish to begin?"

"With my two smiths. I can't run a manor without them."

"Ah, yes. Here are the forge records—from the weekly nail and hinge production to cookpot repairs to the craftsmen themselves, penned in my steward's hand. Are you by chance missing a Hugh McDowell?"

"McDowell?" Dernbrook muttered the name as he ran his finger down his own list, squinting.

"Hugh has been at Faulkhurst not quite three weeks, as you see here. He came from Scotland. Has quite a burr."

"There's no McDowell in your books, Dernbrook." Percy reached across and tapped the Torryhill page with his finger, having taken up a position at her shoulder.

"That proves nothing," Dernbrook said, comparing the two pages against each other. "Could be the same man. Names can be easily falsified."

"Our Hugh is blond, your height, and he's missing the top of his right thumb."

"Hardly evidence. Who else, Lady Eleanor?"

"We have two other blacksmiths here at Faulkhurst, Sir David. Douglas Anders and Wallace Feeney. Are either of the men yours?"

There was more mumbling as Dernbrook compared Faulkhurst's books to his own and came up shaking his head, harrumphing. "The saddler, then."

"We haven't one."

"Then the carpenter?"

"Well, there's Fergus. But he couldn't possibly be your carpenter."

"Fergus, did you say? We had a Fergus! See it here, Arundel: John Fergus—Oh, Ferguson. Could have changed his name; likely has if he's on the run." Dernbrook pointed to his book. "A strapping lad, if I remember—"

"Then he couldn't be our Fergus. He's seventy if he's a day, Sir David. I'm sure he's not in your book. He and his wife Hannah lived all their lives in Berwick. Besides—" she cupped a secret hand toward Dernbrook and said so that all round the table could hear "—Fergus isn't really a carpenter. He's a night-man."

A quick exchange of glances. "You mean the sort who cleans cesspits?"

"Just that. But not anymore. He wanted so much to be a carpenter, so I let him."

"You let him? Are you mad, woman? What does a nightman know of carpentry?"

"As it turns out, Sir David, very little. And as for the rest of my workers, I'm afraid their stories are all quite similar. I doubt that any of these men or women were ever anyone's tenants. At least not for very long. Save perhaps for the king's."

But Arundel had been listening carefully. "The king's tenants?" he asked, shouldering Dernbrook aside to stand over Eleanor. "How is that, milady? Be these men of yours lords in exile?"

"They are not lords, sir. Far from it." And here was where she was taking a chance with everyone's dreams, though she had a keen sense that the earl was genuinely just. "You see, before McDowell arrived at our gate asking to be a blacksmith, he was ... well, an Edinburgh cutpurse."

Dernbrook sputtered, but Percy asked, "Is this the truth, Lady Eleanor?"

"Oh, yes, my lord. And McDowell's not the only case. You'll find that nearly all of my tenants are—or rather were—outside the law, one way or another before the pestilence."

"My lord earl, are you going to believe this woman's malarkey?"

"It isn't malarkey at all, Sir David. Mullock?"

"Aye, my lady?" Mullock stopped midstride with his ever-present wheelbarrow in the midst of the great hall, looking authentically guilty.

"What was your trade before you came to Faulkhurst?"

"Me, my lady?"

Eleanor gently brought the nervous man to stand in the circle of her inquisitors, ready to tell him to run for his life if things got hot and sticky for him. "Just tell us true, Mullock. It's all right."

Mullock shifted his feet and his single eye between the men who were staring at him, then swallowed loudly. "Well, milady, as you know, I used to relieve folks of their excess possessions. This is before I come here."

Dernbrook stuck his face in Mullock's. "What the hell kind of craft was that?"

"He was a housebreaker." And he was blushing like a beet all the way to the tips of his fingers.

"My specialty was digging under walls."

Dernbrook bellowed like a just-castrated bull. "And you let him stay here?"

"Aye, sir. Proudly." Eleanor kept hold of Mullock's arm, though he tugged to be far away, into the hills. "Mullock is the keeper of my stores."

"Are you mad? The lot of them ought to be rounded up and sent back to the king's dungeons. Do your duty, Arundel: Arrest them all."

"I'll do nothing of the sort, Dernbrook. Whatever Lady Eleanor has done to redeem the king's outlaws for honest, law-minding tenants, I applaud. As to your missing laborers, I suggest you ask the kind lady if she can lease you a few for a time."

Eleanor relaxed and let Mullock speed away to his barrow. "If you're in sore need of a blacksmith, sir, I suppose I could spare you one for a week. As long as they agree to it."

"Spare me one of your thieves? I think not."

"I'd love to help you with your troubles, Sir

David, but we are fresh out of regular vassals."

Arundel started laughing. "Regular vassals! Give yourself up, Dernbrook. You haven't a case here. Be damned glad I didn't hear it at the assize, else you'd be fined for filing a nuisance writ."

Dernbrook stomped his foot soundly, grabbed up his saddlebag and his books, and clapped his sagging hat onto his head. "If you'll excuse me, my lady, I won't be staying the night. My lord earl. Percy. Good day to you."

Dernbrook stormed out of the hall, dodging the laundresses and their baskets as though they were hauling the plague. Then he was mercifully gone.

"You see, Uncle? The side trip from Carlisle was well worth the extra day—in all ways, I'd say." Percy was looking directly at Eleanor with a glittering intensity, as though he were trying to see through her, or perhaps past the mud that must still be streaking her from head to toe.

"My lord, I'm sorry to have upset the man."

"Nonsense, Lady Eleanor. He'll not trouble you again. I'm glad I came. You have a fine place here."

"Very fine, indeed!" Percy slipped between

her and his uncle. "I'd love to see what you've done, Lady Eleanor—if you'll honor me with a tour."

Percy was flirting with her! And his uncle was looking on with pride and fatherly encouragement.

She was being courted by the nephew of a very powerful earl. This wasn't right at all.

Damn you, Edward.

And William Bayard, too, since the man had begun it all.

"Well, my lord Percy, I must clean up first. I'm a mess."

"A lovely mess." The young man turned instantly crimson. "I mean that you couldn't possibly be a mess. Ever, Lady Eleanor."

You ought to see my heart just now, Sir Percy. Now, there is a mess.

Chapter 21

Eleanor ran to her chamber for a clean change of clothes and then hurried off toward the grotto for a quick bath, praying she'd run into Nicholas along the way.

After all that blustering about attending to her suit himself, he'd certainly gone out of his way to turn her loose on her own.

Or he'd found more trouble with the weirs, though the sky was cloudless. Still, she had a mind to send Fergus out to find him.

She was nearly undressed by the time she reached the grotto, had hung her kirtle on the peg and was lifting the hem of her chemise, when she felt a shadow in the steam coming off the pool—and felt altogether looked at. The way she did whenever Nicholas was—

"Nicholas?" Oh, yes. Most definitely, Nicholas. All of him. Standing to his knees in the water, without a stitch of clothing, as bare and almighty as a pagan god.

"Good afternoon, madam." Though he was yards away from her she felt his words like a caress, from the top of her shoulders to the very bottoms of her feet and everywhere in between, as though she were the naked one and not he.

There was a quick, heavy rising out of that dark nest of hair at his thighs. She couldn't help her staring, or her disappointment when he slipped a towel around his waist, blocking all that glorious stirring.

"Ah, Nicholas. Sometimes I forget."

"Forget what?" He came toward her through the steam like an enchanter through solid rock, stern and handsome.

"That I'm not your wife."

Nicholas still wasn't used to these double-edged arrows, the sharpness of their tips, the intoxicating heat when they entered his heart. "God help me, Eleanor, but I forget that, too."

"Well, then, you must marry me, Nicholas."

His pulse surged and then ebbed. *What?*

She stepped closer, till he could smell the sunlight on her hair. "Marry me, Nicholas."

No—she couldn't have said that. And yet his heart swayed and stammered to life, soared.

"One more time, my lady. I didn't understand."

"I—can't believe that I'm you asking this, Nicholas. But I want you—need you—to be my husband."

"I can't—"

"No, wait. Please." She put her fingers against his mouth, her eyes glistening with hope she shouldn't feel. "Before you say no, please hear me out. Know that I love you—"

"Eleanor—"

She caught his chin and his gaze. "You are the most"—a sob shuddered out of her, tore at him—"you are the most outstanding man I've ever known."

"I'm not at all. What brought this on? What happened up there with Arundel?"

"Shhh. . . . Please. That's part of it." She put her fingers against his mouth, kissed his cheek, and then the corner of the mouth. He didn't move a muscle. "I must keep and care for my home at any cost. And you are the answer."

"I can't be."

"But you are. Don't you see, Nicholas?" He couldn't see anything more than her mouth and the dear, impossible words she was saying. "Your father was a baron. It would take only a word to Edward about how he owes me far more than he gave me. I have no shame at all; I will blackmail a king if I must. With the stroke of a quill he can grant you a title. He can agree to our marriage, and Faulkhurst will no longer be threatened by the likes of Arundel and his nephew. You are the answer to every one of my prayers, Nicholas, and my heart. You always have been."

"Eleanor, you don't know what you're asking of me." *What a miracle it would be. . . .*

"I think you love me a little, Nicholas. Or you would come to. As I love you."

"Eleanor, in all my days, I've never been so beguiled, or so very sorry."

"Sorry?" She looked woeful and teary and his heart was breaking. "Would it be so awful to be married to me?"

"No—so marvelous. Though I would swim the endless seas for you, for a love like yours, I cannot accept."

"Why? Are you married already? You weren't married to Liam's mother, so I thought that you—"

"I'm . . . pledged, my lady."

Eleanor's heart dropped onto the ground. And way in the distance in some other land, she saw a beautiful young bride waiting for him, waiting for her groom. "Are you betrothed, Nicholas? Because if you are, then—"

"No, Eleanor. There are no other women in my life but you. I am done with that."

"Done how?"

He looked to his hands and then from beneath his brow at her. "I am soon to enter the monastery of St. Jerome, for good."

"What?" Her breath stolen, Eleanor sat hard on the edge of the pool, dumbfounded, trying to make sense of him and having no luck at all. "You're a monk?"

"Not yet."

"You haven't taken holy vows then?"

"No."

"Then you're a novitiate?"

"Not that either. Eleanor, please."

She stood and grabbed those huge shoulders, stopping him. "Then you're no kind of monk at all."

"I've given my word to live my life in poverty, penance, and chastity. I cannot break it."

Eleanor's ears got steamy around their rims. "When?"

"When did I give my word?"

"No, dammit. When did you plan to tell me of these bloody sacred vows of yours?" She felt like a fishwife, but the man had to be daft to think that he could find peace in a monastery.

"I didn't think it necessary to burden you."

"I'm not burdened one little bit, Nicholas—I'm angry! When do you plan to leave for this St. Jerome's?"

"When I'm finished here."

"Finished with what? With me? Finished being my friend? My confidant?"

"Yes. And with—"

But she knew—despite her selfish anger: his son's gravemarker, the chapel. "Liam."

"Yes. Eleanor, I didn't mean to—"

She put out her hand, ashamed to her soul. "You didn't, Nicholas. I did. I've made a fool of myself in front of you. Twice now."

"You're not anything like a fool, Eleanor. If I were free, you would be my wife."

And that hurt worst of all, the hope, the perfect fit of him. Blast! It was better to be done with him now, so her heart would stop breaking. "But that isn't the case now, is it? No matter that I have fallen madly for you. I have a dear castle to protect, though. So if you'll excuse me, Nicholas, I need the bath. I'm a fright, and it seems I'm being courted."

"Courted—by whom?"

"Arundel's nephew."

"Percy?"

"Do you know him, too?"

"Only by reputation. He's a scoundrel, Eleanor. Keep your distance."

"Will you come and sit by my side while they're here? I'll ask nothing more of you than that. My cause will look that much stronger for the presence of my able steward."

And my cause would end the moment I set foot into the great hall, my love.

"You did remarkably well with Arundel earlier. You don't need me."

He saw her swallow back her sob, heard it tear at her voice as he turned away from her undressing. "You couldn't be more wrong, Nicholas."

Nicholas stalked the underpassages while she bathed, not trusting himself to stay. Because there had been one terrifying instant, when she was offering herself to him, when she sounded just like an angel.

Marry me, Nicholas.

The breath of forgiveness and redemption had shoved at his shoulder, nudging him in her direction.

Make love to me.

Aye, that had sounded of divine intercession. And wishful thinking.

And for an even longer moment, the clarity of her logic—ordinarily opaque to him—had rivaled the dawn for the crispness of its hues.

Their marriage unconsummated.

Unsanctioned.

And the proof was in her virginity.

Such a profoundly simple fact to alter.

Blast it all! Thousands of men wandering the countryside, and she had to go and fall in love with a monk.

Aye, and a father who loved his son so deeply that he couldn't see past his sorrow. Nor had she the right to try to sway him from his pledge.

" 'Tis a miracle that you've planted all these acres in so short a time." Percy and his uncle stood with Eleanor just outside the gatehouse, their horses saddled and ready to ride away.

"Aye, Percy," Arundel said, staring out over the village and into the fields, "we'll have to regale the king with Lady Eleanor's pluck."

Great heavens. Not that. "Thank you, Sir Richard. I'm so glad that you came along with Dernbrook."

"As I am, my lady, if only to meet you and tell you that William would be pleased if he knew what marvelous hands his castle was in."

"William Bayard?" Her heart skipped and started, as though a shadow had crossed her grave. How could such a wise man be so very wrong? "I didn't know my husband well, my lord—we weren't married long before he died. But I doubt that he would have cared at all about what happened here at Faulkhurst."

"He would care very deeply."

"Not the man I knew, Sir Richard. William wasn't a very—well, everyone knew of his ruthlessness."

"He was an unmatchable warrior, my lady. The only man I wanted at my back in a battle." Arundel shielded his kind eyes from the sharp, westering sun. "And he was a man of high passions in his youth, reckless and self-ish. Fortunately, some men find their way at the end of their lives. I was glad to see that William had, at the last."

That shadow came again, to cross the sun and loosen her knees. "What do you mean that he found his way?"

"Only that a man can find grace as he grows older. As he learns to temper his life with his better nature." Arundel looked almost wistful. Obviously he hadn't known William as well as he thought he did.

She shouldn't be speaking ill of the dead or contradicting the great earl, but he was dread-fully wrong about her husband. And might use his jaundiced view against her someday, to maneuver Percy into her home, or to stand against her with Edward.

"Sir, William Bayard abandoned Faulkhurst at its worst hour of need. There's nothing of grace in leaving his tenants to fend for themselves."

"Leaving them when?" Arundel straightened and looked her in the eye with surprise. "Gad, woman, he stayed on when other men in his position ran."

The hair rose on her nape; her husband's ghost returned to harass her—though it was Nicholas's face that she saw in the shadows. "Stayed on where, Sir Richard?"

"Why, here at Faulkhurst. Where else would I mean?"

"You're mistaken, Sir Richard. William Bayard hadn't set foot in Faulkhurst in a very long time."

"I'm afraid the mistake is yours, my dear." The earl's frown deepened, defending an undeserving friend with his precise diction. "William left Normandy to come here, just before the pestilence."

The ground tilted madly beneath her feet. "But he couldn't have. That would mean that he—"

"I beg your indulgence, my lady, but I saw William myself in that time."

"Then he must not have stayed long." He couldn't have. He'd have sent for her.

"I had messages from him regularly—word of his losses, the state of his own heath, his condolences, and prayers. Until the messages stopped altogether."

She didn't know what to think next. It was like putting a razor-sharp puzzle together, trying not to slice her fingers. "When was that?"

"A little more than a year ago."

"But—he died in Calais."

"So I understand. I suspected that he might have gone back there after he lost his son."

"His—" *son*. My God. Bright pieces of light spun round in her head, fitting together, but not making any sense.

"He grieved hard for the little lad, I know. Loved him more than a man could bear, I think. I heard nothing more of him after that."

"William Bayard had a son? My husband did?"

"Aye—a bastard, but a son." He suddenly looked as though he'd betrayed a confidence. "Pardon me, my lady. I thought surely you knew of the boy."

A cold lump lodged in her stomach.

"Yes, of course."

Liam.

"Do you mean to marry again one day?"

Nicholas. So rampantly possessive, so startled to find her that day in his tower.

337

His tower.

"Lady Eleanor?"

"Yes?" A muffled roaring filled her ears, her heart shoving up into her throat. Though Arundel was talking, she couldn't hear him. She looked up into the cliff tower, where her dark-hearted gargoyle had stood guard against her, had made his horrible plans.

Had stood fast in his falsehoods—this treacherous husband of hers.

"Oh, this is madness." Eleanor scrabbled over the cliffs at the base of the castle as soon as Arundel left, convincing herself that she'd find nothing in Nicholas's chapel or his work shed to prove that he and William Bayard were one and the same man.

It was preposterous to even think it. This was her damned imagination running wild on a horrible day of disaster and reprieve and disaster again.

So William had had a bastard son—what knight of the realm hadn't a dozen to show for his whoring?

Even Nicholas had a son born on the wrong side of the bed.

Liam. William.

No! Because that would mean the unthinkable: that William hadn't come for her and Nicholas never would.

She searched the chapel first, every niche and alcove, even its tiny undercroft. But there was nothing at all of her husband here; this was Nicholas's project. His joy, his penance, too. That gave her hope and the confidence to scour the shed for evidence, some clue that she hadn't made sense of before, something out of place.

All the while, she prayed that Nicholas wouldn't come looking for her—that he would never see her doubt him, or his honor or his motives.

She found nothing under the workbench, or on the table. Nicholas's tools hung neatly oiled and in their places on the wall; nothing odd or out of place.

She almost dismissed the chest. He kept his drawings there, with their angles and arcs all neatly lettered. She needed to touch them, to assure herself that Nicholas Langridge was just the fourth son of a minor baron.

The rolls of parchment lay on top of each other, as they always had. But something whispered to her to look underneath—and there, lying snugly at the bottom of the chest, were two large books, fashioned as all the

other records had been in wood-bound leather
with the Bayard crest.

"No, Nicholas." Her throat crowded with
tears as she lifted one of the heavy books from
its hiding place.

Her hands trembling, she opened to the first
page: *Faulkhurst, the year of our Lord, 1348.*

She leafed through the thick pages, her fingers quaking, not certain what she was looking for until she found it: two years ago last
March. Rudolphus's aged handwriting gave
way gradually, and then totally, to a firmer,
broader hand: one that was dear and familiar,
because she'd spent hours bent over his broad
shoulder, watching him carefully scribe his
planting forecasts and the harvest yields.

" 'Boon day bread, 100 loaves, from my
bakehouse. *Mea culpa.*' William Nicholas Bayard."

Nicholas.

Her wicked-hearted, pillaging husband. Oh,
God.

Chapter 22

Nicholas had watched Eleanor and Arundel from the cool shadows of the cliff tower, chafing at Percy and his ineffectual courting dance, at Eleanor and her sudden agitation as she paced and gazed up at the castle, at him—although she couldn't possibly know that he stood watching her, his heart rammed up into his throat, aching for her.

Be gone, Arundel. Leave me to my wife. He would gather her up as soon as the two men were gone from Faulkhurst, and then he would tell her of his change of heart. That he understood her plight, that he was willing—despite his vows of chastity—to deflower her.

Willing. Christ, she was his fevered yearning. He burned to taste her, to feel her quaking beneath him, to hear her cry out his name in ecstasy.

The right was his—the obligation, the honor. No man's, but his.

Marry me, Nicholas.

Oh, yes, my love. She'd have her wedding night and all its joys. And he would share it with her to the fullest, would ride her rhythms and be her hunger. A holy joining that God would surely allow him, if only because the bliss of it would leave him aching and repentant forever afterward, through a long, bleak eternity.

Because he couldn't imagine living without her. She'd become part of his breathing, the smile he searched for each morning, his pulse and his hope.

It was a goodness that he would take with him to the grave: that he had been loved by Eleanor.

And that he loved her beyond his life.

Pacing, he watched the gate, her every gesture. Yet somehow, during a blink, his dazzling wife vanished into the afternoon shadows of the castle without a trace, as Arundel and his nephew trotted through the village.

Bloody hell. He felt like a randy bridegroom on the church steps, waiting through the tedious ceremony so that he could get up his wife's skirts.

A smile warmed him deep down inside his chest and sent him down the stairs to the armory, expecting to see her at any moment, expecting her to press him onto a bench and lavish him with tales of Percy and his roving hands.

But she wasn't there, and didn't come. An austere loneliness crept over him, and he tried to ignore the niggling fear in it.

She could have sped off anywhere, on any of a hundred projects. She needed a tether—one of silk, so like the one she'd tied around his heart.

But as supper came and went, as night fell and the great hall grew quiet, and Hannah hadn't seen her either, Nicholas truly began to worry. He'd checked her chamber twice before, and now slowly climbed the stairs with a growing dread that emptied him.

Bloody hell, if she wasn't here now, he'd wake everyone in the castle.

But then he smelled lavender and saffron drifting down the stairs.

Christ, she was here in their chamber, and safe! He reached the landing in great bounding steps.

"Eleanor!" he shouted as he tore through the doorway. And for all his helpless feeling that something had gone terribly wrong, he was astounded by the sight of her.

His stunning wife standing in the middle of the room in a pale gauzy night shift, the shutters open wide to the ocean, every candle lit, throwing dancing ghosts everywhere.

She was looking at him as though she'd never seen him before, her eyes as piercing as day's first light, wide with wonder.

She whispered in astonished awe, "He was here, Nicholas."

God, she was all of his dreams, all the yearnings of his heart. His wife.

And he wanted her in all the possible meanings of the word. He stood there, amazed, anchored by his unspent passion, by this purloined indulgence he'd granted himself in her name.

"Arundel?" he said, taking the breath that had stuck inside his chest. "Aye, a fine man, but he's taken enough of your time with his visit."

She seemed to have gained composure, while he was barely muddling through. "Not Sir Richard, Nicholas."

"Who then?"

She took a deliberate breath that hitched twice. "My husband."

Christ. "Your—" He hadn't air for anything more.

She touched her mouth with her fingers as though testing the words before she spoke them. "William Bayard."

Nicholas managed to shake his head, to unfasten his dagger belt with steady hands, though his nerves crackled. He would listen to every word before he replied, control the situation completely until it became his again.

"What do you mean, he was here?" he asked, hating himself for the fraud, for the anger in her eyes. "Recently?"

She frowned as though he'd purposely asked the wrong question. "How could he have been here recently, Nicholas? He's dead, isn't he?"

She spun away from him and took up a large wooden comb off the side table, then a fistful of her hair, and dug the teeth into the damp tangles.

Arundel must have said something to inflame her. But surely nothing of import. He hadn't communicated with the man for more than a year.

"Did Arundel tell you this, my lady? That Bayard had visited Faulkhurst? Most lords do attend to their distant estates on occasion."

She swung back on him, her stance wide

and challenging, looking ready to charge him. "Yes, Nicholas, the earl told me. It seems that my husband arrived here shortly after we were married, and—damn his eyes—he remained here in our home during the whole of the pestilence."

Our home. Ours.

"Interesting." What else could he say to all that fury, when his heart was slamming around inside his chest?

"Interesting? Oh, yes, Nicholas. Especially when you consider that I never heard from him, though he was little more than a week's journey from me. Not once in all those months."

The truth was his only defense, though it stank of feeble excuses. "Perhaps your husband thought you were dead."

She arched a brow, nearly spitting. "Why the devil would he think that, Nicholas? Did he just decide that I was? Was I more convenient that way?"

Truly, I didn't know, love. Word had come that the de Laceys were gone, Glenstow in other hands.

"You said yourself that communications broke down completely, that your father's estate had been hit very hard. The reports that your husband heard from his sources were mistaken."

"And not pursued or verified."

Guilty, madam. He took her anger full force because he deserved it, and wanted nothing more than to assuage her anger.

"Your husband obviously didn't care to, my lady, or think to. But what could you expect from a blackguard like William Bayard?"

She plopped the comb onto the table and threw out her hip, a pose that outlined the smooth, round slope of her bottom. "That's another point, Nicholas. That 'blackguard' reputation of his. My scourge of a husband . . ."

She was biting the inside of her cheek, waiting for him to make some kind of reply to this new path and its blind, treacherous curves, but she'd completely befuddled him.

"A rotter to the bone, indeed," he tried.

"Not according to the earl."

What the devil did the man say about him to rouse her passions? He felt the sand being sucked out from under his feet, unbalancing him.

"Meaning what, my lady? Had Bayard a few undiscovered virtues in his character?"

Oooooo, Eleanor wanted to throttle the man. For the startled pain in his eyes, the guilty con-

347

fusion, the stunning fact that he *was* her husband—that he was alive and hers.

She loved him for all those things. But she
was still reeling with the pain of his betrayal.

And she refused to let the man hole himself
up in a monastery for the rest of their lives.

A monk, be damned. He was her husband.
He was and would be a father to all their children. The plowshare to her furrow, the vigilant steward of her heart. He just needed a bit
of tender guidance.

And a long night of seduction.

Which wasn't the mood that she'd managed
to create here. A court, more like, with the befuddled defendant unaware that he had already been convicted of high crimes and was
in the midst of taking his punishment.

So, seduction first. Then she'd lecture him
on the finer points of marriage, the trusting
and the cleaving. And the forgiving.

She clasped her hands behind her neck and
lifted the mass of curls, letting her breasts
strain against her gown.

He followed the fall of her hair with his
eyes, then sucked in a breath through his
teeth, his gaze arrested on her breasts—which
seemed to heat and expand with his regard,
leaving her breathless and dizzy.

"Oh, never mind me, Nicholas."

"What's that?"

She dropped the rest of her hair abruptly and crossed her arms beneath her breasts, which lifted them nicely, making more of their roundness than they actually were. "This has nothing to do with you."

His eyes found hers briefly. "But it—"

"No, truly. The matter is between me and my husband, should we ever meet up." Double meanings all around. Let him squirm a little more. "But I was wondering if—"

"If what?"

She didn't have to pretend her shyness; her heart was fluttering madly. She'd never seduced a man before. "If you had reconsidered my request?"

"Your—"

"If you could set aside your vow of chastity long enough to relieve me of my virginity."

He scrubbed his hair off his forehead, turned away and then back again. "Jesus God, Eleanor, you are very free with yourself."

"I have to be expedient, Nicholas. I may be taking a husband soon." An excellent double meaning. She meant to have the man tonight. To take her wedding-night revels on her own terms, and at long last. Because she felt so married to him already.

Nicholas looked delightfully apoplectic.

"You're taking you a husband?" He caught her arms and peered down at her with those dark, possessive eyes. "Who? Percy?"

She caught her lip to keep from smiling. This was jealousy, plain and simple, a welcome sign that he himself might be willing to fight to keep her after all. A sign that he loved her as she did him.

"Well, he really wasn't such a bad fellow. You maligned him."

"Eleanor, he's an ass."

"That's neither here nor there. I only need to know if you will deflower me, Nicholas. Soon. Tonight, preferably, else I'll have to risk blisters on my toes and hie me off to Ravensglass to find me a willing stranger." She left him for the candle on the blanket chest and pinched out the flame.

"You'll do nothing of the sort."

"Then you'll do the deed, Nicholas? Tonight?"

"The deed? My God, Eleanor, this is your virtue that you're so quick to give away. I would think you'd hold it in better esteem."

"I hold myself in great esteem, Nicholas. That's why I offer it to you—in my husband's stead."

That stopped him, had him scratching pensively at his beard, silent and staring.

"Well, sir? What's your answer? Or do you want to see the goods first?" It took only a bold breath and she was naked, letting her gown drop to the floor.

"No." Nicholas knew that his answer had come eons too late to stop her. She was splendid and willful in her nakedness, his teasing wood nymph, her arms spread at her elbows with a soft, sideways pressure that lifted her small perfect breasts to him, and framed the gilded shadow at the lithe joining of her thighs.

Ah, my love, will you call my name when I kiss you there?

"No, *what*, Nicholas? That you don't want to see the goods first—in which case, you're too late, or no, you aren't interested."

He couldn't help his diabolical smile as he grabbed up her fallen night shift.

"No, madam, I don't need to see the goods to know that you are lovely beyond my imagining."

"Am I?"

"Oh, yes." He kept his eyes on hers as he found the neck hole, as he settled the gown over her head with a soft kiss against her temple to keep himself from sliding his hands down her soft flesh.

Too soon. Too lush.

"Oh, Nicholas." He felt the rush of her breath beneath his chin as he dutifully stuck her arms back inside the gaping sleeves, trying to ignore the scent of her bath—that downy lavender she brought each night to their chamber to make him senseless with wanting.

And now here she was, inches from him, her eyes huge and suddenly teary, her mouth a glistening pout as she watched him tug the hem of her gown slowly down the length of her. It took all of his resolve not to stay and play there.

But there was more to this night than that, and he would have to restrain himself at every turn—else he'd become that man he used to be, would plunge and thrust mindlessly, and be done far too soon.

Tonight was for his love, his Eleanor.

"You do want me then, Nicholas?" She frowned at him as though she could possibly doubt it, when his hands were hot and quaking as he threaded his fingers through her hair; when he was breathing her scent, deeply, his senses spinning out of control.

"Oh, my lady, I want you as I've wanted no other woman in all my life." The moment was a stolen, blazing miracle that he meant to see through to the end with his wits intact. But she cupped his chin with her soft hand, moistened her lips with the tip of her tongue, then grazed his mouth—a gentle, exploring pressure that grew bolder, hotter, until he was aching.

"And do you plan, Nicholas, to—" Another kiss, just under his ear, drawing a long, lingering hiss from him.

"Breach your maidenhead?" *To drown in your embrace, to hear my name on your lips.* "Oh, yes, madam."

"Tonight?" All that unnecessary pleading, breathed against his mouth.

"God, yes, Eleanor." *Tonight and always, you'll be in my heart.*

She smiled and looked up at him with eyes that promised magic. "But then, why—"

"The gown?"

"Mmmm." She made a slow pivot, holding out the hem, making a silhouette of her curves.

"Because I want to start again. At the beginning."

"Ah, Nicholas, that would be at my father's house."

"What?" He heard only the sweep of his pulse through his ears.

"At our wedding."

"Ours?" His heart thundered against his chest. But she looked like peace itself, the dangerous sort that beckoned from the shore when one was standing to the neck in rising floodwaters.

"Aye, if you're to stand in my husband's stead in the matter of my virginity, Nicholas, then you ought to know all that you missed at this proxy wedding of ours."

Well. There was some logic here, and his curiosity to be appeased. Sorrel had never been forthcoming about the details of the wedding and Nicholas had never asked, beyond the success of gaining the dowry.

"Yes, of course." He sat down on the edge of the table, one foot on the bench, his ardor simmering for the moment.

She poured a cup of wine and handed it to him. "I suppose I must begin earlier, when I was kidnapped from St. Catherine's in the dead of night by a half dozen men I'd never seen before."

"What?" He set the cup down hard on the table, took hold of her shoulders, and brought her against his thighs. "Say that again, Eleanor. You were kidnapped?"

For all the violence of her tale, she wore a glint of mischief in her eyes and at the corner of her mouth. "Aye, three of my father's guards and three of Bayard's, I learned later."

This was madness. He hadn't ordered her kidnapped. "The bloody bastards didn't tell you that you were being taken to be married?"

She shook her head and toyed with the ties at his cuff, her touch light and inviting. "I knew nothing until I arrived at Glenstow."

Christ, no wonder she reviled him. "You didn't have to agree to the marriage. Why did you?"

Now she was at his other cuff, running her fingers delicately between his. "Spoken like a man who's always been allowed to decide such things for himself. My dear father threatened his dungeon for me. I was too fond of my gardens to survive that kind of punishment."

Outraged, he pulled her close. "Your own father threatened you?"

Her eyes softened as she met his with all her trust, and admiration that he didn't deserve. "It takes more than blood and bone to be a father, Nicholas. You know that as few men do. But I was resigned and hopeful—despite what I knew of the man I was marrying. I hoped to discover some goodness in William Bayard that I could love unconditionally. So I said my vows, Nicholas."

But not to me, my love. His heart filled up with longing for what might have been. She was summer honey coursing through him, pouring into his loins, heating and hardening him.

"And then?"

She slipped out of his arms and drew him toward the parted curtains and their marriage bed. "And then I was escorted to my chamber, where my attendants stripped me and put me under the counterpane in my bed."

"Why? You had no bridegroom to come to you." He almost felt sorry for himself, that he hadn't been there to bed her then—but she was here now, tugging on his belt. She'd somehow relieved him of his leather jerkin sometime back, and his sleeves were hanging loose.

"What are you doing to me, madam?" He shucked off his tunic and tossed it aside, to his wife's approving smile.

"What was done at my proxy wedding. The lack of a bridegroom made the bedding ritual that much more important, so John Sorrel joined me there."

"The bastard got in bed with you?" he roared. "He saw you without your clothes?"

"Oh, my." She looked down at his chest, and lower, at the bulge at the top of his breeches.

Wanting to kill Sorrel with his bare hands, he tilted her chin to him and found her blushing and bright-eyed, her gown drooping off the shoulder again. "Did Sorrel get into bed with you?"

"Partially." She stepped back from him, appraising him from head to foot. "Oh, but Nicholas, he wasn't nearly the man that you are."

"What the hell does 'partially' mean? Did he come to you naked?"

"Only his leg, when he shoved it beneath the counterpane next to mine—as is the custom in these matters." That same lithely naked leg came out of the folds of her gown like a pagan offering, slim and pink-toed and *his*.

And John bloody Sorrel had been naked with her in *his* marriage bed? Sorrel was a man who would take a mile when offered an inch. "Did he touch you further?"

"He tried to."

"And?"

Her smile was wicked, worldly, and he wanted her. "He never tried again. But I do wonder, Nicholas, when you mean to begin our wedding night. I have a craving to touch you everywhere, and to be touched by you."

Eleanor recognized that singularly masculine look in her husband's eyes: hunger and longing, lighting her pulse and sending it soaring, making her wonder what she was going to do with him, this steward that she loved too much.

This husband that she would die for.

He was the resonance of her heart, the thunder that slipped through her veins and into her belly when he whispered against her ear. "Oh, my love, may this wedding night forever erase the first."

"This *is* the first, Nicholas. Never doubt it."

"Christ, Eleanor, you are my heart." He finally came to her, his bay and woodsmoke surrounding her completely. His kiss was deep and lasting, made her crazy and writhing with need for him—a slow, molten exploration of her mouth, then down her throat to the cleaving of her breasts, where he met the limits of the linen and moaned, as though he were starving to taste beneath it.

"The gown, Nicholas. Now?" She reached down to rid herself of the barrier between them, but he caught her wrist and made love to it and then her fingers, before he looked into her eyes.

"Not yet, my love." He kept calling her "love" and "sweet," whispering his heart, making her wish that she wasn't deceiving him in this. Still, she ached for his great, scalding hands to hold her, and pressed herself into his splintering kiss wherever it wandered.

He slid the gown off her shoulder, letting it droop to her elbow. Then, his eyes glittering, he gently lifted her breast from its cradle of linen, holding it in his palm like a gem. Slowly, maddeningly so, he lowered his eyes to look, to admire; then he breathed his magic against her nipple, dashing it with his searing breath. And then he took it into his wondrous mouth.

"Oh, Nicholas. Oh, that's—" She felt a gentle, flickering tug that sent stars into the sky. Then he nibbled, tugged again, and possessed her completely with his startling kiss—an insistent pressure that made her arch into him, made her hips writhe as she rose up on her toes, to be closer to his rioting.

"Now the gown, Eleanor." But he took long delicious minutes raising the hem to her thighs, nuzzling her toes, then the back of her knees. He steamed his kiss through the linen to find the peaks of her breasts, his hands finally tugging the fabric over her head so that she felt free and new.

He stood away from her, looking wolflike and hungry, his body hard flesh and golden shadows.

"You are beautiful, wife."

Wife. Oh, God! She prayed that he hadn't heard himself, that he so often used the word in his thoughts that he wouldn't notice his slip. Because this was all becoming too tangled, too sweet. She didn't want to hurt him. Didn't want to stop.

He smiled, lighting little fires inside her, at the ends of her fingers and across her breasts.

"You're not undressed, Nicholas." She found the ties at the front of his breeches, and he sucked in his breath.

"You're killing me, you know."

"I was hoping so. You feel very good here, Nicholas. Mysterious, and warm." She cupped the marvelous shape of him with her hand.

"Great bleeding saints, woman!" He scooped her into his arms and carried her back against the mountain of pillows on the bed, his eyes wild and glittering.

"I only wanted to touch."

"Not yet, love. I'll not make it through the night."

Through the night, and all the rest of her days with the man she adored, who cared for her people as she did, who held Dickon's esteem and Pippa's heart. Feeling wicked and possessive, she pushed at the center of his chest when he would have gone back to his kissing. "Yes, but you still have your breeches on. And your boots."

She felt tightly coiled and aching, and even

more so when he raised a brow and then left to shuck his clothes. Following him to the end of the bed, she clung to the bedpost and watched him undress—something she planned to do every night, every day of her life.

She gasped, nearly lost her balance and fell off the bed when he turned back to her. He was magnificent, his large tarse standing proud and quick, the rest of him rippling muscles.

She knew exactly what all that maleness was for, exactly where it was meant to be, for that opposite part of her was aching for him now, hot and damp. And she wondered how he would taste, and if he would like to be kissed there.

Nicholas was striving with all of his might not to drive his wife back into the bed and take her swiftly. He could barely think beyond the shapes of her: her breasts set free, and ready for his hands, his mouth; the shadowy triangle, dark red and scented for him.

She was utterly irresistible, waiting for him on her knees, clinging to the bedpost, looking at him in wanton appraisal.

"You're astounding, Nicholas."

"And you are beyond all my dreams." He knelt on the bed in front of her, pulled her against him, and drew her sigh into his kiss.

She arched against him, measuring his arousal with the rhythm of her hips, until she was his pulse and his heartbeat, and he was making new bargains with God. Just one more moment with her, one more day. Then he'd spend all the rest of his life in penance.

"It feels so wonderful, Nicholas. Large and just right and just there."

"And here, my love." He took her sigh deep into his heart as he slid his palm down her stomach, and then watched her astonishment as he spread his fingers and sifted through her damp curls, softly, lightly, until she was pressing herself into his hand, gasping.

"Oh, Nicholas, what you're doing!"

He parted her with his fingers, taking her mouth at the same time, plunging into both fevered slicknesses, reveling in her crooning, in her clutching at him, delving deeply to meet the rising, primitive tilt of her hips. Her eyes were glassy and the color of an October forest.

"Oh, Nicholas—our wedding night is quite wonderful, don't you think?"

It's heaven and hell, my wife. He lifted her against the pillows and knelt between her legs, then trailed his caress down her silky belly, kissing her. He was so hungry for her he had to taste her there just once, even knowing the firestorm that it would unleash inside him. He prayed that he could weather it.

Eleanor could hardly breathe for the pleasure, for her husband's intimacies, and her battered heart. She was open to him, and glad of it, her thighs spread and the great man kneeling between them. So husbandly, so familiar, and so unaware of the way that she was looking at him—as the man she had married. Her blood was on fire, her skin ached for him to hold her, and to be just where he was, trailing his mouth down her belly toward the fever that had gathered between her legs.

"What are you going to do, Nicholas?"

"I plan to kiss you."

"Do you mean there?" He couldn't.

"Oh, yes, my love." He slipped his hands beneath her hips, raised them, and then, mother of all sweet mercies, he kissed her. Right there, lightly but with great attention. "And here." He parted her with gentle fingers and found the center of her with his tongue and then his ravenous mouth against her, and she was sure that the sunlight had come streaming into their midnight chamber, or the brilliant end of the world.

She was soaring upward toward some glorious heaven, leaving the earth, leaving Nicholas behind. And that suddenly felt all wrong.

There were too many lies between them.

She'd intended to lead him down a tortuous path of near misses, to torment him for his deceit and to confuse him, to make him twist in the wind while she held the tether. But she couldn't do that now.

"I can't do this, Nicholas." She shoved him away, and flung herself off the bed and through the curtains to the outer room, shaking to her bones, wondering how she'd let it get this far.

Nicholas followed, starved for her, terrified that he'd frightened her, unsure what to do next. "Eleanor, what?"

"I'm sorry." He reached for her, but she scurried to the other side of the table, put her hands up, and turned from him. "I can't go on. I thought I could, but I'm not very good at this."

She was quaking, her skin goose-fleshed, and he draped a blanket over her shoulders. "You've been marvelous, love. I am stunned and aching for you. And though we've come far, you're still a virgin."

"Yes, Nicholas. But we can't do this now." She dragged in a hiccupping sob, harrowing tears welling in her eyes and then falling down her chest, making gleaming trails that he wanted to follow with his mouth and kiss away. "Because I can't deceive you any longer. I thought I could trick you into this."

He sighed, knowing that he wouldn't have missed this for anything—his wedding night with his remarkable wife. "My eyes are wide-open, Eleanor."

"No, they're not, Nicholas. They can't be." She pointed toward the bailey. "Do you know what Sir Richard told me today, just when he was leaving?"

A chill swept across his shoulders: the end of the world, the beginning of his forever without her. "More about your husband?"

Her eyes glittered wetly. "Oh, Nicholas, that he had a son."

Nicholas swallowed and battled his own tears, that everlasting grief. "Did he?"

"Yes. Don't you see what that means? *We* had a son. His and mine."

He felt her accusation bubbling inside his chest, sending his thoughts into circles, the past, the present all tangled and tied together. "I'm sorry for your loss, Eleanor." *For ours.*

"I would have loved him, Nicholas—I love him now. I would have held him in his pain. I would have been a comfort beside his father who adored him, who would have laid down his life for him. But don't you see? I was never given the chance to mother him, never given

365

a chance to love my husband as I should, as I want to."

He turned from her, feeling the light slip away, the familiar darkness at the edge of his vision. His chest filled up with sorrow, that fierce aching that never went away. "He wasn't that kind of man."

"Oh, but he *was* that kind of man, Nicholas. He was good and honorable and devoted."

"You have the wrong man."

"And the most remarkable thing about him was that he hadn't always been that way. He changed, Nicholas. He wasn't the man I married—not the William Bayard who came to live at Faulkhurst, who selflessly cared for his tenants, who found his bastard son and cherished him, who carved little bears for him out of scraps of pine. And who came to love a wife who overran his sanctuary."

"Eleanor, stop."

"No." The room grew quiet, just his heartbeat and hers. "You are my husband. William Nicholas Bayard."

His throat closed up, and he went to the window to find more air. "I can't be that man to you."

He could feel her heat at his back. "Why can't you?"

"You don't know me." He closed off his

366

heart. *All those battlefields, all those bloody churchyards.*

"You don't know yourself at all, Nicholas."

"Don't you see that it's too late?"

"For what?"

"Madam, my soul is black and unchangeable—God's least favorite."

"No." She came around him with her clean scent, her goodness, put her warm hand in the middle of his chest. "You're His best kind of work, Nicholas, His proudest. Look at what you've done with your life in such a short time."

"You're wrong—I learned that the hard way. I know what it's like to feel God's coolness on your cheek, the breath of His laughter when you think that He's forgiven you all your sins. But you see, they pile up and begin to spill over into other parts of your life, into the whole countryside."

Eleanor's heart was breaking into tiny pieces for this wonderful man, whose broad shoulders carried the weight of the world. "The plague wasn't God's judgment on you."

"No. But it was His means to condemn me. I did everything He asked of me, gladly and with an honest heart, because I believed that I'd found redemption. After all, the world was falling apart, yet I had Liam. We had each other, the best of friends, father to son, my little boy and I. And then he was gone. Just gone."

He was looking out at the dark sea, his eyes full of tears that he was too stubborn to blink away.

"I'm sorry, Nicholas," she said through a sob.

"I've done my best here. I'll finish the chapel roof, and see that your grain barrels are full before I leave." He grabbed his breeches off the floor and looked as though he would just walk out.

"You'll do nothing of the sort, Nicholas." She caught his arm and stood in his path. "You're needed here, where you've always been."

"So that I can watch the crops fail and the tenants die and my wife taken from me because I love her with all of my heart? I won't have it."

"Liam wasn't taken from you out of retribution."

"You don't understand. We had six months together—six months to fill my heart to bursting with a love that I'd never known existed. I was terrified, Eleanor, and I was astonished, and I was—" His voice broke, and he raked his fingers through his hair, his hands shaking.

"Nicholas, you were a father."

"Oh, God, Eleanor, I couldn't save him." A keening sound tore from his chest. He dropped onto the chair and put his head in his hands. "I can't stop it from hurting."

Eleanor didn't know what to say, only knelt at his feet and feathered her fingers through his hair, sitting there for long minutes while he sobbed quietly.

"I don't want you to leave, Nicholas. I need you. Pippa needs you. Little Toddy thinks the world of you."

"You don't know what you're risking." He stood abruptly, still startlingly naked, her caged lion, so vital, so very much alive.

"Only my love for you—and you have it all."

"Christ, Eleanor!" He came at her, as fierce as she'd ever seen him, and cradled the back of her head roughly so that all she could see was the terrible sorrow in his eyes. "Do you know how much I love you? And how helpless that makes me feel? I knew the ways of this God. I understood the proposition the first moment you and I met. You couldn't be plain, or timid, or dull. No, you were fashioned for me to love until the end of my days. And I'm terrified." He held her to him, brushed his lips across her ear and her lashes, as though he couldn't get enough of her.

"You've got it all wrong, Nicholas. I'm not plain or timid or dull, because I was sent here to save you—and you're an awfully stubborn man when it comes to opportunities. We have so much to do. A chapel to build, a life to celebrate, a whole village, rolling fields of barley and pease to tend." Eleanor thought she heard his heart shift as she took his face in her hands. "How many chances does one man get, my love?"

He looked down, his tender heart reluctant to the end. "I've had many in my life."

"Aye, Nicholas—but you've never had *me*."

Nicholas felt his chest fill again, and he fought it, struggled against the coming pain and the emptiness—until he realized that the feeling was radiant and spiraling upward. His wife was mad and wonderful and warm, and if there were bright, persistent angels, she must be his—his redemption come to earth, as undeniable as the coming of spring.

"Will you marry me, Eleanor?" He picked her up into his arms, and her blanket fell away.

"Oh, my love, as often as you ask me."

His heart soaring, he carried his wife to their marriage bed. There he settled her back against the pillows and knelt in the joining of her legs.

"Do you know, wife, that this bed was given to us as a wedding present?"

She smiled and lifted her arm. "Mmmmm. Time we put it to good use, husband."

He groaned from deep inside, made love to her mouth, and to her throat, took his time with the backs of her knees and her fingers. Her eyes were smoky and daring, and while he plied his mouth to her breast, imagining the children they would have, she slid her stealthy fingers down his stomach until she reached the root of him.

"Woman, you—" But he hadn't been prepared for her boldness, for her fingers wrapped around him.

"Please, Nicholas. Inspecting the goods."

"Please, Eleanor." He ground his teeth and rode the sensations, the fluting of her fingers, until he was whispering for her to stop. "I'm too fond of this."

"Now, Nicholas. Please." She tilted her hips to meet him, and he met that place she'd offered him so boldly. He was at the end of his tether, could last no longer.

"I don't want to hurt you, my love." She was tight and tender and writhing against him.

"Just come to me, husband. Join with me." She arched her back and pressed her heels to his backside—and took him just inside.

"Oh, my love." Without another breath, Nicholas propelled himself mindlessly, heard her shocked sigh, and then her crooning.

"Married, Nicholas."

"Forever."

Her husband held himself above her, smiling broadly, his eyes misted, their corners crinkled, and she felt a quiet pulsing rhythm begin to build within her, matched within him.

"Are you all right?"

"Oh, my, Nicholas. I've never in my life been righter." She loved the hot pleasure that licked between them, like the currents off the sea. She couldn't get enough of him—held him and encouraged him and strained toward him, with him, feeling ripe and wanted, her skin made of sunlight.

"You are magnificent, wife. *My* wife. I will say that a thousand times a day." His voice was jubilant as he roared out his joy, rocking her in his slow, pounding rhythm toward a place she'd never been before.

"Come with me, sweet." Nicholas's voice was a kiss, sweet and tucked against her ear.

"Anywhere, Nicholas." This wondrous feeling of being part of Nicholas, which turned her limbs light and languid, was a maddening, never-quite-far-enough euphoria—then a surge of pure, white-hot pleasure began where she was joined to him.

"Nicholas, I—Oh, my—I—" The pleasure grew and spread and became wave after cresting wave of bliss, and had her gasping, calling out his name until she was weeping.

Nicholas came up on his hands, her amazing husband, her miracle, thrusting himself into her while she pulled him deeper, nearer, until he finally thickened inside her and went still, his muscles flexed—

"I love you, Eleanor!" And then he was pouring his seed into her, their child, the rest of their lives. The thought sent her over another cloud, through another rainbow. She drifted from there, calling out to Nicholas.

And he was waiting there with his lopsided smile, his eyes damp, making her feel so well loved.

"Well, my dear wife, what shall we say to Edward?"

She nuzzled his chin and settled into his shoulder, marveling that they fit together so perfectly, in their hearts and in their marriage bed.

"I'll tell him that I found my husband in my castle, and that I'm going to keep him."

He rolled atop her, holding his weight on his elbows, sheltering them both. "*Our* castle, my love."

"Oh, Nicholas, our home—forevermore."

Avon Romantic Treasures

*Unforgettable, enthralling love stories,
sparkling with passion and adventure
from Romance's bestselling authors*

Dear Reader,

Whether I finish a book, I love I begin to look for another that I'll enjoy just as much. And now that you've turned the last page of the book you have in your hands, I know you'll be keeping an eye out for another story to fall in love with.

Historical romance readers need look no further than next month's Avon Treasure by Connie Mason, *A Taste Of Sin*. Set in romantic Scotland, Lady Christy has been claimed as a bride—but in name only. Now, it's up to her to seduce the dashing rogue who has taken her as is wife . . . and to have her wedding night at last!

Patti Berg has charmed contemporary readers with her dynamic heroines, sexy heroes, and sassy humor. Now, the bestselling author of *Wife for a Day* brings us another rollicking love story, *Bride for a Night*. Cairo McKnight never wants to see her husband-for-one-night, Duncan Kincaid, again. But now he's back in her life . . . and just as irresistible as ever.

Ana Leigh's *The McKenzies* are some of the best-known characters of our time. Now, they make a spectacular return in *The MacKenzies: Josh*. Josh MacKenzie is hot on the trail of Emily Lawrence, who has fled her stuffy, wealthy home for the freedom of the west and life as a Harvey Girl. His mission is to get Emily back to Boston, but the beautiful spitfire fights him at every turn . . .

Susan Sizemore is a rising star of historical romance and the author of *The Price of Innocence*. Now, don't miss her latest sensuous page-turner *On a Long Ago Night*. Years ago, Honoria Pyne was forced to make a bargain with a mysterious rogue, and now he's come to claim her . . . as his bride. She has sworn to hate James Marbury forever . . . but some promises are meant to be broken.

Enjoy!

Lucia Macro

Lucia Macro
Senior Editor

AEL 0400